Praise for the novels of Candace Camp

"…entertaining, well-written
Victorian romantic mystery."
—*The Best Reviews* on
An Unexpected Pleasure

"This one has it all: smooth writing,
an intelligent story, engaging characters,
and sexual tension that positively sizzles."
—*All About Romance* on *Swept Away*

"Camp brings the dark Victorian world to life.
Her strong characters and perfect pacing keep you
turning the pages of this chilling mystery."
—*Romantic Times BOOKclub* on *Winterset*

"From its delicious beginning to its
satisfying ending, [*Mesmerized*] offers
a double helping of romance."
—*Booklist*

"Camp shows the ability of love to help people
overcome something out of the ordinary."
—*Romantic Times BOOKclub* on *Mesmerized*

"A smart, fun-filled romp."
—*Publishers Weekly* on *Impetuous*

"One of Camp's best."
—*Publishers Weekly* on *Indiscreet*

"Candace Camp is renowned as a
storyteller who touches the hearts of
her readers time and time again."
—*Romantic Times BOOKclub* on *Impulse*

"…will leave you breathless with laughter
and eagerly anticipating the next mishap."
—*Affair de Coeur* on *Suddenly*

CANDACE CAMP

AN
Independent
WOMAN

HQN™

ISBN 0-373-77097-9

AN INDEPENDENT WOMAN

This edition published by arrangement with Harlequin Books S.A.

® and TM are trademarks of the publisher. Trademarks indicated with
® are registered in the United States Patent and Trademark Office, the
Canadian Trade Marks Office and in other countries.

www.HQNBooks.com

Printed in U.S.A.

CHAPTER ONE

JULIANA HAD NOT EXPECTED to see him again.

She had heard that Nicholas had come into the title and returned to England, which had surprised her. All her life, she had thought that it was Nicholas's uncle who was the heir, not him. Certainly, no one had ever treated him like the future earl. She had assumed that their paths would never cross. After all, he was an earl now, and wealthy, and she was a paid companion to a woman who moved only on the edges of that rarefied circle of society to which he belonged.

There had been an instant, when she had first heard the murmurs of Nicholas's return from America and his sudden elevation into the inner sanctum of polite society, that she had thought with an upsurge of an almost painful excitement that she would see him once more. Time, and an application of reason, had led her to realize that was unlikely.

Even though they had once been close, it had been many years ago. If he even thought of her, it would be only as a dim memory from his past, a person from a time and place he doubtless recalled with little fondness. Her time at Lychwood Hall had been unhappy, but his had been even bleaker. Juliana suspected that he had done his best to put the past behind him. He would not seek her out. Only a foolish romantic would hope that he would.

And there was little chance that they would accidentally run into each other. Her employer, Mrs. Thrall, however much she might like to think she was a member of the upper echelon of London society, was in reality a very small fish swimming in the outer, eddying rings of that pond. The family was at best acceptable country gentry come to the city, and it was only the undeniable beauty of Clementine, Mrs. Thrall's daughter, that got them any sort of notice.

Tonight, however, the Thralls had received an invitation to Lady Sherbourne's ball, a huge crush of an affair, so large that it pulled in many lesser members of Society. Juliana understood that it was only the sheer numbers of invitees that had made it possible for them to be here. Mrs. Thrall, of course, did not. She had been crowing for the past week about Lady Sherbourne having taken them under her wing.

Because of the size of the party, Juliana had harbored a small flicker of hope, barely acknowledged, that Lord Barre would appear. But she had not really believed it, deep down. After all, from the gossip she had managed to glean, sitting quietly listening to Clementine and her giggling friends, Nicholas rarely attended any party. His reclusiveness, of course, simply added to his mystique.

But there he was. Juliana looked up from her perusal of Clementine sweeping around the floor in the arms of one of her many admirers, and there, standing at the top of the wide staircase leading down into the ballroom, was Nicholas Barre.

Her heart skittered in her chest, and for an instant, she felt as if she could not breathe. He was handsome, more handsome even than she remembered—filled out now into a man, with broad shoulders that needed no extra padding from his tailor, and long, muscled legs. He stood, looking out coolly over the mass of people below him, confidence, even a certain arrogance, stamped on his features. His hair was thick and a trifle shaggy, jet-black in color and falling carelessly beside his face. His eyes appeared as black as his hair, accented by the straight slashes of his black brows.

He did not look like other men. Not even the black formal coat and snowy white shirt could camouflage the hint of wildness that clung to him.

Wherever he went, Juliana thought, he must immediately be the center of attention. She wondered if he was aware of that.

Perhaps he had become accustomed to it. He had always been one set apart. Dangerous, they had called him. And wicked. Juliana suspected that the same appellations were still directed at him.

She realized suddenly that she was staring, and she glanced quickly away. *What was she to do?* She swallowed hard, her hands curling into fists in her lap.

She remembered the last time she had seen him—the planes and angles of his face stark white in the moonlight, his eyes great pools of darkness. He had been only sixteen then, leanly muscular in a way that suggested the powerful male body he would grow into. His hair had been longer and unkempt, tousled by the wind and his impatient fingers. There had been a hardness to his face even then, a certain wariness that bespoke much about his past.

Juliana had clung to him, holding his arm with both hands as though she could make him stay, her twelve-year-old heart breaking within her. "Please," she had begged. "Don't go...."

"I can't, Jules," he had replied, frowning. "I have to go. I can't stay here anymore."

"But what will I do?" she had asked plaintively.

"It will be so horrid here without you. No one but *them*..." Her voice invested the word with disgust.

"You'll be all right. You'll get through it. They won't hurt you."

"I know," she had whispered, tears filling her eyes. She knew that no one ever harmed her as they did him. There were no angry cuffs of the hand, or days spent without meals or companionship, alone in her room, as there were for Nick. But the thought of life without him beside her was dull and flat, almost unbearable.

From the time she and her mother had come to Lychwood Hall when she was eight, Nicholas had been her only friend, her closest companion. They had been drawn together naturally, the two outsiders on the Barre estate, disdained by Nicholas's aunt and uncle and their children. Charity children, both of them, and often reminded of it, they had formed a firm alliance, closer than a boy of twelve and a girl of eight would normally have been. And if, as he had grown up, racing toward adulthood, he had moved farther from her in interests and activities, there had always remained that special bond between them.

"Can't I come with you?" she had asked without hope, knowing that his answer would be a refusal.

He shook his head. "They'd come after me for

sure if I took you with me. This way, perhaps, I have a chance of getting away from them."

"Will you come back? Please?"

He had smiled then, a rare wondrous smile that few besides her had seen. "Of course. I'll make lots and lots of money, and then I shall come back and take you away. You'll be rich, and everyone will call you 'my lady.' And Seraphina will have to curtsey to you. How's that?"

"Perfect." Her heart had swelled with love for him even as she knew, deep inside her realistic soul, that he was unlikely to return, that he would disappear from her life just as her father had.

"Don't forget me," she had said, swallowing her tears, refusing to act like a baby in front of him. She reached up, taking the simple leather thong from around her neck, and held it out to him. A gold signet ring dangled from it, simple and masculine.

Nicholas had looked at her in surprise. "No. Jules—that was your father's. I can't take that. I know how much it means to you."

"I want you to have it," she had replied stubbornly. "It'll keep you safe. Take it."

Finally he had taken it from her hand. Then, with a last halfhearted smile, he had vanished into the night, leaving her alone in the darkening garden.

She had not seen him again for fifteen years.

Juliana cast another glance toward the top of the staircase. Nicholas was no longer there. Cautiously she looked around the room, but she could not spot him anywhere in the crowd. She returned her gaze to her lap, wondering how she could manage to get out of here without his seeing her.

Her stomach was twisted into knots, partly with excitement, but mostly with fear. She did not want him to see her, did not want to have to face the fact that he might snub her…that he might not even recognize her.

Nicholas Barre had meant too much to her for her to bear a snub. She had loved him as only a child can love. After he ran away from the estate, she had not let her memories of him fade. For a long time she had held his promise in her heart, hoping he would reappear and take her away—from her mother's sadness, from Crandall's cruelties and Aunt Lilith's petty sniping, from Seraphina's casual assumption that Juliana was there to do whatever she asked. As Juliana had grown into womanhood, it had been Nicholas's image that had fueled her adolescent dreams, becoming the hero on a white charger who would come riding up to Lychwood Hall and sweep her up before him on his horse, carrying her away from the life she disliked and bestowing upon her his name, as well as fabulous jewels and fashionable clothes.

Of course, she had not been so foolish as to keep those dreams long. She had grown up and had made her own life. Long ago she had stopped believing— and then finally stopped even wishing—that Nicholas would return and seek out his childhood friend. Even when she had heard that he had returned to London from whatever far-flung place he had been, she had not thought he would come for her…or at least she had firmly squashed the little germ of an idea before it even grew full-size in her mind.

After all, when he had promised to return, they had been of more or less equal station—unwanted relatives, living on the Barres' charity—or, at least, so she had thought. But now he was Lord Barre and reportedly quite wealthy in his own right, as well as having inherited his grandfather's estate. It would be foolish in the extreme, she knew, to even hope he would look her up. Promises made at the age of sixteen rarely lasted.

She had experienced the bitter reward of being proved right. It had been two months since she had heard that Nicholas was in London again, and he had not come to her. She was too realistic to think that if he ran into her tonight, he would greet her with cries of delight. Heavens, he probably would not even recognize her as the child he had once known.

But Juliana did not want to have to face that situation. She did not want to see him look at her with the blank expression of lack of recognition. Worse, she did not want to see him see her, recognize her, and then turn away, not acknowledging the bond. Almost as bad would be having him converse with her with the stiff formality of a stranger, or the faintly harassed look of someone caught in a social situation he wished he could get out of.

She must get away from the party, she thought, but that was far more easily said than done. Mrs. Thrall had hired her as a companion primarily because she wanted help watching over her lively, headstrong daughter. Clementine was both beautiful and spoiled, accustomed to getting her way. She was also foolish enough to think that she could ignore the dictates of Society. Unwatched, she was likely to flirt more than was considered proper, or to dance with the same bachelor more than twice. Juliana had even once caught her attempting to slip out an opened French door into the darkened gardens beyond with an ardent suitor.

And since Mrs. Thrall was a rather indolent woman, she used Juliana as Clementine's primary chaperone. Mrs. Thrall liked to think that this tiresome duty was a gift she bestowed upon her companion, pointing out to Juliana how nice it was that she got to attend all these balls. Frankly, Juliana would have preferred spending the evening curled up with a book or playing games with the Thralls' younger—and far more likeable—daughter, Fiona. It was no pleasure to sit, as plainly dressed as a wren among peacocks, against the wall with the mothers and wallflowers, watching people dance and enjoy themselves.

Mrs. Thrall would be highly displeased if Juliana were to plead a headache or other illness and wish to leave the party, and she certainly had no desire to listen to her employer complain that she was attempting to ruin the grandest ball of her daughter's career. Moreover, she had little hope that Mrs. Thrall would send her home, even with a lecture. She was far more likely to tell Juliana to simply bear up like a proper British gentlewoman…and then send her off to fetch a cup of punch.

The best course, she thought, would be to simply keep her eyes glued on Clementine. That way her gaze could not happen to meet Nicholas's, and she would be able to avoid seeing the expression that would come over his face. It was unlikely that Lord

Barre would look over at the duennas watching their charges, and even if he did, if she was not watching, at least she would not know if he then turned away without speaking.

"Juliana?" A deep masculine voice cut through the air, filled with surprise and—surely she could not be mistaken—delight, as well.

Juliana's head snapped up. Despite the years between them, she knew the voice immediately. Nicholas Barre was walking rapidly toward her, a smile lighting his handsome face.

"Nicholas!" The word came out breathlessly, and without realizing it, Juliana rose to her feet.

"Juliana! It *is* you!" He stopped in front of her, so tall she had to tilt her head back to look up at him, his dark eyes alight, a smile curving his full, firm lips. "I can scarcely believe it! When I think of all the time that I have looked for you..." He reached out his hand and, somewhat shakily, she gave hers to him.

"I—I'm sorry. I should say Lord Barre," she went on hastily.

"I beg you will not," he replied. "I would think you no longer counted yourself my friend."

Juliana blushed, unsure what to say. She felt un-accustomedly shy. Nicholas was at once so familiar and so different, the traces of the boy still evident in the man, yet far removed from what he had once been.

"I am surprised you recognized me," she told him. "It has been so long."

He shrugged. "You have grown up." His eyes swept briefly, almost involuntarily, down her form. "Still, your face is much the same. I could scarcely forget it."

There was a loud, admonitory clearing of a throat from the chair beside Juliana, and she started. "Oh, I am so sorry. Lord Barre, please allow me to introduce you to Mrs. Thrall."

Juliana half turned toward her employer. "Mrs. Thrall, Lord Barre."

The middle-aged woman simpered, extending her hand to Nicholas. "Lord Barre, what a pleasure. No doubt you wish to meet Clementine, but I am afraid she is out on the dance floor. Her dance card is always full, you know."

"Mrs. Thrall." Nicholas gave the woman a polite bow, his dark eyes summing her up quickly before he turned back to Juliana. "I hope that you will give me the honor of a waltz, Juliana."

Juliana knew that her employer would doubtless frown on her shirking her duty in that way, but she wanted quite badly to accept his invitation. She never got to dance at any of the parties they attended; she could not count the number of times she had sat, toes tapping, heart aching, watching the other couples swirl merrily around the floor.

"I would love to," she said recklessly, then turned toward her employer. "If you will excuse me, Mrs. Thrall."

She expected at best a scowl from the other woman, with a deferred lecture about the impropriety of her taking to the floor with young bachelors when she should be overseeing Clementine. But she hoped that Mrs. Thrall would not have the gall to flatly refuse, right in front of one of the peers of the land.

To her surprise, the older woman smiled benignly at her and said, "Yes, of course. That sounds like an excellent idea. No doubt Clementine will be back when you return."

Nicholas bowed toward Mrs. Thrall and extended his hand to Juliana. She took it, letting him lead her out onto the dance floor, struggling to control the happy excitement fizzing within her.

"Who the devil is Clementine?" he murmured, bending his head closer to hers.

Juliana could not suppress a giggle. "She is Mrs. Thrall's daughter. She is making her debut this year."

"Good Gad, another one," he commented darkly.

Juliana, more accustomed to listening to the gushings of the besotted suitors of Clementine Thrall, could not help but feel a small spurt of amusement.

Nicholas turned to her, putting his hand lightly on her waist and taking her other hand in his. She felt a little breathless, her nerves jumping with excitement, as the music began and they swept out onto the floor. There had been few times when Juliana had waltzed—there had been no Season in London for her, and paid companions were rarely asked to dance—and she was eager, yet scared that she would make a mistake.

For the first few moments she was too aware of following the steps to pay much attention to anything else, but gradually she gave herself up to the rhythm of the music and found herself swirling about the room quite easily. She cast a glance up at her companion. It seemed like a dream, she thought, to be here with Nicholas after all these years.

As if he had read her thoughts, Nicholas said to her, "You know, I've had the very devil of a time trying to find you."

"I'm sorry," Juliana replied. "I did not realize you were looking for me."

"Of course I was. Why would I not?"

"It has been a long time," she replied. "I was only a child when you left."

"You were my only friend," he told her simply. "That is difficult to forget."

His words were true, of course. When she had met him, she had thought that he was the most alone person she knew. At twelve years of age, his reputation as a rebel and troublemaker was firmly established, and even then, there had been a certain hardness in his face that closed out others. But Juliana, herself feeling cast adrift in the world after the death of her beloved father, had felt an affinity with the dark, brooding boy. She had glimpsed in his onyx eyes a lurking loneliness, a vulnerability, that had spoken to her.

"We were the outcasts of Lychwood Hall," she agreed now, keeping her voice light.

"I told you I would come back, you know," he reminded her.

"So you did." And she had lived on it for years, she thought, until she had grown old enough to be wiser. "But I did not hear from you."

"I was not a very good correspondent," Nicholas admitted wryly.

Juliana chuckled. "That, sir, is an understatement of the grossest sort."

"I did not want them to know where I was," he said, shrugging.

"I know." Even as a child, she had understood that. "I never expected you to write," she told him honestly.

"Somehow I thought you would still be there," he went on.

"At Lychwood Hall?" Juliana asked, surprised.

"Foolish of me, I know. Of course you wanted to get away from them, too."

"My mother died while I was away at school with Seraphina," Juliana told him. "After that, there was little to hold me there."

"I inquired there after you," he went on. "My uncle is dead now, but my aunt replied. She told me you had gone abroad to live several years ago, and she did not know where you were."

Juliana raised a brow. "Her memory must be shockingly short, then. I have been back in England for some years now. I send Aunt Lilith a courtesy note every year at Christmas."

"I suspected her lack of knowledge was terribly convenient. I set my business man to looking for you. Of course, I told him you were in Europe, so it is little wonder that he got no results." He gave her a quizzical look. "If you have been in London, why have I not seen you anywhere?"

Juliana smiled faintly. "Companions, I'm afraid, are rarely seen."

"Companion?" Nicholas frowned. "You? Juliana, no…"

"What would you have me do?" Juliana lifted her chin a little defiantly. "I had to make my way in the world somehow, and I did not like the idea of being a governess. My sewing is not good enough to make a living as a seamstress. And call it unseemly pride, but I did not want to seek employment below stairs."

His mouth tightened. "Don't be absurd. None of those positions are worthy of you."

"I could not remain living on Trenton Barre's charity. Surely you, of all people, can understand that. You set out on your own. So did I."

"It is different for a woman," he pointed out.

"Alas, I am quite aware of that. There are very few ways by which a female can support herself—and even fewer that are considered respectable," Juliana replied tartly. "Believe me, I would much rather have done something exciting—or even just somewhat interesting. Women, however, are given little choice in the matter."

He smiled a little. "I had forgotten how fiery you can be about one of your causes. Nay, please, do not bristle at my words. I meant no criticism. I am very glad of your passion and dedication. After all, I was once one of your causes."

Juliana relaxed, smiling. "No, 'tis I who should apologize. You expressed only concern about me, and I became as prickly as a porcupine. I am well aware that I cannot change the world. I am also well aware that none of the fault lies at your feet."

"I wish that I had known. I should have. I should have realized."

"And what could you have done?" Juliana asked him, her tone light and teasing.

"I should have helped you. I should—" He stopped, unexpectedly at a loss.

"You see? It was not in your hands. If you are going to say that you would have sent me money to help me live, I am sure you can see that that would scarcely have been considered proper. I should not have cared for any of the labels given to a woman who lives off a man's largesse."

"None would dare think that of you," Nicholas said decisively.

Juliana chuckled. "I am glad you think so. In any case, there is no reason to feel sorry for me. My life has been mostly pleasant. I was companion for several years to a most intelligent and generous woman, Mrs. Simmons, until she became too frail to live alone and moved in with her son and family. She treated me more like a niece or a ward than an employee. I dined with her and slept in a very nice room, and in return I had to do little more than spend several hours a day in enjoyable conversation and help her keep track of her correspondence. We traveled to the continent—and I can tell you that it was far more enjoyable than when I accompanied Seraphina and Aunt Lilith on their tour after she finished school."

Nicholas winced. "I should think so. That sounds more like torture than travel."

"Yes, and all the more so given that Aunt Lilith kept reminding me of my good fortune in being given the opportunity to broaden my horizons with them."

"No good deed is left unheralded with them," Nicholas agreed.

"It is so good to talk to you!" Juliana blurted out. "No one else would understand exactly how it was. How obligated one was made to feel for every mouthful of food and every stitch of clothing."

"And how ungrateful you were for the wonderful opportunity of being allowed to associate with them," he added.

"Just so." Juliana smiled at him.

It was odd, she thought, that she should feel so instantly comfortable with him again, as if all the years that had separated them meant nothing. He was once again Nicky, her protector against Crandall's mean tricks and bullying tactics, her confidant and friend.

And yet, at the same time, she was very aware of how different it all was. They were no longer children. He was a man now, large and hard and almost overpoweringly masculine. Being swept around the room in his arms was a far cry from sitting beside him on the bank of the brook, dangling their bare feet in the water. There was an elemental excitement in being so close to him, feeling his hand spread upon her waist. She could not help but think that he was virtually a stranger to her now, someone whose thoughts and deeds she had no knowledge of, whose past fifteen years were a mystery to her.

The music finally swept to a close. They stopped and stepped apart. Juliana looked up at Nicholas. She was a little breathless, and she knew it was not just from the exertion of dancing.

He offered her his arm, and they walked back to where Mrs. Thrall sat waiting for them. Juliana saw with a flicker of irritation that Clementine now stood with her mother. The girl was the picture of English beauty—dainty and dimpled in her demure white ball gown, blue-eyed and blond-haired, her dewy complexion touched with soft pink color along her cheeks.

Men were drawn to her china-doll loveliness, and

Clementine had achieved a certain success this Season. However, she had not yet caught the eye of any titled gentleman, and Juliana suspected that she and her mother were hoping to correct that omission right now. Mrs. Thrall had obviously been gleeful at meeting Lord Barre, and Juliana felt sure she had drawn her daughter off the dance floor so that she could meet Nicholas when he brought Juliana back to her seat. One glance at the young gentleman waiting with them, scowling, confirmed Juliana's suspicion.

"Juliana!" Mrs. Thrall said, beaming at Juliana as if she were her dearest friend. "And Lord Barre. Please allow me to introduce you to my daughter Clementine."

Clementine looked up at Nicholas with a fair semblance of girlish shyness, dimpling into an enchanting smile. "My lord. 'Tis a pleasure to meet you."

Juliana clenched her teeth, somewhat surprised by the stab of dislike she felt for the girl.

"Miss Thrall." Nicholas smiled and bowed to Clementine, casting a glance and a nod toward the young gentleman behind her.

Clementine opened her fan and plied it gently, gazing limpidly at Nicholas over the top of it.

Nicholas turned back to Juliana. "I hope you will allow me to call on you, Miss Holcott."

Juliana smiled. "Of course—that is, I mean…" She turned toward Mrs. Thrall. "If you will permit it, madam."

"Of course, of course." Mrs. Thrall bared her teeth in a smile so wide it was almost frightening. "We would be honored for you to visit our house." She told him the address, adding with a deprecating titter, "Not the most fashionable address, I fear. 'Tis Clementine's first Season, you know, and I did not realize how far in advance one must let a house to obtain a truly good address."

"I am sure that the presence of such fair ladies makes any place fashionable," Nicholas replied diplomatically.

Clementine and her mother simpered at this remark, and Juliana was aware of a strong and no doubt childish resentment. Nicholas was hers, she wanted to cry out.

But, of course, that was absurd. Nicholas was not, could not be, hers.

Nicholas took his leave of them, with a bow and impartial smile to them all. As soon as he was out of sight, Clementine and her mother swung to Juliana.

"You did not tell me you knew Lord Barre!" Mrs. Thrall exclaimed, her tone a mixture of accusation and delight.

"I was not sure he would remember me," Juliana

replied. "It has been many years since we have seen one another."

"But how do you know him?" Clementine pressed, moving closer to Juliana and turning her back rudely on the young man who stood with them.

"We were friends as children," Juliana explained. "I…lived near his family." It was, she thought, too complicated to explain the relationship between them, and, moreover, she had little desire to expose her history to their curiosity.

"It is generous of him to seek you out," Mrs. Thrall went on, unaware, as she usually was, of the rudeness of her words.

Juliana, accustomed to the petty stings of being employed as a companion, ignored the disdain inherent in the other woman's words. "He is a generous man," she allowed dryly.

"Of course, he doubtless wanted to meet Clementine," the older woman went on placidly, explaining the oddity of a nobleman acknowledging someone of as little status as Juliana. "It is quite fortuitous, really, that he knew you and could gain an introduction."

Juliana swallowed her anger, looking away from her employer. She reminded herself that Mrs. Thrall was a woman of little sense and a deficient upbringing. She did not mean to be rude and hurtful—frankly,

Juliana thought, she did not consider Juliana's feelings enough to intend to hurt her—and she did not know what she was talking about. Nicholas had come over because he was glad to see her, not because he wanted to meet Mrs. Thrall's daughter.

But as the evening wore on and Juliana watched Clementine flirt with her bevy of admirers, and take to the floor time and again to dance, her certainty began to erode. The girl was obviously devastatingly appealing to men, whereas she herself…

She looked down at her plain dark gown and sighed. She was dressed like a governess, her hair pinned into a plain knot. A companion was not paid to attract attention—especially in this case, where Mrs. Thrall would have squelched any semblance of a beauty that might compete with her own daughter. How could any man's eyes not be drawn to Clementine rather than to her?

CHAPTER TWO

JULIANA FOUND HERSELF brooding over the matter the rest of the evening. She did not believe that Nicholas had merely used her to get an introduction to Clementine. But she was realistic enough to think that he must have noticed the girl's beauty when he was introduced to her. Nor could she help but wonder if his desire to call on her had as much or more to do with Clementine's appeal as with his friendship with Juliana.

It wasn't that she thought Nicholas was interested in her in a romantic way, she told herself. She had long ago given up those girlhood dreams. She was a grown woman and well aware that she did not even know the man; all she had known was the boy. But he had been very dear to her at one time; it hurt to think that his motivation for calling upon her might be only interest in the silly but beautiful Clementine.

All the way home, Mrs. Thrall and her daughter pelted Juliana with questions about the handsome and highly eligible Lord Barre. How old was he? Did he have a London residence? Was he as wealthy as everyone said?

"He is thirty-one. But as to the rest, I really don't know," Juliana replied, gritting her teeth. "We did not speak about any of those things while we were dancing. And I have not seen him since we were young."

"They say he is fabulously wealthy," Clementine said, her eyes shining.

"I heard that he made a fortune in the China Trade," Mrs. Thrall said. "Not an occupation for a gentleman, of course, but, then, his lineage is impeccable."

"And the fortune is great," Juliana murmured.

"Exactly," Mrs. Thrall agreed, nodding her head, blissfully unaware of any sarcasm in Juliana's words.

"I heard he made his money in smuggling during the War," Clementine put in. "Sarah Thurgood says her aunt told her that he was a spy, as well."

"Did she say for which side?" Juliana asked.

"No one knows," Clementine told her, her eyes wide. "He is reputed to be a very dangerous man."

"Very wild in his youth," Mrs. Thrall added knowledgeably.

"He has been much maligned," Juliana started hotly. This was the sort of statement she had heard about Nicholas from the time she met him.

"Everyone says…" Clementine began.

"Everyone doesn't know him!" Juliana snapped.

"Really, Juliana…" Mrs. Thrall gave her a dark look.

Juliana stifled her anger. Her quick tongue was what had most often gotten her into trouble as a paid companion. It had been a hard lesson, but over the years she had learned not to argue with her employers.

"I'm sorry, ma'am," she said now. "I did not mean to contradict you. It is just that I know Lord Barre has often been adjudged much more wicked than he really is."

Mrs. Thrall smiled at her in a condescending way that made Juliana's fingers curl into fists in her lap. "You must take my word for it, my dear, as one who knows a bit more about the world than you—where there is smoke, there's fire."

Fortunately, Juliana's ready sense of humor came to her rescue, overcoming her anger. The woman stated the old adage as if she were imparting the greatest wisdom.

"Of course," Juliana choked out, and pressed her lips together to keep from chuckling. What did it matter, anyway, what someone as foolish as Elspeth Thrall thought about Nicholas Barre?

She settled into her corner of the carriage, only half listening to Clementine chatter on about what dress she should wear on the morrow and what hair-style would look best. When they reached the house, she went upstairs to her bedroom, a small, sparely furnished room at the end of the hallway closest to the servants' stairs. As a genteel companion, she was not tucked away in an attic room with the servants, but her bedchamber was hardly what one could consider comfortable. Juliana thought with some longing of her accommodations when she had lived with Mrs. Simmons.

Ah, well, she reminded herself, even a small room and putting up with employers like Mrs. Thrall was preferable to continuing to live on the charity of Lilith and Trenton Barre.

With a grimace, Juliana began to undress, her mind going back to her life at the Barre estate. She supposed it was seeing Nicholas tonight that made her think of it, for she had managed to bury such memories long ago and normally did not even think about that time.

Juliana had been eight years old when her beloved father, the scholarly youngest son of a baron, had died. She remembered lying in her bed at night, listening to the soft sounds of her mother weeping in the room next door. Juliana had been too frightened to cry herself.

Overnight, her world had been turned upside down. Not only was her father gone, but the smiling, warm mother she had known all her life was gone, as well, replaced by a pale, sad, anxious woman who paced the floors, twisting her handkerchief between her hands when she wasn't collapsed on the sofa or her bed, crying. First the maids had left, and then, finally, their housekeeper, and angry men had come knocking on their door at all hours. Those visits invariably left her mother crying.

Finally they had left the small house in which they had lived all Juliana's life, packing only their clothes and her mother's jewelry, and moved into a set of rooms in a house where several other people lived. Her mother, Diana, spent her time staring dully out the window and writing letters. Periodically Diana would take out her small jewelry box and open it, then search through the contents, finally selecting a set of earrings or a bracelet. She would leave their rooms, admonishing Juliana to be quiet, and return a few hours later, her eyes red and a bag of sweets for Juliana in her hand.

Only years later had Juliana come to understand the terror that her fragile, pretty mother had faced— a woman with a young child and no money or skills, eking out a living for them by selling her small stock of precious jewelry, aware that before long this source of money would run out, too, and they would be left utterly penniless. The family's sole source of money had been a small trust left to her father by a grandmother, added to by the small sums of money he brought in from his scholarly articles. Both incomes had died with her father.

One day a tall dark-haired man had come to visit them. He had spoken briefly to Juliana's mother, who began to cry, sitting down on a chair. Juliana had run to Diana, furious with the man for hurting her mother.

But Diana had reached out an arm and encircled Juliana, pulling her close, and said, "No, no, darling. This is Cousin Lilith's husband, and he has saved us. They have very kindly invited us to live with them."

The next day they had traveled to Lychwood Hall in a post chaise, with Trenton Barre riding alongside the coach. Lychwood Hall had been a grand and imposing place, built of gray stone, with alternating narrow strips of black slate. Fortunately Juliana and her mother were not to be living at the estate house itself, but in a smaller cottage on the grounds. Juliana found the cottage rather cheerless and cold, but her mother simply said over and over again how wonderful it was that they had found a home.

Diana had explained to her daughter that her

cousin, Lilith, had married Trenton Barre, and that the couple were not only giving them a house in which to live but were also generously allowing Juliana to be educated with their own children at the main house. Carefully she had instructed her daughter on how she was to act around the Barre family—always polite and respectful, never contradicting them or making herself a nuisance in any way. They were there on the Barre family's sufferance, she had told Juliana, and Juliana must always remember that. She was to play with the Barre children, but only if asked to, and she was to let them have their way in all things, whether in play or at work in school.

Such admonitions grated on Juliana, who had always had a mind of her own. It galled her to be a "charity case," and the idea of having to always give in to another's wishes appalled her. However, because of her desire to please her mother and ease her obvious anxiety, she had promised to follow her orders. Then she had been taken over to meet the Barres, who by that time had assumed somewhat legendary proportions in Juliana's childish mind.

Lilith Barre was an icy blonde, attractive in a long, slender way most unlike Juliana's small, curvaceous mother. She did not seem, Juliana thought, the sort whose lap one could climb onto to lean one's head against her shoulder. And she certainly did not display any sort of affection for either Juliana or Juliana's mother. The young girl found it hard to believe that she was related to them in any way.

Lilith looked at Juliana in a cool, assessing way, then instructed one of the maids to take the child up to the nursery to meet the governess and the other tutors.

The governess was a woman who seemed to be of varying shades of gray, from her iron-colored hair to her charcoal-hued dress. She was, she told Juliana, Miss Emerson, and these were Master Crandall Barre and Miss Seraphina Barre.

Crandall was a sturdy boy a year or two older than Juliana, with a haughty expression and cold dark eyes. "You're another poor relation," he had announced and stuck out his tongue.

Juliana, unused to other children, had been rather shocked, but she gave him the polite curtsey her mother had taught her and turned to his sister. Seraphina was about Juliana's age and took after her mother in looks, tall for her age and slender, with long blond hair carefully woven into braids and coiled on her head.

"Hullo," Seraphina said in a rather friendlier

manner than her brother. "Mummy said that you would play with me."

"Yes, if you'd like," Juliana had replied, relieved that this girl, at least, did not seem to actively dislike her as her brother did.

Juliana's eyes had gone past the two children to another boy who slouched against the bookcase behind him, his hands thrust into his pockets and a closed, sullen look on his face. He was a few years old than Juliana, with thick black hair, messily tumbled about his face, and black eyes. He looked at Juliana without expression as Juliana studied him curiously.

"Hullo," she had said finally, intrigued by the boy, who seemed to her much more interesting than the other two. "I am Juliana Holcott. Who are you?"

"What do you care?" he had replied.

"Nicholas!" the governess exclaimed.

"He lives with us," Seraphina volunteered.

"He's an orphan," Crandall had added with a sneer.

The boy cast a dark look at Crandall but said nothing.

"He is Nicholas Barre," the governess had explained to Juliana. "The children's cousin. Mr. Trenton Barre is his guardian. Mr. Barre is, as you know, a most generous man and kindly took him in after his parents' sailing accident. However, your question was quite rude. You must learn to mind your tongue."

Juliana had looked at the woman in surprise, saying, "But how else was I to learn who he was?"

Miss Emerson had frowned at her and cautioned her once again to curb her tongue. Juliana, remembering her mother's strictures, had swallowed her protest. She had glanced over at Crandall, who was smirking at her, then at Nicholas, who was watching her impassively.

They had begun their schoolwork. Juliana, whose scholarly father had taught her in the past, found their schoolwork easy enough and frankly boring. When Miss Emerson read to them from a book that Juliana herself had already read, it had been a struggle to keep her eyes open. A glance across the table told her that Nicholas, head down on the table, was not even pretending to listen. Juliana secretly wished she could be so bold.

Later in the afternoon, as Miss Emerson stood at the chalkboard on the wall, writing math problems, Crandall squirmed and twisted in his chair, obviously bored. After a moment he pulled out the contents of one of his pockets; then, after putting the rest back in his pocket, he picked up a small, smooth stone. Looking around, he noticed Juliana watching him, and he grinned, waggling his eyebrows at her, then turned and lobbed the pebble at the governess. The small stone missed her, cracking into the blackboard, and Miss Emerson jumped in surprise.

The governess whirled around, her eyes blazing. "Nicholas! That was a dangerous thing to do. Hold out your hands."

She marched across the room to him, grabbing up her ruler.

"I didn't do it!" Nicholas shot back furiously. "It was Crandall."

"And now you are adding lying to your sins?" the governess asked. "Hold out your hands this instant." She raised her ruler.

"I didn't do it!" Nicholas repeated as he rose to his feet and faced their teacher pugnaciously.

"How dare you defy me?" Miss Emerson cried, looking a little frightened. "Go to your room."

"But he's telling the truth," Juliana protested. "It was Crandall who did it. I saw him."

Nicholas's cold dark gaze turned to Juliana. The governess whirled to look at her, too, her face alight with anger.

"Don't lie to me, young lady," she told Juliana sternly.

"I'm not lying!" Juliana exclaimed, incensed. "I don't lie. It was Crandall. Nicholas didn't do anything."

Her words seemed only to infuriate the woman even more. "Has he corrupted you already? Or are you simply of the same sort of seed? No doubt that is why you, too, have been cast upon the world. Having to depend on others' generosity…"

Tears sprang into Juliana's eyes, and she was filled with a desire to fling herself at the woman, kicking and hitting.

"It's a good thing we don't have to depend on *your* generosity," Nicholas told the governess, his hands clenching and unclenching at his sides. "It's clear you haven't any."

"Go to your room. Right now. Let's see how defiant you are tomorrow after no supper tonight."

"That's not fair!" Juliana cried.

"And you, miss, will go stand in the corner until I tell you otherwise. I suggest you think over your actions just now and ask yourself whether a proper lady would say and do the things you just did."

Nicholas strode out of the schoolroom and into a small room adjoining it, slamming the door behind him.

Juliana took up her place in the corner, and later, when Miss Emerson allowed her to return to her lessons, she kept her mouth shut and ignored Crandall's smug looks. During luncheon, she sneaked a few bits of food into her pocket. Later, when the children were supposed to be reading but Miss Emerson had nodded off in her chair and the others had taken the opportunity to lay their own heads down on their desks to nap, Juliana crept over to Nicholas's door and eased it open.

Nicholas was standing on a chair, gazing out the high window, and he whipped around at her quiet entrance. Frowning, he hopped lightly down from the chair and came over to her.

"What are you doing here?" he asked in a none-too-friendly whisper. "The Dragon'll punish you if she catches you."

"She's asleep," Juliana whispered back, reaching into her pocket, then pulling out the napkin and passing it across to Nicholas.

He looked down at the roll and ham that Juliana had secreted there. He looked up at her questioningly. "Why are you doing this?"

"Because I thought you would be hungry," she replied simply.

He looked at her for another moment, then began to eat.

"You shouldn't do that, you know," he told her.

"Give you food?"

He shrugged. "And contradict the Dragon. Crandall

is always right, you see. And I am always wrong. That is the way to get along at Lychwood Hall."

"I don't understand. That's not fair."

Again he shrugged, the look in his eyes far older than his years. "Doesn't matter. That's how it is." He jerked his head toward the door. "You'd better go now."

Juliana nodded and crossed the room quietly. As she reached for the doorknob, Nicholas said quietly, "Thanks."

Juliana turned and smiled at him. He had smiled back at her, that rare, sweet smile that transformed his face. In that moment, the bond between them was formed.

The lessons Juliana learned on the first day were confirmed in the days that followed. Crandall and Seraphina Barre were never wrong and never punished. Nicholas was invariably held to blame for whatever misdeed occurred.

Juliana complained to her mother about the governess's unfairness, but her mother shook her head, the anxious frown that was becoming more and more familiar to Juliana forming on her forehead.

"Don't argue with your governess," Diana warned Juliana. "Obey her and be a good girl. Do you really think she would act that way on her own? She is hired by Mr. Barre. She would never do anything to cross him. No one here would."

Juliana had not understood at first exactly what her mother meant, but the very mention of Trenton Barre's name was enough to still her protests. Juliana found him to be a frightening man—quiet and calm, not a man who raged, but with a cold, flat look in his eyes that could quell anyone. Even Crandall's whining and tricks would stop short when his father turned that gaze on him.

Nicholas was the only person who would face his uncle's gaze, his back straight and his head raised, even when he knew that his "impertinence" would inevitably lead to a caning in Trenton Barre's study.

Juliana had never understood where Nicholas found the courage. However able she was to fight back with Crandall or to stand up to Miss Emerson's strictures, her spirit always quailed in front of Trenton. Though she called Mrs. Barre "Aunt Lilith," as Nicholas did, she found herself unable to address Trenton as anything but "sir." He dropped by their cottage periodically on a courtesy call, and Juliana dreaded the times when he came. Her mother would call her in to greet Mr. Barre, and she would have to join them in the parlor and give him a polite curtsey. Juliana was rarely able to lift her head and look him in the eye, which he seemed to find amusing, and as soon as he waved her away dismissively, she fled to her room and shut herself in for the remainder of his visit.

She knew her mother worried about these visits; she could see the tension in her mother's face when she heard his voice at the front door. Diana would look Juliana over anxiously, tugging at her braids and retying their bows, smoothing down her skirts, and Juliana was certain that her mother was afraid she would embarrass her or offend Mr. Barre somehow.

When Juliana complained about having to make her polite appearance, her mother would rebuke her. "Don't say that. The Barres have been very generous to us. We have nowhere to go if they don't let us stay here. You cannot offend Mr. Barre. And, please, do not say anything to him about that wicked boy."

"Nicholas is not wicked! It is Crandall who's the wicked one."

But the sight of her mother's pale face, stamped with anxiety, would make her stop. She schooled herself to be polite and endured her hours with Seraphina and Crandall.

At the time, Juliana had not thought about why the Barres had been so generous as to take her in. She had simply accepted it as a part of her life. As she grew older, though, she had wondered at Trenton and Lilith's generosity. They were not kind-hearted people, by any means, and while it was little enough expense for them to allow Juliana and her mother to live in the empty cottage on the estate, even such a small act of kindness seemed out of character for them. She had once asked her mother about it, but her mother had looked pained and a little frightened, as she always did when their precarious position at the Barre estate was discussed, and had told Juliana that she should not question their good fortune.

Looking back on it years later, when she was grown and had moved away, Juliana decided that Lilith and Trenton had invited them to live on the estate only because it would have looked bad in the eyes of Society if they had callously left a penniless, widowed cousin to starve. She was certain that their actions were not from some sudden upsurge of human generosity. And, when she found out that it was really Nicholas who would inherit the estate, with his uncle merely holding it in trust for him, Juliana realized that even *that* bit of generosity had been out of Nicholas's pocket, not their own.

During those first few years at Lychwood Hall, it was only her friendship with Nicholas that made her life bearable. Even though he had been four years older than she, he had allowed her to tag along after him, and he had more than once protected her from Crandall's malicious words and pinches. Even though Crandall could ensure that Nicholas would be punished for anything he did or said, still Crandall was scared of him. There was something about Nicholas's cold, implacable stare that made Crandall back down.

With Nicholas as her ally, Miss Emerson and the Barre children could be ignored. Even the fact that her mother never regained her once-happy personality could be endured.

It had devastated her when Nicholas left. Juliana had understood it, of course. His life was miserable at Lychwood Hall. He wanted to return to Cornwall, where he had lived as a boy with his parents. But his departure had left her chilled and alone.

Now, after all these years, Nicholas had come back. She could not help but wonder what impact his return would have on her life. Juliana sat down on the side of her bed, frowning. She picked up her hairbrush and began to brush out her hair as she thought.

Obviously Mrs. Thrall and Clementine thought that they could use her friendship with Nicholas to snare Clementine the Season's prize marital catch. Juliana sincerely hoped that her old friend would not be foolish enough to be taken in by Clementine's beauty. But neither was she so naive as to revive her own long-moribund dreams of love and marriage.

Indeed, she was not sure what she hoped for with Nicholas. She only knew how delightful it had felt to sweep around the dance floor in his arms, how her heart itself had seemed to warm at his smile. And, for the first time in a long time, she was looking forward to the morrow with excitement.

JULIANA WAS IN the sitting room early the next afternoon, embroidering fine stitches on a handkerchief, when the parlor maid announced the arrival of a visitor for her. Juliana took the engraved calling card and stood up, her heart picking up its beat, as the maid ushered Nicholas into the room.

"Nicholas!" She could not stop the delighted grin that spread across her face.

"Juliana." He crossed the room and took the hand she extended. "You look surprised. Did you think I would not come?"

"Of course not. I just…" She gave a little shrug. She could not really explain her surprise and pleasure that he had found calling on her important enough to do it so soon after seeing her last night. "Please, sit down."

She sat back down on the sofa, and Nicholas took the chair across from her. His tall, masculine presence somehow made the rather small sitting room seem even more cramped. Juliana was aware of a flutter of nerves in her stomach. She looked at him, suddenly unsure of what to say.

He removed his gloves, and she noticed the ring on his right hand, a plain gold signet ring. It was small and simple; she had not noticed it the night before. But now she stared at it, recognizing the ornate *H* engraved upon it.

"My father's ring!" she said in amazement.

"What?" Nicholas followed her gaze down to his hand. "Oh, yes, it is the ring you gave me when I left."

"You kept it all this time?" Strangely, she felt her throat close with tears.

"Of course." He grinned. "It's been my good luck charm."

Juliana swallowed hard. She felt inordinately pleased to learn that he had kept the memento of hers close to him for so long, yet at the same time she felt uncomfortable.

"I—it has been so long, I scarcely know where to start," she told him with a little laugh. "Where did you go? What have you been doing? The town is full of rumors about you, you know."

He made a wry face. "And what do they say about me?"

"Oh, that you have been everything from a

smuggler to a pirate to a spy. I suspect that the truth was probably something more prosaic—a sea merchant, perhaps."

His dark eyes lit with amusement. "All of them, perhaps, have some truth to them. Although I do not think I have ever actually stopped a ship and demanded chests of gold and gems."

"How disappointing," Juliana commented. "I shall not let all the young girls know. It will quite spoil the picture they have built up of you."

"Please," he said in a heartfelt manner. "I wish you *would* spoil their view of me. I should very much like to go somewhere without finding an empty-headed chit and her odious matchmaking mother determined to cast their lures at me."

"There is little hope of that," Juliana retorted. "You are reputed to be quite wealthy. And with a title, as well… I am afraid you will find your path quite littered with them until you finally decide to marry one of them."

"Never," he remarked, with a grimace.

"Then I should warn you that you should not linger here," Juliana went on.

Nicholas's dark brows rose, and then understanding dawned in his eyes. "The blond girl?"

Juliana nodded. "Clementine."

He opened his mouth to speak, but just at that moment, as if the conversation had called them, there was the sound of hurried steps outside, and Mrs. Thrall swept into the room.

"Lord Barre! What a delightful surprise! I am so sorry I was not here to greet you when you arrived."

With a rueful glance at Juliana, Nicholas stood up and made a polite bow. "Mrs. Thrall. We were just speaking about you."

The woman tittered, casting a flirtatious look at him. "Flatterer! I'll warrant I know who it is you are interested in seeing, and it is not me. Don't worry. Clementine will be down in a moment." She turned toward Juliana. "Juliana, dear, why don't you ring for tea? Let's have it in the drawing room." She turned back toward Nicholas with a smile. "It is much roomier, my lord. I cannot imagine what Juliana was thinking of to receive you in here."

Nicholas cast an indifferent glance around the room. "I was more interested in talking to Juliana than in the room."

"Prettily said, sir, but, still, I think we will find it more pleasant to converse in the front room."

There was little to do except go with Mrs. Thrall as she ushered Nicholas out of the room and down the hallway to the more formal drawing room at the front of the narrow house. Juliana rang for tea, as her employer had requested, and sat down, resigned to having her chat with Nicholas spoiled.

Clementine came rushing in a few minutes later, breathless and attractively flushed, and Juliana noted that she had paused to put on a different dress than she had been wearing earlier, and tie a new blue ribbon through her curls.

"Lord Barre!" She came forward and dropped him a pretty little curtsey, extending her hand and smiling at him. "I was so surprised when Mama told me that you had come to call on me."

Nicholas raised one brow at this bit of news. "Actually, I called on Miss Holcott."

Clementine's eyes widened a bit at this unexpected rebuff, but her mother jumped in to cover her momentary silence.

"Yes, we were so surprised to hear that dear Juliana was acquainted with you," Mrs. Thrall said. She wagged a playful finger at her employee. "Such a naughty girl you are, keeping your news a secret."

Juliana was tempted to reply that who she knew or didn't know was no business of Mrs. Thrall's, but Nicholas intervened, saying smoothly, "No doubt

Miss Holcott did not deem knowing a reprobate like me worthy of your attention, madam."

Mrs. Thrall's response to this was a shrill whinny of laughter. "Oh, you…" She snapped open her fan and covered the lower half of her face in a girlish way that looked bizarre, given that she was well into middle age.

Clementine, annoyed at not being the center of attention for so long, jumped back into the conversation. "Your life must have been so fascinating," she said to Nicholas, gazing at him with wide, limpid eyes. "You have seen so many places. I can scarce imagine what you must have done."

"Oh, yes," Mrs. Thrall agreed. "You must tell us about your travels, Lord Barre."

Juliana could envision the woman storing up tidbits to drop into her future conversations. "As Lord Barre was saying to me the other day…" or "Lord Barre told me he found India quite…"

She glanced at Nicholas, whose expression indicated that he had little desire to conduct a travelogue for Mrs. Thrall and her daughter. He glanced toward Juliana, then turned back to Mrs. Thrall, saying, "You must forgive me, madam. I am afraid I haven't time to stay and chat. I just came by to invite Miss Holcott to come riding tomorrow in my curricle." He looked over at Juliana. "If you would like to, I could come by in the morning."

"That would be lovely," Juliana replied quickly, not even looking toward Mrs. Thrall for permission. She was not about to let the woman ruin another visit with Nicholas by giving her a chance to thrust Clementine into their party.

"Excellent." Nicholas rose to his feet. "Now, if you will excuse me, I must take my leave of you ladies. Mrs. Thrall. Miss Thrall." He sketched a brief bow in their direction. "Miss Holcott."

"My lord."

Clementine stared after Nicholas as he left the room, too astonished for a moment to even say anything. Then she whirled around to face Juliana, her face contorting with anger. Juliana had a sudden, wicked desire that the girl's suitors could see her as she looked now.

"No!" Clementine exclaimed. "You cannot go. I won't allow it."

CHAPTER THREE

JULIANA'S BACK stiffened. "I beg your pardon?"

"Mama!" Clementine whirled around to face her mother. "You cannot allow Juliana to go with Lord Barre. I should be the one to ride in his curricle."

It took all Juliana's strength of will not to snap at the girl that *she* was the one Lord Barre had invited, not Clementine.

"Oh, no, dear," Mrs. Thrall assured her. "Don't you worry about that. Of course he had to invite Juliana. It would not do for a young girl like you to ride out with a man alone. You have to have Juliana as a chaperone."

"No, I don't," Clementine insisted. "It's perfectly all right for a lady to go for a ride in a vehicle with a gentleman alone, especially an open-air one like a curricle. Juliet Sloane told me ladies and gentlemen do it all the time."

Her mother looked uncertain. "Well, I know that it's unexceptionable for older ladies and gentlemen, but a girl your age, new to the Town, I'm not sure...."

She glanced toward Juliana. "What do you think, Juliana?"

"I think that it scarcely matters in this instance, since Lord Barre has already invited me to ride with him."

"That's true." Mrs. Thrall brightened. "And you can count on it, Clemmy, that if as highborn a gentleman as Lord Barre asked Juliana to come along, as well, then that is the way it should be."

Juliana had to grind her teeth together to keep from pointing out that Lord Barre had not invited Clementine along at all. It galled her to think of the tiresome girl inserting herself into her ride with Nicholas. She would chatter and giggle and flirt like mad, and Juliana would have no more chance to chat alone with him than she had had today. It was, she thought, the outside of enough. But she could scarcely tell her employer that her daughter was not welcome to come with them. Mrs. Thrall would all too likely forbid Juliana to go, as well.

Clementine pouted for a few minutes, flashing a look of intense dislike in Juliana's direction, until finally Mrs. Thrall suggested that the two of them go to a millinery shop and purchase a fetching new bonnet for Clementine to wear on the ride tomorrow. Juliana, she said, could take Fiona to the bookshop, as the tiresome girl had been begging to go.

Mrs. Thrall would have been surprised to learn that Juliana much preferred doing almost anything with her younger daughter Fiona than with Clementine or her mother. Fiona, at thirteen, had a livelier wit and more charming personality than Mrs. Thrall and Clementine combined. Juliana had spent a great deal of time with the girl, as Mrs. Thrall found Fiona's questions tiring and her interests peculiar, so she often shoved her younger daughter off into Juliana's capable hands.

Fiona, it turned out, was finding Clementine as obnoxious today as Juliana. "If I hear one more word about Lord Barre, I think I shall scream," she told Juliana as they strode up the street in the direction of the bookshop.

Juliana glanced down at the young girl and smiled. Fiona's coloring was much like her sister's, her hair pale blond and her eyes blue, but there the resemblance ended. Fiona was already as tall as her petite sister and showed no signs of stopping growing yet. Her face was squarish in shape, with a firm chin, and none of the soft, dimpled look for which Clementine was well-known. In sharp contrast to Clementine, her blue eyes were sharp and gleaming with intelligence.

"She has done nothing but talk of the man the

whole day," Fiona went on in irritation. "How handsome he is, how wealthy he is, how respected his name is."

"Lord Barre is a…remarkable man," Juliana told her.

The younger girl made a face. "No one could be the paragon that Clementine describes."

Juliana chuckled. "Well, that is probably true. But he is a friend of mine. We grew up together, and long ago he was the best friend I had."

"Really?" Fiona looked up at her in astonishment. "You are friends with the man Clemmy is going to marry?"

Juliana raised one brow skeptically. "Is that what she said?"

"Oh, yes. She said he would be head-over-heels about her in a few days." Fiona grimaced. "And she's usually right about men, even if she is abysmally ignorant about everything else. Men seem to be disgustingly taken with her."

Juliana automatically started to remind Fiona that she should not talk so disparagingly about her sister. But on second thought, she decided that it was wrong to reprimand the girl for speaking the truth. "I'm not sure that she will have the usual success with this one."

The evening before Juliana *had* wondered if

Nicholas might become attracted to Clementine's beauty. He had, after all, smiled and conversed with her. But his actions today had left little room for misinterpretation. He had left, pleading lack of time, shortly after Clementine had entered the room and taken over the conversation, and, whatever Mrs. Thrall might choose to think about Nicholas's invitation, he had *not* included Clementine in it. Mrs. Thrall and her daughter might be able to arrange it the next morning so that he had to take Clementine along, but Juliana was quite certain that he had not intended for Clementine to go.

Juliana, too, had seen Clementine wrap men around her finger, and she could not say with certainty that she might not be able to eventually work her wiles on Nicholas, but she did not think it would be easy.

"That would be wonderful," Fiona said, grinning. "He must be smarter than most of the men Clemmy sees."

"Yes, I rather think he is. Nicholas was always perceptive."

"How did you know him?"

"He was orphaned and had to live with his uncle. My mother was a cousin to his uncle's wife, and we lived in a cottage on the estate. Nicholas and I formed a—well, a sort of alliance of outcasts."

"Why was he an outcast? I mean, he is a lord now," Fiona pointed out.

"It was odd," Juliana agreed. "He wasn't treated like a future lord. I never even realized until I heard that he'd come into the title that he was the heir. His grandfather was ill and lived in Bath, and Nicholas's uncle was his guardian. The way everyone acted… well, I never asked, but I assumed that his uncle Trenton was the one who would inherit the title and the estate, and that after him, Trenton's son Crandall would. Trenton Barre ran the estate for his father, and everyone acted as if he were the lord and master."

"Why?" Fiona asked.

"Trenton Barre was a tyrant. I think probably everyone was too scared of him to cross him. There were people—some of the servants and some of the farmers who lived around there—who were nice to Nicholas. But in a secretive way, not in front of his uncle. I never understood why Uncle Trenton disliked Nicholas so. Now I can see that it was because he knew that Nicholas would inherit the title, not him or his son. It must have galled him terribly to know that one day he would have to turn over the estate he ran to Nicholas. That he would have to call him 'my lord.'"

"Well, he can't have been terribly smart. I mean,

wouldn't it have been better to be kind to him? Maybe then he wouldn't have had to lose everything when Lord Barre came into the title."

"I don't think Uncle Trenton thought that way. It seemed to always be all or nothing with him. He had to be in command. I think he viewed the estate as his and hated Nicholas for being a reminder that it really was not." Juliana shrugged. "At any rate, he didn't have to see Nicholas succeed to the title. He died several years ago."

"It sounds as if he was a terrible man," Fiona commented.

"He was. I was glad I was in Europe with Mrs. Simmons at the time he died and couldn't be expected to return for the funeral. I would have found it difficult to honor him."

They walked on in silence for a few more minutes, and then Fiona said, "Well...if Lord Barre is a friend of yours, then I suppose I cannot dislike him. As long as he does not fall in love with Clementine, that is."

"Yes," Juliana agreed. "I think that I would have a hard time liking him, too, if he did that."

Fiona began to talk about the book she had just finished reading, and Juliana listened to her chatter, her mind only partly on what the girl was saying. The rest was occupied with mentally sorting through her small wardrobe, trying to find a dress that was not horribly dull to wear on her ride the next morning.

That, she soon realized, would be an impossible task. All her dresses were plain and sewn of sensible fabrics in dark shades of gray, blue and brown, chosen for their durability and practicality, with an eye to giving Juliana the appearance of dull reliability that people sought in a paid companion. Companions, after all, were not usually hired in the hopes that they would be entertaining and interesting people to have around. They were there to provide a certain respectability for a woman on her own, or to fetch and carry and respond to someone's boring conversation with apparent interest.

Juliana found that she could not bear to appear the next morning looking dowdy, so that evening she took out her best bonnet and re-attached the saucy little cluster of cherries that she had removed from it in order to dress it down. There was little she could do to the dress to improve it other than add a small ruffle of lace around the modestly high neck and long sleeves.

She thought of sitting beside Clementine, who would be wearing a doubtlessly fetching new hat, and she could not help but feel a stab of jealousy. She had spent her life around people who had more than she did, and Juliana thought that she had done very well at not feeling envious. She had always tried to think instead of the graces of her life —good health and reasonably attractive looks, and her ability to make her own way in the world without being at the mercy of others, as her mother had been. She was free and had at least a small amount of savings, and she had made some very good friends in her life. These things were much more than some people had, she knew, and she normally felt grateful for them and did not hunger over what others possessed.

But this time she could not shrug off the black resentment that crept over her as she thought of Clementine wedging her way into this moment that belonged to Juliana. Clementine would talk and preen and spoil the moment. There was nothing she could do, however, except hope that Clementine would, in her usual way, be so late that they could leave without her.

Unfortunately, the next morning Clementine was in the sitting room ready to go only minutes after Juliana. She was flushed with excitement, her eyes sparkling and her cheeks rosy, looking, Juliana had to admit, quite lovely. And the hat she had bought yesterday was indeed fetching, a chip straw with a shallow brim that showed her face to full advantage and tied with a great blue satin ribbon that accentuated the blue of her eyes.

When Nicholas was announced a few minutes later, he strolled into the room, his eyes sweeping over Clementine and her mother. "Mrs. Thrall. Miss Thrall."

His gaze came to rest on Juliana, and a faint smile lightened his dark visage. "Juliana. Are you ready?"

"Yes." Juliana rose, glancing toward Clementine, who also stood up.

"My lord," Clementine said, smiling prettily and coming forward, reaching out to tuck her hand into his arm. "I am all aflutter. Is your curricle terribly high-seated? I shall be quite frightened if it is." She let out a little chuckle, inviting him to share in the amusement of her charmingly silly feminine fear.

Nicholas looked back at her, his face wooden, and did not move to extend his arm to her. He said only, "I am sorry, Miss Thrall, there must have been some sort of misunderstanding. My invitation this morning was for Miss Holcott."

Clementine's jaw dropped at the obvious snub, and Juliana had to press her lips together tightly to keep a smile from forming on them.

Mrs. Thrall, too, stared in astonishment, but she recovered more quickly than her daughter, saying, "I—I presumed it was a general invitation. After all, it is scarcely proper for a gentleman and lady to jaunt about the city alone in a carriage."

Nicholas turned his flat dark gaze on the older woman. "It is gratifying that you are so concerned about Miss Holcott's good name, madam, but I assure you, it is perfectly acceptable. It is an open carriage. And quite small. I fear only two people are able to ride in it at a time, which is the reason that my invitation was specifically to Juliana."

Mrs. Thrall could think of no reply, but simply stood, looking at him. Nicholas seized the opportunity to turn and offer Juliana his arm. Juliana hurried forward and tucked her hand through his. She was not about to dawdle and give her employer time to recover her wits and forbid her to go.

Nicholas was apparently of the same mind as she, for he swept her down the hall and out the front door at a fast clip, scarcely giving Juliana even a moment to appreciate the gleaming new yellow curricle before he handed her up into it. Taking the reins from his groom, who had been walking the horses to keep them warm while he was inside, Nicholas climbed up onto the seat next to Juliana.

"Abominable woman!" he exclaimed, slapping the reins to set the horses in motion.

Juliana let out a laugh of delight at having eluded

Mrs. Thrall's schemes. There would be the devil to pay when she got back, no doubt, but for the moment, she did not care. It was too wonderful to be out with Nicholas, free for the next hour, perched in a vehicle that was the height of fashion, and from which she had a wonderful view of all the hustle and bustle of London. Juliana set her hat firmly on her head, tied the ribbon beneath her chin and looked over at Nicholas with a smile.

Nicholas grinned back. "How the devil did you wind up with those two, anyway?"

Juliana shrugged. "It isn't always easy to find a position as a companion. People usually want someone older than I am and more…well…"

"Unattractive?" Nicholas hazarded a guess.

Juliana cast him a sideways glance, smiling. "Why, thank you, sir." *Was she actually flirting with Nicholas?* Somehow she could not bring herself to care about that, either. "But I was about to say 'obsequious.'"

He let out a bark of laughter. "I can see that you have not changed. I cannot picture you at someone else's beck and call. How did you ever seize upon the idea of being a companion?"

"It seemed a natural avenue, after living with Seraphina and your aunt Lilith all those years," Juliana replied. "They sent me to finishing school with Seraphina." She remembered her mother's pleasure at Juliana's being given the opportunity to go to a good school for girls, something they obviously could never have afforded. But she, of course, had known the reason behind Trenton and Lilith's apparent generosity.

"They needed someone to keep an eye on Seraphina and make sure she didn't get into any trouble. Which was not an easy task, I can assure you. Seraphina was just as flighty and silly a young woman as she was as a child. And then, after we finished, Seraphina had a tour of the continent. The war was over by then. So, again, I went along to help, and when that was over, I saw that I was amply prepared to be a companion. I knew all about fetching and carrying, and listening to boring conversation and flattering someone."

"Did Aunt Lilith turn you out?" he asked, a dangerous note in his voice.

"Oh, no. I could have stayed. I didn't flatter myself that Aunt Lilith liked me, but she would have liked my help in getting Seraphina through her debut, and she would not have wanted the gossip about her throwing a poor young girl upon the world. But I could not stand living in that prison any longer, and with my mother gone, there was really no reason to. Lilith was just as happy that I decided to leave, I think. If I had stayed, she would have had to bring me out, as well, at least in some small fashion, and that would have galled her."

Juliana did not add that Crandall had begun to change his tactics when she grew up, from pulling her hair and playing mean tricks on her to trying to corner her in the library and sneak a kiss, or run a caressing hand over her body. His pursuit had been one of the major reasons that she had been determined to leave Lychwood Hall. Aunt Lilith, she thought, suspected that something was going on, but Lilith had been convinced that the situation was the other way around, even accusing Juliana on one occasion of trying to ensnare her son.

"So Aunt Lilith wrote a letter of recommendation for me, and I set out on my own. It took a little while, but then someone hired me to take care of his aging mother." She also did not add that that bit of employment had ended when the man who had hired her showed up at the door of her bedroom one night, drunk and leering and making fumbling advances to her. "After a time I met Mrs. Simmons, and it was actually quite pleasant after that."

Nicholas frowned. "I dislike your being at that Thrall woman's beck and call."

"Nor do I like it," Juliana agreed candidly.

"However, it is a price that I am willing to pay for my freedom. At least this is a straightforward business transaction. I am not dependent on anyone's charity."

Nicholas had maneuvered through the streets as they talked, and they had reached the sylvan paths of Hyde Park, where there was far less traffic, and he could relax and turn his attention away from controlling the horses. He looked over at Juliana.

It was still a little something of a surprise to him each time he looked at her. He had known she would be older, of course, though he had been able to recognize the child he had known in her face. But still, somehow, it was disconcerting to see the woman she had become, the sweetly familiar face of his childhood turned into a beauty.

Hers was not the pale, insipid beauty of one such as the Thrall girl, whom Nicholas found crushingly boring. Juliana's beauty lay not just in her thick dark-brown hair, sternly constrained in a firm knot at the base of her neck, although it was the sort of hair that made a man's fingers itch to pull out her pins and release it in a luxuriant tumble around her shoulders. Nor was it only the well-modeled features of her face. Hers was a beauty that shone out of her lively gray eyes and blossomed in the smile that curved her lips, a loveliness born of strength and personality, and the multitude of small things that made Juliana uniquely herself.

He knew her, and yet he did not know her, and he found the combination compelling. Gazing at her now, Nicholas was aware of a sudden desire to lean over and kiss that softly curving mouth, to taste what he was sure would be the piquant sweetness of her lips.

His eyes darkened, straying to her mouth, and it was only with some inner firmness that he was able to pull his gaze away. He stared straight ahead above his horses' heads for a few moments, pondering the instant of desire that had just flashed through him. This was not the sort of feeling he should be having about Juliana, he told himself.

She was the beloved companion of his childhood, the girl who had provided the only warmth he had known after his parents' deaths. He had been eager to find her when he returned to England, but it had been the eagerness of an old close friend...of a brother, say. He loved her, he thought, as much as he found himself able to love anyone, but it was a small, pure, uncomplicated love, a deep fondness for a childhood memory.

Yet here Juliana was, not at all a memory, looking very much like a desirable woman, and the feeling that had just speared through him was not years-old devotion but the swift lust of a man for a woman.

The feeling shook him. It seemed perverse to experience this sort of sensation about someone almost a sister to him. Had any other man expressed feeling such a thing for her, he would have taught him a quick, brutal lesson.

This unexpected desire was certainly not something upon which he could act. Juliana trusted him; he could never take advantage of her, even in the smallest way. There were many, he knew, who considered him unscrupulous, even wicked, and he admitted that he was not a good man. But he would never do something so dastardly as to take advantage of Juliana's kind feelings for him.

Moreover, aside from the importance of not violating Juliana's trust in him, there was the matter of her reputation. She was a lady, and her reputation must be above reproach. It was even more imperative that nothing besmirch her name, given that she had to make her own way in the world. It was far too easy for even unproved black marks to attach to the reputation of a woman who had no family to protect her and no high name to bolster hers. He could and would, of course, defend her name, but it was a sad truth that merely the defense of a man of his uncertain reputation would probably only damage her name further.

Nicholas knew, therefore, that he could not even pay her particular attention without causing scandalous talk about her. He should not call on her too often nor take her out on the dance floor more than every once in a while. It would have been more politic, he was sure, to have taken the annoying Thrall chit with them today in a larger vehicle. It would have deflected attention from Juliana onto Clementine, and he frankly had little regard for whether tongues wagged about that girl. However, he had selfishly wanted Juliana all to himself, at least this once.

There were far too many looks being cast in their direction from the carriages and riders they passed, and Nicholas knew that the gossip circuit would soon be buzzing about the woman with whom Lord Barre had been seen in the Park. He would have to refrain from going out riding with Juliana again for a week or two, and it would be wise not to even call on her again for a few days. Nicholas despised having to kowtow to such arbitrary constraints, but he could not jeopardize Juliana's reputation.

Juliana, looking up at Nicholas, had seen the subtle change in his face, the way his eyes flickered involuntarily to her lips. Her breath had caught in her throat, and her stomach had tightened. He was about to kiss her, she had thought.

Then he had looked abruptly away. She relaxed, not quite sure whether she felt relief or disappointment. Indeed, she was not quite certain anything at all had happened. *Had she mistaken the look in his eyes*?

Surely she was not wrong. There had been a spark, an infinitesimal tightening of his face, and something inside her had responded. She could not deny that response—eager, yet also a trifle wary, a tingle of warmth that moved through her with the speed of lightning. It had all been faster, more subtle, than thought. Instinctive, but beyond doubt.

She cast another sideways glance up at Nicholas. He was staring straight ahead, his jaw set. She wondered what he thought, what he felt. *Had he regretted that momentary impulse*? With a certain disappointment, she realized that he probably had. *Why else would he have turned away so abruptly*?

It was a lowering thought. If he had felt a flash of masculine interest in her, he had clearly and immediately regretted it. He was right, of course. Even though they had once been close, she was clearly someone whom he would not think of courting and marrying. The difference in their stations in life was now vast. All she could hope for was friendship from him, and desire would only hinder that.

He had been correct, and if it wounded her pride a little, that was simply something she would have to get over. It wasn't, she reminded herself, as if she had *wanted* him to kiss her. He was, after all, virtually a stranger to her after all these years. And she was much too mature and practical now to give weight to the romantic adolescent dreams she had had about him. It did not matter that she had felt some sort of reaction when she thought he was about to kiss her, that there had been a flash of warmth in her midsection and a sudden tingling awareness of seemingly every inch of her skin. Why, she was not entirely sure whether what she had felt had been eagerness or fear.

And whatever she might have felt, she was, after all, the master of herself and her emotions. A kiss would have been highly improper, and she was glad—yes, glad—that Nicholas had turned away without giving in to his impulse.

Still, she could not help but be very aware of Nicholas now—of his warmth, his size, his very presence beside her on their high perch. She looked up at his face, sharp in profile, his skin taut across the slicing arc of his cheekbones, the only softening feature the thick brush of his lashes.

He must have felt her gaze upon him, for he turned his head toward her. Juliana glanced quickly away, a blush rising in her cheeks at having been caught staring at him. She would hate for him to think that she was overly bold.

Her eyes strayed to his hands, large and firm on the reins, encased in supple kid driving gloves. She remembered the touch of his hand on her waist as they danced, warm and strong. There was something about the memory of his touch that made her a trifle breathless.

A breeze caressed her flushed cheeks and lifted a few stray tendrils of her hair. She felt as if her skin was more sensitive than normal, more alive to the warmth of the sun or the brush of air against it.

Juliana clasped her hands in her lap and looked down at them. These sorts of thoughts would never do, she told herself. And Nicholas would think her a tongue-tied dolt, the way she was sitting here, saying nothing.

They passed an open landaulet, occupied by two middle-aged ladies who eyed them sharply. Juliana felt sure that by this evening, the word would be all over fashionable society that Lord Barre had driven

out in the Park this morning with an unknown girl—
and one of such plain dress and demeanor, too.

"They will be gossiping about you, you know,"
she told him. "It will cause great speculation that you
are with a female whom none of them recognize."

Nicholas shrugged carelessly. "They always gossip about me. Or, at least, that is what people tell me.
The good thing about it is that *I* never hear it." He
glanced at her. "Will it bother you?"

She smiled at him. "Oh, no. As I said, they won't
know who I am. And even if they did…as you said,
I won't hear it. What worries me more is what Mrs.
Thrall will say when I return."

"Perhaps I should come in with you. A few minutes
spent with that tedious girl might improve her mood."

"No, I shan't ask you to subject yourself to that."
Juliana smiled. "I am sure that you will find yourself
plagued by having to talk to her far more times than
you will wish—that is, I mean, if you intend to call
at the house again." She stumbled to a halt, realizing
that all unintentionally she had put herself forward,
assuming that he intended to continue his visits with
her. "I'm sorry. I have put you in an awkward
position. Aunt Lilith always told me I was far too
blunt in my speech."

"Nonsense. I find plain speaking refreshing. Of

course I intend to call upon you again…even if it does mean having to put up with the Thrall women."

"Do not come too often," Juliana warned him.

He lifted his brows, amusement touching his dark eyes. "Do you find my presence so tedious?"

"No." Juliana chuckled. "Of course not. But Mrs. Thrall and Clementine will be convinced that you are madly in love with her if you call very often."

"Perish the thought," he responded. "Although… mayhap I could use her as a ruse. That way 'twould do no harm to your reputation if I called upon you often."

Juliana was aware of a twinge of jealousy at the thought of Nicholas pretending to court Clementine. "Yes, but then you would be expected to propose to Clementine or else be considered a cad."

He shrugged. "I have been considered far worse things. Indeed, I have *done* far worse things."

"If you think that, then you have not spent day after day in conversation with Clementine."

Nicholas laughed. "Ah, Juliana, I cannot tell you how relieved I am that you have not grown up to be dull."

Juliana could not help but smile. "And I am glad to be around someone with whom I need not rein in my tongue."

"I suspect that in the Thrall family, much of what you say is not even understood."

"No, Clementine has a younger sister who is quite bright. Her name is Fiona, and I cannot imagine how she came to be in that family."

"Is there a Mr. Thrall?"

"Oh, yes, but he had the good sense to remain in Yorkshire during Clementine's Season."

"Then perhaps that is where this Fiona gets her intelligence."

"You are probably right."

They continued to chat in this light way as they made their way through the Park. They passed a number of other people, some in vehicles, others on horseback. It was the fashionable thing to ride in the morning—though how so many of them managed to be up by this hour after the late nights at various parties, Juliana was not sure. Some of the people nodded to Nicholas or spoke to them. Others clearly hoped to catch his eye and perhaps receive a nod from him.

"A number of people seem to want to know you," Juliana remarked.

"It is remarkable how popular a title makes one," Nicholas retorted.

"Oh, it takes more than a title," Juliana said. "Money helps."

Again his grin flashed, softening the hard lines of his face. Neither of them was aware of how others' interest in Juliana's identity was heightened by the look he turned toward her.

"Cynic," Nicholas told her. "Don't you know that you are supposed to protest that it is my wonderful qualities that others admire?"

"It has been my experience that most people never bothered to look for your wonderful qualities," Juliana answered truthfully. "I am sure none of these people are aware of them, either."

"Indeed, I think you were always my only champion."

"Not much of one, I'm afraid. I never managed to save you from punishment, as I recall."

He shrugged carelessly. "No one could have, much less a nine- or ten-year-old girl. My fate was sealed the day my father and mother died."

"Your grandfather could have taken you in," Juliana pointed out. "He should have taken an interest in you, at least."

"His only interest was in his various aches and pains, real or otherwise. There may have been some estrangement between him and my father. I don't remember visiting him or his coming to us before my parents died. The first time I remember seeing him was at my parents' funeral, and then he turned me over to Uncle Trenton. And from my uncle's reports of me, I feel sure he felt little desire to see me."

"'Twas no excuse," Juliana maintained stoutly.

He looked at her, his dark eyes unreadable. "I think that you don't remember me as I was. You were a better friend to me than I deserved."

"Nonsense," Juliana retorted. "I knew you were not a saint. You were quite often sullen, and you were rude to our governess and frequently bloodied Crandall's nose."

"Ah, then you do remember."

"Yes. I also remember that few people deserved having their noses bloodied as much as Crandall. He was a vile boy who grew up into a vile young man. And Miss Emerson was not merely strict, she was unkind. Perhaps you should have been less hard on Seraphina. She wasn't really mean, I think, merely selfish and silly. But how could you not have hated your uncle? He was a terrible man. When I heard that he died, I can tell you that I felt not the slightest bit of regret."

"Nor did I." He slanted a smile at her. "Are we villains together, then?"

"I think not. Merely human."

"You do not know what else I have done," he

reminded her, watching her steadily. "It's been many years that I've been gone."

Juliana looked into his eyes, deep and black, and she saw in them, as she had seen those many years ago, a terrifying aloneness. Impulsively, she put her hand upon his arm, saying, "I think that whatever you have done, Nicholas, you did because you had to."

"And does that make it right?"

"I don't know. But I think it means you do not have a wicked heart."

He gazed at her for a long time, unspeaking, and the lines of his face softened subtly. He shifted the reins to one hand and placed his free hand over hers on his arm. For a moment they remained that way, unspeaking, and then he moved, letting his hand fall away.

"And your heart, I think, is a generous one," he said lightly, and the moment was past. "Now, we had best get you home before your Mrs. Thrall starts breathing fire."

Juliana's hand tingled where his hand had touched it, and her cheeks were suddenly warm. It took a great deal of restraint not to lay her other hand on the spot where he had touched her; such a gesture would, she was sure, reveal too much of what she was feeling. She wished, with an intensity that both surprised and shook her, that he had not taken his hand away. That he had, instead, leaned closer to her and kissed her.

Juliana pressed her lips together tightly and directed her gaze out onto the street—anywhere but at Nicholas. He considered her a friend. She could not let him know that what she felt for him was something different.

CHAPTER FOUR

WHEN JULIANA RETURNED to the house, she found Fiona loitering in the hallway just inside the front door. The girl had obviously been waiting for her, for she turned to her with a sigh of relief and, taking her hand, pulled Juliana into the empty front drawing room. Juliana opened her mouth to ask the girl what she was doing, but Fiona held her finger to her lips, glancing upstairs in a rather dramatic fashion.

Fiona closed the door behind them softly and turned to face Juliana. "You had best stay out of Clementine's way. She has been storming about the house for the past hour, ranting about you. She's in a rare snit."

"Oh, dear." Juliana sighed. She had thoroughly enjoyed the ride alone with Nicholas, but as she had expected, she would have to pay for it now.

"What happened? She talks as if you'd ruined her life," Fiona remarked. "It's much worse than when I lost her favorite comb last month."

"I'm afraid that Lord Barre took me for a ride in his curricle without inviting Clementine to come along."

Fiona let out a laugh. "Is that it? I wondered what she was talking about. She kept saying you had stolen something from her, but I knew you wouldn't have done anything like that."

Juliana grimaced. "I suppose I'd best go face the music."

"I wouldn't, if I were you. I've always found it's better to let her calm down a bit. She'll still be quite angry, but she'll be less likely to slap you. Why don't we go for a stroll?"

Juliana was frankly tempted, but she replied, "No. Better not get *you* into trouble, as well. But I appreciate the forewarning."

She left Fiona and went out into the hall, starting toward the rear sitting room. Fiona was doubtless right about giving Clementine a chance to calm down, and while Juliana was not about to hide from the girl, it only made sense not to provoke her.

However, Clementine apparently heard the sound of Juliana's footsteps on the floor, for she appeared at the head of the stairs. "There you are!"

"Hello, Clementine," Juliana said pleasantly, nodding to her.

"How could you?" Clementine exclaimed.

"I am afraid I don't know what you mean," Juliana replied calmly. "Why don't we retire to the sitting room and talk about it?"

"Talk about it? Talk about it?" Clementine's voice dripped disgust. "Do you think that you can try to steal Lord Barre from me and then make it all right by talking about it?"

Juliana kept a firm grip on her own temper, saying, "Clementine, I assure you that I did not try to steal Lord Barre from you."

"What else would you call it?" Clementine retorted, color flaring in her cheeks. "You cut me out! You—"

"I did no such thing, I assure you. Lord Barre explained that there was room for only two in his curricle, and—"

"And I should have been the one to go with him." Clementine clattered down the stairs, stopping on the second step from the bottom—acting from, Juliana presumed, a desire to loom over her, since she was taller than the girl.

"Lord Barre invited me," Juliana pointed out. "I could scarcely have made him take you instead."

"You connived against me. You inveigled him into inviting you."

"Clementine, please calm yourself. This is non-sensical," Juliana protested.

Clementine's mother came down the stairs like a battleship in full sail, and Juliana turned toward her. "Mrs. Thrall, I—"

The older woman held up her hand peremptorily, saying, "Don't think you can get around me, now, miss. You have overstepped your bounds, and that's clear."

"I beg your pardon?" Juliana had not expected Mrs. Thrall to be pleased with her, but this patently unreasonable charge got her back up.

"I'll not have you working your wiles on men while you're under my roof, I'll have you know."

"What?" Juliana stared at her employer, too stunned to think how to reply to this.

"Oh, don't think I don't know what you're about," Mrs. Thrall told her, nodding her head. "Clemmy is too innocent and naive to realize what you've been up to, but I'm not. I know what you did, how you seduced Lord Barre into taking you out alone—the promises you must have made. Where did you go while you were out?"

"How dare you?" Juliana shot back, her face utterly pale except for two furious spots of color that flared in her cheeks. "You have no reason to say such things about me! I would never—"

Mrs. Thrall waved away Juliana's protests. "Oh, I know all right. Why else would a man choose to invite you and not my Clementine? It doesn't take a genius to figure out the lures you were casting out…the sort of enticements that no man, even a gentleman, could resist. And I won't have it, miss, not in my household, with two impressionable young girls here."

"Mama! No!" Fiona gasped from where she stood at the doorway to the drawing room, watching the scene unfold before her.

Juliana stalked forward to Mrs. Thrall, towering over the squat woman. She had managed over the years to hold her temper under all sorts of provocation, but this accusation was too much for her.

"There has never been the slightest stain on my name," Juliana said fiercely, her voice trembling with the force of her indignation. "My reputation is unblemished."

"Hah!" Clementine responded. "Mama has the right of it. You knew that he admired me, and you seduced him into taking you for a ride."

"Don't be any more foolish than you already are, Clementine," Juliana snapped, the words tumbling out of her. "Nicholas did not admire you. He didn't even know who you were. He was my friend from many years ago, and he asked me to go out with him in his curricle because he wanted to talk with me. And he did not ask you to go because he didn't want you to. Not every man in the world is going to fall at your feet."

Before Clementine could do anything more than gape at her, mouth opening and closing like a fish, Juliana swung toward her mother. "And as for casting out lures or staining her precious reputation, I would suggest that you look toward your daughter first. Clementine is an outrageous flirt, and I have to keep my eye on her the entire time at every ball to make sure she does not slip out onto the terrace with any man who asks her. If you don't put some reins on her, she is going to come a cropper, and I can assure you that if she makes a serious misstep, she will be ruined in Society. And no amount of beauty will overcome that. However attractive she might be, any closer acquaintance with her will show just how spoiled, selfish, vain and foolish Clementine is, with the result that over the course of time, a great number of her conquests will drop away. If you expect her to marry well, you had better make sure that she is the sort of girl that a gentleman's mother will accept as a daughter-in-law, not just the sort of beauty that callow youths dangle after."

Juliana stopped and drew a long breath, a great sense of calm falling over her. She realized that she had doubtless just lost her position there, but she could not regret it…at least, not just yet. She was too filled with a sense of well-being at having at last been able to express her true feelings.

"Leave this house!" Mrs. Thrall rasped, rage suffusing her face. "Right now! Do you hear me?"

"Gladly," Juliana responded, stepping around the woman and starting up the stairs.

"And don't expect any reference from me!" Mrs. Thrall called after her.

"I wouldn't dream of it." Juliana continued up the stairs and down the hall to her room. Behind her, she heard Fiona run past her sister and mother and up the stairs after her.

"Miss Holcott! Wait!" Fiona called.

Juliana turned at the door of her room and looked back at the girl. She felt a twinge of regret when she saw Fiona's unhappy face.

"Please do not leave, Miss Holcott," Fiona went on, drawing close to her.

"I am sorry. I have no choice. I'm afraid your mother has let me go." Juliana turned the doorknob and went into her room.

Fiona trailed after her. "She is just angry. She will calm down, and then I am sure she will regret it."

"I'm not so sure, after what I said." Juliana looked down at Fiona, then sighed and said, "I am sorry. I should not have said what I did about your sister."

"No." Fiona stood and watched as Juliana opened the small chest at the foot of her bed and began to fill it with clothes from her drawers. "I am afraid you are right. Clementine is a very silly creature, and quite selfish. And you should not have to endure her scolding you because Lord Barre did not fall at her feet. I hate to see you go."

"I shall miss you, as well," Juliana assured the girl honestly, then went over to curl an arm around Fiona's shoulders affectionately. "Perhaps your mother will let you visit me sometime."

"Perhaps," Fiona replied doubtfully. "Where will you go?"

Juliana realized that she had not even thought about where she would go or what she would do now. She had indeed acted hastily. Still, she could not regret it.

"I think I will go to my friend's house. Eleanor Townsend—well, Lady Scarbrough now, since she has married. Here," she said, turning and taking a pencil from her pocket, and a piece of paper from one of the dresser drawers. "I shall write down her address for you, so that you may come to see me. We went to school together, and she has always extended me an open invitation to stay with her."

It did not take long to pack her belongings, and Juliana was soon ready to leave. She rang for a footman to carry down her trunk, then turned and hugged Fiona goodbye.

The girl's eyes filled with tears, and Juliana felt a tug at her own heartstrings. Even though she had been here only a few months, she had developed a deep fondness for Fiona.

"I will come see you," Fiona promised, her voice muffled against Juliana's shoulder. "Even if I have to sneak out of the house."

"Don't get into any trouble," Juliana told her. She knew that the "right" thing to tell the girl was to obey her mother, but she was also quite sure that Fiona was far smarter than Mrs. Thrall and better able to judge what should be done.

Juliana left quickly after that, picking up her small bag and going lightly down the backstairs to bid farewell to the household staff. When she came around to the front of the house, she found that the footman who had carried her trunk downstairs had already hailed a hack for her and strapped her trunk on the back of it. He helped her up into the cab, closing the door after her, and the vehicle rattled off.

Here she was, once again, without employment and with no prospect of any. Juliana leaned back with a sigh against the seat, and for the first time in the last two hours thought about her situation.

It was then that she realized Nicholas no longer knew where she was.

CHAPTER FIVE

LADY SCARBROUGH'S HOUSE was an elegant white Queen Anne-style mansion that took up a good third of one of the most fashionable blocks in Mayfair. As Juliana climbed down from the carriage, she heard the driver let out a low whistle, and he hopped down to get his money, tipping his hat to her more respectfully than he had when she got into his vehicle.

While he removed her trunk from the back of the cab, Juliana walked up to the door and used the large brass knocker. The door was opened a moment later by a short, square man with the misshapen ears and oft-broken nose that betokened a bare-knuckle fighter. He was not the sort of person one expected for a footman and even less for the butler who ran the household, but Juliana knew that was his position. Like many of her friend Eleanor's employees, he was unorthodox, competent and intensely loyal.

"Miss Holcott!" he said now, his rough face lightening into a grin. "It's good to see you. Miss Eleanor will be so happy. Come in, come in."

"Hello, Bartwell," Juliana replied, following him inside and handing him the small bag she carried. "Sorry to arrive on the doorstep this way. I hadn't time to send Miss—I mean, Lady Scarbrough—a note."

"Never worry about that, miss. There's always a room ready for you," he assured her, then turned to say to a young man approaching them from the rear of the house, "You, Fletcher, get the young lady's trunk and take it up to the blue bedchamber."

Like Bartwell, Fletcher was dressed in neat black and white, but he did not wear livery, another oddity of Eleanor's servants. They were a mixture of nationalities, Bartwell American like Eleanor herself, as was Eleanor's personal maid, while Fletcher and most of the other servants were English, and the cook was decidedly French.

The servants were not the only oddities about Eleanor's household. She was in the habit of helping others—indeed, there were some caustic souls who deemed her an inveterate meddler—and she had in the course of the past few years acquired two orphaned children, one an energetic young French girl named Claire and the other an American lad named Seth, as well as a young woman from India whom Eleanor had rescued from being thrown on a funeral pyre along with her dead husband, and who had become the children's nanny. Her business manager was a well-spoken black man whom Eleanor's father had bought out of slavery and sent to school. It made for a lively and sometimes noisy household, but everyone in it was devoted to Eleanor.

"Miss Eleanor is in her study," Bartwell told her. It was clear, Juliana thought, that despite her marriage to Sir Edmund, Eleanor would never be Lady Scarbrough to Bartwell, but always the Miss Eleanor she had been since he had been employed by her father when Eleanor was only a child. "Would you like me to take you to her, or would you prefer that I show you to your room, so that you may freshen up?"

Juliana replied that she would see Eleanor first, feeling it incumbent upon her to at least go through the formality of asking to stay, even though she knew her friend would never think of refusing her hospitality.

She and Eleanor had been friends for twelve years, and despite the different paths their lives had taken and their frequent separations, their friendship was still as fast as it had been from the first. They had met at the finishing school to which Juliana had been sent with Seraphina Barre. It had been the intention of Seraphina's parents that Juliana watch over the girl, helping her with her studies, as she often needed, and making sure that she didn't get into any scrapes. Seraphina had accepted Juliana's help as her due, but she had not considered her a bosom friend. That position was reserved for other girls of similar wealth and consequence.

Juliana was, therefore, left largely alone at the school by Seraphina and her group, as well as by most of the other students. All were aware that Juliana's friendship would do nothing to improve their position in Society. But she had quickly become friends with another girl who was also considered an outsider. Eleanor Townsend, although very wealthy, was an American and, according to the general opinion at the Miss Blanton School for Girls, decidedly odd. Juliana, of course, had liked her immediately.

As Bartwell led Juliana down the hall to Eleanor's study, she heard the sound of a piano being played, the music ending abruptly, starting again hesitantly, then stopping.

"Sir Edmund is in the music room," Bartwell explained in an aside. "Composing."

Juliana nodded. She did not know Eleanor's husband well. Eleanor had married him only two months earlier, in a small wedding that Juliana had attended. He was a slender, quiet man who seemed, as best Juliana could tell, to live on the periphery of Eleanor's life. When she had called at the house since the marriage, Sir Edmund had usually been sequestered in the music room or upstairs in his bedroom, nursing another of the coughs and fevers that apparently plagued him. He was a musical genius, Eleanor had assured her, and Juliana sometimes wondered if Eleanor had not married him simply to make sure that his life was properly managed, allowing him to occupy himself with his music and not worry about other, lesser, things such as food or medicine or bills being paid.

Managing things was, after all, what Eleanor did best.

Bartwell tapped on the study door, then opened it at Eleanor's reply. "Miss Holcott is here to see you, ma'am."

Eleanor, who had been busy running down columns of figures, pencil at the ready, looked up in surprise and saw Juliana. She jumped up with a pleased cry and came forward, reaching out to take Juliana's hands.

Eleanor was a tall woman, taller even than Juliana, but possessed of a statuesque figure, rather than Juliana's willowy slenderness. Her hair was jet-black, her skin pale, and her eyes a vivid blue. She was a commanding woman, sure to draw attention in any crowd, and Juliana had always thought her quite beautiful, though detractors were wont to say that her features were too large, her cheekbones and jaw too angular, for true beauty. She dressed as she pleased, as well, favoring clean, simple lines and vivid colors even before she had married, when girls were generally relegated to the whites and pastels that Eleanor termed insipid.

"Juliana! What a wonderful surprise," she said now, her voice warm with affection. "Bring us some tea, why don't you, Bartwell?"

"Of course, Miss Eleanor."

Eleanor kissed Juliana on the cheek, then stepped back, still holding her hands, and searched her face, her own brow knitting in a frown. "What brings you here at this hour on a weekday? Is something wrong?"

Juliana sighed. "I fear I am throwing myself on your mercy, Eleanor. I have been dismissed."

"Let go?" Eleanor's expressive face filled with gratifying indignation. "By that toad of a woman? Thrall?"

Juliana could not help but smile at her friend's description of Mrs. Thrall. "Yes."

"Good Lord. I knew she was foolish, but really… Come, sit down and tell me about it."

Juliana did as she ordered, spilling out the entire

story of meeting Nicholas again and all the events that followed. Eleanor listened intently, stopping her only once to say, looking intrigued, "Nicholas—the boy who was Seraphina's cousin? The one you used to talk about?"

At Juliana's nod, she pursed her lips thoughtfully and told her to go on. Juliana did so, finally winding down just as Bartwell wheeled in the tea cart.

"What a thoroughly stupid woman," Eleanor commented, pouring tea into their cups. "Here is her entrée into the very Society where she longs to place her daughter, and she cuts herself off from it. If she had instead kept you on and treated you well, her daughter could have been invited to all the best parties because of her connection with Lord Barre."

"Do you know Lord Barre?" Juliana asked.

Her friend, Juliana knew, moved among a certain part of London Society. Eleanor had established herself as a patron of the arts and maintained an eclectic salon, where artists and pundits mingled with those of wealth or noted lineage who were drawn to intellectual stimulation.

"No, I have never met him. I have heard about his return—it is one of the more popular stories among the *ton*, but I did not realize that he was *your* Nicholas. I would have made an effort to meet him if I had known." She smiled at Juliana. "Although I suppose I will now."

"He doesn't even know what happened or where I am," Juliana admitted. "I cannot send him a note telling him where I have gone. That would be far too bold."

Eleanor shrugged. She knew as well as Juliana of the restrictions placed on ladies of quality. She was fond of flouting them, but she knew that her friend's position was far more precarious than her own.

"Don't fret. We will think of something."

Juliana shook her head. "It does not matter. 'Tis not a friendship I can keep up. A paid companion does not have men—or anyone, for that matter— calling on her. And while I can visit you or Mrs. Simmons when I have a day off, I can scarcely call on a gentleman. When would I ever be able to see him?"

"Then stay with me," Eleanor offered. "You needn't get another position. You know that you are welcome here. I have asked you many times. There will be no problem with Lord Barre calling upon you here. I am sure that I can find a way to let him know that you are staying with me. Edmund and I are going to Italy in three weeks—it is better for his health and his music, you know—but I could delay our departure a bit."

"No, do not do that for me. You are very kind, but I cannot impose on you so," Juliana responded. It was an argument that she and her friend had held many times before, the only bone of contention between them.

Eleanor grimaced. "You and your stubborn pride! It is no more than you would do for me if our situations were reversed."

"And you know that if our situations were reversed, you would feel exactly as I do," Juliana retorted with a smile. "I cannot live on your charity."

"Then I will hire you. I need a companion. Things are ever so much more enjoyable when there is a friend with whom to share them. I shall pay you what Mrs. Thrall did, and then you will be independent."

"You do not need a companion, and we both know it. It would still be charity, whatever guise you give it—only then it would be compounded, for you would be paying me money, as well." Juliana reached over and took her friend's hand, giving it an affectionate squeeze. "I know you fairly itch to take me in hand."

Eleanor laughed. "Unfair, unfair. Though I will admit to a desire to arrange things." She gave Juliana a droll look, then added, "But all I want is for your life to be easier. You deserve far more happiness than you have had."

"I don't know what I deserve. But surely you see that however my life goes, I must manage it for myself."

"Of course. I realize that," the American woman agreed. "You are quite independent."

"I have to seek employment. And…I have to be realistic about Lord Barre." Juliana looked at her friend sadly. "I thought about it all the way over here. I have been living in a fool's world the past few days. 'Tis an impossible situation. I cannot continue to see Nicholas."

CHAPTER SIX

NICHOLAS TROTTED up the steps to the Thralls' rented house, humming lightly under his breath. He had waited what he felt was a very circumspect two days before calling upon Juliana again. He had found the interim rather dull, frankly, and had thought more than once what nonsense it was that when he wanted to talk to someone, he had to cool his heels for several days before he could do so, just because she was a woman.

Still, he was accustomed to the fact that the rules of polite society made little sense to him, and it was not for his sake but for Juliana's that he had to follow them. So he had spent the last couple of days doing the sort of things that gentlemen of leisure did in London and finding them thoroughly boring. He had sold off most of his businesses when he decided to leave America and accept the title, knowing that it would keep him bound to England, and the rest of his concerns his business agent kept in good shape, so that they required no more than a visit from him now and then. The bulk of the money that came with the title was tied to the estate at Lychwood Hall and was managed by the estate manager under the eye of Crandall Barre. Nicholas had yet to travel to the Hall, avoiding, he knew, the inevitable meeting with his relatives.

His knock at the door was greeted by a parlor maid, who smiled and showed him into the front drawing room when he asked to see Miss Holcott. After a few minutes, Mrs. Thrall bustled into the room, all smiles.

"Lord Barre! What a pleasure. Clementine will be down in just a moment. You know how girls are. Perhaps you'd care for a cup of tea?"

"Thank you." Nicholas resigned himself to spending his visit with Juliana with the Thralls in attendance. It was a nuisance, of course, but he did not wish to get Juliana into trouble with her employer…however much it grated on him that she should have to worry about this woman's opinion. He wondered where Juliana was—probably helping that wretched girl primp.

Mrs. Thrall engaged him in idle talk for the next few minutes, and Nicholas grew increasingly impatient. Then Clementine fluttered into the room, and he rose to say hello, looking beyond her in vain for Juliana.

"And Miss Holcott?" he asked, as Clementine sat

down on the chair closest to him. "Where is she? I hope she is not indisposed."

"Oh, no. I fear you must make do with Clementine and me this afternoon," Mrs. Thrall simpered. "Miss Holcott is not here."

"I see," he replied, although he did not. "Will Miss Holcott return soon?" It seemed the worst of luck that he had managed to arrive while Juliana was gone on some errand or other. He wondered if he should endure the Thrall women's company for a few minutes in the hopes of Juliana's return, or simply leave and return another day.

"No, I shouldn't think so. Shall I pour you more tea, my lord?"

"No." Nicholas found that his patience was wearing thin. "Where is Miss Holcott?"

Mrs. Thrall glanced around the room as if the answer to Nicholas's question might spring up before her. Finally, with some reluctance, she said, "I am afraid that Miss Holcott is no longer employed here."

"I beg your pardon." Nicholas's eyes narrowed as he looked at the squat woman. "She has left your employ?"

"Yes. Yes, she has," Mrs. Thrall nodded.

"Where did she go?"

"I am afraid I don't know," Mrs. Thrall responded.

"She did not leave a forwarding address?" Nicholas asked in some disbelief.

"No. No. She did not. I was, frankly, astonished at her behavior. I would have expected more from Miss Holcott," Mrs. Thrall told him, warming to her story.

"Why did she leave?" Nicholas asked, fastening Mrs. Thrall with his flat dark gaze.

She swallowed and shifted uncomfortably in her seat. "Ah, well, that is, I'm not quite sure. Um…"

"She was stealing from us," Clementine declared. "Mama had to let her go."

Nicholas swung toward her, and she felt the full force of his black stare. "Stealing from you? Juliana? I suggest you rethink that answer. If I hear that story spread around Town, I will deal with it—and you—summarily."

Clementine flushed an unbecoming red, her hands suddenly turning damp with sweat. "What are you—how dare you threaten me?" she finished weakly.

"I do not threaten, Miss Thrall. I am telling you straight out that if I hear that lie about Miss Holcott, I will know from whence it came, and I can guarantee you that any hope you have of making an advantageous marriage will be at an end." He turned from the gaping Clementine to her mother. "Am I clear on that, madam?"

Mrs. Thrall nodded, unable to speak.

"Now, I will ask you once again. Where did Juliana go?"

"I don't know," Mrs. Thrall wailed. "That's the truth. She packed her bags and left. I don't know where she went."

"The devil take it!" Nicholas jumped to his feet.

It was no good asking the women why Juliana had left, Nicholas knew. He felt sure that the blame fell on the Thralls, but he was equally sure that he would be unable to get an honest answer out of them. Not that it mattered; he thought they were speaking the truth when they said they didn't know where Juliana had gone, and that was all that mattered. He had lost her once again.

He strode out of the room, across the hall to the front door, scarcely hearing Mrs. Thrall's and Clementine's voices rising in protest.

"Lord Barre!"

"No, wait!"

Nicholas went out the front door, barely restraining himself from slamming it behind him. He was furious, all the more so because he knew that he was the cause of her firing. He had at best ignored the Thrall girl; at worst, he had been rude to her the day he had taken Juliana out for a drive in his curricle—

all because he had been thinking only of himself. The chit was irritating, and he had wanted to be alone with Juliana, so he had given her a decided set-down. He had not thought about how his actions would affect Juliana; he had not considered that the idiotic woman would take out the humiliation of his snub on her.

Juliana had been tossed out of the house and was alone in the world, without any means of support, because of his hasty words. And he did not even know where she was.

He stood for a long moment on the Thralls' front doorstep, thinking his black thoughts. Finally, with a sigh of disgust, he went down the steps and out onto the sidewalk. He had not gotten far when a voice stopped him.

"Lord Barre! Lord Barre! Wait!"

It was a girl's voice, a little breathless, and it came from the side of the house. He turned to see a girl running toward him up the narrow walkway that led from the side door. It was the servants' entrance, but this girl was clearly not a servant. She was still an adolescent, for her hair was tied back in girlish braids, but her simple muslin dress was of good quality.

He remembered that Juliana had said that there was another girl in the Thrall household whom she had liked, and hope began to rise in him.

"Miss Thrall?" he asked.

She came to a breathless halt in front of him. "Yes. I—my name is Fiona Thrall. I know what really happened."

"To Miss Holcott?" Nicholas was all attention now, and he moved a step closer to her.

Fiona nodded. "Yes. It wasn't the way Mother said. Miss Juliana didn't just leave. She wouldn't have."

"I am sure of that. Mrs. Thrall turned her out?"

"Yes. There was a huge argument. My mother and Clementine were furious. Clemmy said that Miss Juliana had tried to take you away from her, and Mother said…" The girl stumbled to a halt, her cheeks flaming with embarrassment. "She accused Juliana of…of using her 'wiles' on you."

"I can well imagine what she said," Nicholas told her grimly. "You needn't describe it further. Just tell me that you know where Juliana went."

"I do," Fiona told him, looking pleased to leave the subject of her mother's absurd and slanderous accusations. "Miss Juliana left me her address so that I could visit her. She went to her friend's house. Lady Scarbrough. She said she knew her from school." Fiona held out a scrap of paper. "Here, you may copy the address if you like."

He took the paper from her. It was merely an

address, which he quickly committed to memory, and he handed the paper back to Fiona.

"Thank you, Miss Thrall. I am in your debt. And should you wish to visit Miss Holcott…" He reached in his pocket, withdrew his card case and handed her one of his calling cards. "You need only send round to me, and I will send my carriage to take you to see her."

"Really?" Fiona took the card from his hand and flashed him a dazzling smile that made him think to himself that one day Fiona would quite outshine her older sister.

With a tip of his hat to the girl, Nicholas set out toward the fashionable Mayfair address that had been written on the scrap of paper. He walked the distance, deep in thought, his mind ranging over his part in Juliana's troubles and what he could do about them. By the time he reached the elegant white Queen Anne house where Lady Scarbrough lived, he had come to a satisfactory conclusion.

The door was opened by a servant—or so he presumed, although the man was dressed not in livery, but in a simple black suit. The man took in Nicholas's measure in a glance and led him up the stairs to a spacious, gracefully decorated drawing room that managed to be at once warm and elegant.

Juliana was seated with another woman, a statuesque brunette with arrestingly blue eyes, and they were laughing over something with the ease and affection of old friends. The black-haired woman looked up at their entrance into the room, and Nicholas was pierced by her intelligent, vivid gaze. Juliana's face remained bent down to the sewing in her lap, and she did not glance up until the servant announced him.

Then her head flew up, and Juliana looked at Nicholas, her mouth forming an O of surprise. "Nicholas! How did you find me here?"

"Were you hiding from me?" he retorted quizzically. "If so, you did not do it well enough. Your friend, Miss Fiona Thrall, let the cat out of the bag."

Juliana's cheeks warmed. "No, I did not mean that. Of course I wasn't hiding. I merely—I did not know how to let you know. It was, um, rather sudden."

"So I heard."

"Lord Barre." The other woman stood, then crossed the room to him, holding out her hand. "I am Eleanor Scarbrough."

"I'm sorry," Juliana said quickly, rising also. "Lord Barre, pray allow me to introduce you to my friend, Lady Scarbrough. Lady Scarbrough, Lord Barre."

Juliana felt unaccountably flustered by Nicholas's presence. When he had stepped into the room, joy had shot through her, throwing her off balance. She had convinced herself just two days ago that she would have to give up his friendship, yet the moment she had seen him, her heart had leapt in her chest, and she had felt breathless and all aflutter.

"I am pleased to meet you, Lord Barre," Eleanor said now. Then, with a quick sidewards glance at Juliana, she went on smoothly. "I am sorry, but I'm afraid I have some business I need to attend to in my study. However, I am sure that Miss Holcott will be pleased to chat with you. If you will excuse me…?"

Juliana knew that her friend was discreetly giving her a chance to talk with Nicholas alone, but, given the tumult in her insides, she rather wished that Eleanor had not been quite so accommodating. She wasn't sure what she should say to him. She knew that she should explain the futility of their continued friendship, but she was terribly afraid that if she started talking about it, her voice might clog up with tears. She was equally alarmed that he would sense in her voice her inappropriately great pleasure in his visit. It simply would not do to display such emotion, especially given the fact that Nicholas's face was set in a grim expression. Was he angry with her? she wondered.

"I must apologize for what happened," Nicholas began abruptly, as soon as Eleanor had left the room.

"For what?" Juliana asked blankly.

"For that doltish woman's behavior," he replied shortly.

"Mrs. Thrall? She is scarcely your responsibility," Juliana replied wonderingly.

"No, but you are. And she would not have given you the sack if I had not given her and her daughter a set-down the other morning. I should have had more care. I did not think how it would affect you."

"It's all right," Juliana replied, stiffening. She did not care to think that Nicholas regarded her as a responsibility, especially not the onerous one that his expression seemed to indicate. "It's not your fault. And I will find another position soon."

She had already visited the employment agency, and though there had been no openings available for a companion, she hoped there would soon be one.

Nicholas's expression darkened. "No."

He seemed to realize how flat and dictatorial the single word sounded, and he added, "You should not have to be someone's companion."

Juliana started to speak, but before she could get a word out, he went on quickly. "I have come up with the answer to your dilemma."

"You have?" Juliana stared at him, wondering what in the world he was talking about.

"Yes. It's quite simple. You shall marry me."

There was a long moment of silence. Juliana stared at him, at first too stunned to speak. She was taken aback by the sudden fierce uprush of longing inside her. She realized that she wanted desperately to accept his offer. But immediately on the heels of that emotion came the sharp sting of anger and humiliation.

It could not be clearer that Nicholas had no desire to marry her, that he was asking her—no, not even asking, *telling* her!—strictly out of some skewed feeling that he was somehow responsible for her.

"Excuse me, my lord," Juliana said icily, lifting her chin defiantly. "You may have a title now, but that does not give you the right to order me around. I am not one of your servants."

"Of course you are not," he replied, with some impatience. "I'm not trying to order you. But this is the clear answer."

"Answer? I did not realize I had a question," Juliana retorted. "This is my life we are discussing, not some 'problem.'"

"I know I am talking about your life," he responded, looking baffled. "I am asking you to marry me."

"Asking? I heard no question. All I heard was your declaration that I was to marry you. Have you grown so arrogant in the years since I've known you?

Did you expect me to swoon at your feet because you deigned to say you would marry me?"

"Arrogance?" His brows contracted, and his dark eyes glittered. "You call it arrogance to offer you my name?"

"I call it arrogance to assume that marriage is the only thing that can save me. That my life is a…a problem because I am an unmarried woman. Yes, I have to earn my way, but at least I am independent. I choose what I do."

"You call it independence when you are at someone else's beck and call?" he shot back.

"At least I am paid to be at someone's beck and call. I have a day off every other week, and if my duties become too much, I am free to leave. I am not at some man's beck and call twenty-fours hours a day, every day of the week, with no money of my own and no possibility of leaving!"

"And that is what you think marriage to me would be?" Nicholas thundered. "That I would seek to control your life? To force you to obey me? I offer you a chance to escape from a life of drudgery, and you toss it back in my face, as if I were trying to harm you."

"I did not ask for your help!" Juliana exclaimed, knotting her hands into fists at her sides. "You thrust it upon me. Without any by-your-leave, you tell me I will marry you. You tell me my life is a misery, and you will mend it." She stalked forward until they were nearly toe-to-toe, looking up into his face pugnaciously. "Well, thank you very much, but it is *my* misery, and I will thank you to keep your nose out of it."

"Of all the suspicious, ungrateful—" Nicholas broke off, his eyes fiery.

For a long moment they simply stood, glaring at each other, too angry to even speak. He faced her, his fists on his hips, head thrust forward, and she stood in an almost identical pose, practically quivering with her indignation.

Then, suddenly, to Juliana's surprise, humor glinted in Nicholas's eyes, and he relaxed, his hands falling to his sides and a laugh escaping his lips. "You were always a Hotspur, weren't you?"

Juliana tried to maintain her fury, but she felt it slipping away from her, and after a moment *she* had to chuckle, as well. "I am not the only one."

"Ah, Juliana, please, don't be angry with me. I meant no insult to you. If I was arrogant, I apologize. 'Tisn't the title, I'm afraid, but the fact that I have grown accustomed to giving orders. I meant nothing but to help you. But, as you know, I was never one who allowed good manners to be drummed into me."

"Perhaps your manners would have been better if

they had not tried to drum them in," she responded. With a sigh, she moved away, saying, "I know you have my interests at heart, Nicholas, but…"

"But what?" he asked. "Please, Juliana, just listen to me. I am not trying to force you into anything. I have no wish to control you, and I mean no disrespect. I am merely offering you a…an easier life. Think of the advantages. You would have money, clothes, the freedom to do whatever you like. It would be a marriage in name only. I would not expect you to be my wife in all ways."

"But, Nicholas, this is mad. Why would you want to offer such a thing?"

"It would be advantageous to me, as well," he argued. "I need a wife. I have a title now, and there are certain social obligations that come with it. And you know me—I am thoroughly unskilled in the social graces, as you have just witnessed. I would blunder through Society, alienating everyone."

"Do you care?" Juliana asked skeptically.

He chuckled. "Perhaps not much. But it might be, as I grew older, that I would regret having earned the enmity of all the peers of the land." He paused, and his face fell into more serious lines. "I know what people think of me. Wild and wicked. Most of the time, it does not bother me.

But there are times…" He shrugged. "I am not completely inured to it. I think that I might wish not to be a…a creature beyond hope." Something flickered in his eyes and was gone. "You could make me respectable. You would know what to say and do, how to hold parties, and who to invite so I would not want to howl at the moon rather than listen to them."

Juliana half smiled. "I am not sure there is anyone in Society who would fit that description. Besides, I am just as much an outsider as you."

"Mayhap. But you, at least, are a good person. You know what is right and wrong."

"So do you, Nicholas. If you were not good, you would scarcely be offering to give me all this."

"Not so good. We both know I need a wife. I have two households to manage. And I need someone to soften my rough edges."

"But surely you need someone more your equal. A girl from an excellent family."

"There is nothing wrong with your family. Your father was merely a youngest son."

"Of a younger son," Juliana added. "Yes, our name is good enough, but we have no wealth. No stature."

"Do not let Aunt Lilith hear you so denigrate her family."

"I am merely her cousin."

"You are worth a hundred of her, however. That is what is important to me. I have no interest in wealth; I have enough of that. Who should I marry, Juliana? Tell me that. One of those silly chits who chases me? Whose mothers lay traps for unwary bachelors on the marriage mart? Perhaps a beauty like Clementine Thrall?"

"Nicholas! Of course not. But there are other women…."

"Who? I am not interested in giggling girls. I know you, and I know that you would do an exceptional job of everything that is required of a nobleman's wife. And if you marry me, I will no longer be pursued by every nubile young lady of the *ton*, which will be, I can assure you, a great relief to me."

"Nicholas…this is ridiculous."

"Not at all. Just think, I have to travel to Lychwood Hall soon and face my relatives. Surely you would not be so cruel as to make me meet Aunt Lilith and Crandall on my own, would you?"

Juliana looked at him. Despite his joking manner, she sensed that deep down there was a serious element to his plea.

Then, with a wicked grin, he went on. "Come, tell

me the truth now. Wouldn't you like to face Aunt Lilith as the new mistress of the house?"

"But what about love?" Juliana blurted out. In all his careful arguments, he had not spoken once about it.

Nicholas cast her a sardonic look. "What about it?"

"Wouldn't you want to marry the woman you love? Isn't that the whole purpose of getting married? To be with the one you love for the rest of your life?"

"Is it?" he retorted, and moved away, his face falling into its usual hard lines. "I don't believe in love."

"Don't say that!"

"Why not? It's the truth." He turned to face her. "Love is mostly a fairy tale, with little purpose except to make people feel better with their lot. Certainly I have seen little of it in marriages."

"But your parents…"

"I scarce remember my parents." Nicholas's face was closed, and he seemed, for the first time, very much a stranger to her. "But I remember my aunt and uncle, and there was nothing between them but pride and dislike."

"You cannot use Lilith and Trenton Barre as an example!" Juliana cried. "They were a good example of nothing—not husband and wife, or parents, or even people. My mother and father loved each other. They were happy together."

"And your mother was a ghost all the years I knew her," Nicholas responded.

Juliana knew that his words were no less than truth. Her mother had lived the last of her life in a sad, remote fog, and nothing that Juliana did could make her happy again.

"At least she had love for a time," Juliana said stubbornly.

"Juliana…" Nicholas crossed the room to her. "You are the one person in the world whom I trust. You are as close to real family as I have ever had. I want to see that you are taken care of. I have the means to do it, and the desire, but there is no other way to see to it that would not dishonor your name. Marriage is the only way that I can give you what you deserve, what I want to see you have. Beyond that, I have no feelings for any woman. I have never felt anything more than lust, easily satisfied."

Juliana's eyes widened at his blunt words, and she could feel heat creeping into her cheeks.

"I know," he said with some impatience. "I should not speak of such things to a lady. But I must be honest with you. I have to make you see—I care not for love. I will not regret marrying without it. I will deal quite easily with an impassionate relationship. Desires of the flesh can be taken care of outside the marriage. Discreetly, of course. I would not embarrass you."

"Well, what about me?" Juliana shot back, ignoring the fiery blush that stained her face. She would be every bit as straightforward as he. "Am I to find love in affairs, too—discreet, of course?"

A cold light flashed in his eyes, and for a moment Nicholas's face was cold and dangerous. He looked every bit the pirate some claimed he had been.

Then, with a visible effort, he relaxed. "I will trust your judgment, of course."

He sent her a challenging look, one brow raised, and Juliana knew that he was fully aware that she would never seek out an illicit affair, even in a loveless marriage.

A little miffed that he had called her bluff, she snapped back, "Well, whatever your feelings on the matter, perhaps *I* still hope to marry someone I love someday."

"And how are you to find that person?" Nicholas asked sardonically. "Be practical, Juliana. Who are you going to meet while you are fetching and carrying for silly girls or wealthy old ladies?"

Tears stung Juliana's eyes at his words. Nicholas was depressingly correct. In all the years that she had been a companion, she had met no eligible man, or, at least, none that would consider marrying her. And she was realistic enough to admit that during the years ahead, she would only grow older and therefore more unlikely to be asked to marry, even if she did find a man whom she could love. It was a bleak prospect, and one that had more than once made her shed tears into her pillow late at night.

She turned away, fighting the tears that threatened even now to choke her voice. "I am aware that I have no prospects. Still…" She squared her shoulders proudly and turned back to face him, her chin going up. "At least I alone control my life."

His face softened, his eyes suddenly touched by regret. "I am sorry if I have hurt you. My words were too blunt. I never meant to bring pain to your eyes."

"'Tis not your fault you speak the truth," Juliana replied.

Nicholas reached out and took her hands, gazing down into her eyes. "You are a brave and wonderful woman. If the world were fair, you would be a duchess, and all the Mrs. Thralls and Clementines of the world would be waiting on you. I cannot change what has happened to you. But I am offering you what I can. You will have money to do what you wish, buy what you want. You will have servants to take care of you, and there will be no one who can look down on you or order you about. I would not be a controlling, demanding husband, I promise. We would be, as we always were, friends. And you would be quite free and independent. I would never put a rein on you."

Juliana's heart ached within her. She was overwhelmingly aware of Nicholas's closeness—the faint roughness of his hands upon her skin, the cool metal of his ring, the masculine scent of shaving soap that teased at her nostrils, the warmth of his hard body so near to hers. If only he were offering her his heart as well as his hand. If only it was love she saw in his dark eyes, not just kindness.

"What about children?" she blurted out, surprising even herself.

"What?" Nicholas looked startled.

Embarrassed, still Juliana plowed ahead. "What if I grew to want children? 'Tis a natural enough thing for a woman to wish for a baby. A family to love and nourish."

Nicholas gazed at her for a long moment. Juliana waited, the flush of her embarrassment beginning to mingle with an entirely different sort of heat.

"When that time comes," he said at last in a husky voice, "then you need only to tell me."

He leaned toward her, his face looming ever closer. Juliana's eyes went involuntarily to his lips. "If you should decide you want a different type of marriage," he murmured, "that can be arranged."

Juliana's breath caught, and she closed her eyes. His lips touched hers, soft but firm, moving ever more insistently against hers. Her head whirled, her senses suddenly, vividly alive. His hands came up to rest on her arms, fingers pressing into her flesh, and the heat from his body was a palpable thing, touching and warming her.

She trembled a little in his grasp, her head falling back and her lips parting under his. The taste of his mouth was honeyed, intoxicating. Juliana could not breathe, could not protest; she felt as if she were teetering on the edge of some vast precipice, and she knew that she wanted only to tumble over it, to fall forever into this dark chasm of desire.

Nicholas pulled back and looked down into her face. His own eyes blazed with a dark fire.

"Think about it," he said hoarsely. "That is all I ask."

With that, he turned abruptly and strode out of the room, leaving Juliana staring dazedly after him.

CHAPTER SEVEN

JULIANA DID THINK ABOUT IT. Indeed, for the rest of the day, she did little but think about the scene that had taken place between them. Nicholas's kiss had left her rattled and disturbed, filled with strange sensations and random, clattering thoughts—and thrilled down to her toes.

What had he meant by that kiss? There was a part of her that wanted to think his kiss had been an indication that he felt more for her than he had expressed, that despite his declarations of not believing in love, deep down he felt it for her.

But, sternly, she turned herself from such thoughts. She knew enough about the world to know that there was a distinct difference between love and lust. And men seemed to quite easily feel desire without any sort of deeper connection. It would be the height of folly for her to allow herself to believe that Nicholas's offer was anything other than what he had stated: a marriage in name only, without any love.

Nor could Juliana deny that it was a very desirable offer indeed. Many women would have leapt at the opportunity to be Lord Barre's wife, even without the slightest hint of affection. To be Lady Barre, the mistress of two households and a large number of servants, automatically given a great deal of status in Society, would be the dream of many a marriageable girl. For a twenty-seven-year-old spinster with no fortune, forced to earn her own way in the world, it was an almost unimaginable gift.

All her life, Juliana had been on the fringes of the world of wealth and privilege, always looking on, but never actually participating. She had helped some girl, like her cousin Seraphina or Clementine Thrall, dress and do her hair, then watched, stuck in her own drab clothes, as that girl sallied forth to dance or attend the opera or go to some soiree.

Marriage to Nicholas would change all that. The clothes she would buy would be her own. She would be giving elaborate parties and attending others as a welcomed guest. She would wear jewels and rich fabrics. And she would never again have to placate an employer or worry about what she would do if she could not find another position. It would give her, just as Nicholas had said, an immense freedom.

But, still, she could not help but recoil from the idea of a loveless marriage. She had always believed that she would marry for love. She carried the memory of her parents' love—the laughter and affection they had shared. Money had never been plentiful, but they had not minded; their love had made up for any lack. That, she knew, was what she wanted for herself.

Nicholas had been the man who figured in those dreams as she grew up. Of course, as she had gotten older, she had realized how foolish and unlikely such dreams were. But she had clung to the hope that somewhere there was a man who would love her, that she would find the sort of love her parents had shared. It seemed the most terrible irony that when at last she was offered marriage, it should be one that was the very antithesis of what she had longed for—yet offered to her by the very man who had once occupied those romantic dreams.

How could she bear to tie herself to such an arrangement, so tantalizingly close to her dreams, yet so harshly removed from them?

On the other hand, she knew how absurd it would be to throw away such an opportunity. There was little likelihood of her marrying for love in her present situation. Nicholas had been correct in saying that, given her position, she rarely met eligible men, and if she did, certainly none of them would think of offering for a nobody like her.

If there was no possibility of marrying for love, was it then so terrible to marry where there was at least true affection? Nicholas did care for her in his own way. He had said that she was as much family as he had. Surely it said something about her place in his life that he was willing to marry her to give her a better life instead of marrying any of the young beauties he could have taken to wife.

And even if that was far from love, it seemed to her that it could still be the basis for a lasting marriage. They shared a past; they were friends. And he was a good man, whatever he or others might say about his wicked nature. Only kindness could have made him offer to bind himself to her for life.

Oh, there was, no doubt, a little roguish desire in him to figuratively spit in the eye of the relatives who had so mistreated him—it was galling enough to see him take over the house and title they had so wanted. How much more galling would it be to have her, another undeserving creature in their eyes, be the mistress of that estate? He would indulge in a mild laugh at the consternation of all the Society maidens—and their mothers—who had chased him when they heard that he had preferred a penniless girl to them.

But those wishes were not enough to make him marry, Juliana was sure. It had to be, at the heart of it, his generous nature that had prompted his offer. And such a man, surely, would be a kind and generous husband. If some other woman in the same position had asked her for advice, Juliana knew she would have urged her to accept the proposal.

Indeed, Eleanor said as much later that day, when Juliana told her about Nicholas's offer, "Of course you should accept. You deserve the life he can give you, and he sounds like a very intelligent man to choose you for a wife."

Juliana suspected that her friend did not share her own feelings about the sacred bond of marriage. Eleanor and her husband seemed to have a rather odd sort of relationship, more that of a brother and sister, really, fond, but lacking in any passion. Still, she also knew that Eleanor had Juliana's best interests at heart. Perhaps she was right in what she said.

She went to bed that night without having resolved the issue in her mind, and when the morning light came, and she awoke from a restless and dream-filled sleep, she found that she was still unsure of her course of action.

After breakfast, Eleanor went to work in her office, as she did most mornings. Juliana went for a walk with the children and their nanny, an attractive young dark-skinned woman from India, who was still somewhat shy around Juliana. After that the children went upstairs for their lessons, and Juliana was left alone with her thoughts.

She should, she supposed, go to the employment agency and inquire whether any new positions had opened up. Yet she could not bring herself to. She had to be here for Nicholas's visit.

She started to work on some mending that Eleanor needed done, but she could not concentrate and found she had to tear out half the stitches she had put in. Finally she put it aside as a waste of effort.

It was time, she knew, to make up her mind. Nicholas would be here soon, and she must give him her answer.

Her prospects were not good, she admitted. It was unlikely that she would find the love she sought, so if she insisted on waiting for it, most likely she would never marry. She would spend the rest of her life on the edge of someone else's life. Would it not be better to marry Nicholas? To have the security and the advantages that marriage to him would bring? Yet she could scarcely bear to think of resigning herself to a husband who did not love her, who carried on affairs, discreet or otherwise. She wanted a true marriage, yet when she thought about turning him down, her heart quailed inside her.

There was the sound of a knock at the front door. Juliana's stomach twisted in anticipation, and she clenched her hands together in her lap. She listened to the sound of steps coming down the hall, and a moment later Nicholas strode into the room.

She stood up, suddenly breathless, as he crossed the room to her. He bowed over her hand, then straightened, looking into her eyes.

"Well?" he asked, his face serious. "Have you decided?"

She could not do it, she thought; she could not shackle herself to such a life. Juliana opened her mouth to say so, but to her surprise, the words that came out were, "Yes, I will marry you."

NICHOLAS SEEMED almost as surprised by her acceptance as Juliana was. Then his face broke into a wide grin, and he pulled her into his arms, hugging her. For an instant she relaxed against him. It was almost easy to believe that their engagement was a normal one, that he was happy because the woman he loved had agreed to marry him.

But that was not the truth, she told herself, and the sooner she learned to live with that idea, the better. She pulled back, smiling at him a trifle awkwardly.

"I was certain you were going to be stiff-necked about it," he told her, "and I would have to work to convince you. You have made it much easier."

"I—it was the sensible thing to do," Juliana replied carefully.

"I have to go to Lychwood Hall soon," he told her. "Why don't we have the wedding there? They are all we have of family, either of us, little as I like it."

Juliana nodded. She had little desire to see her cousins again, but that would be one of her primary duties as Nicholas's wife. However strong and successful he was, he could use a buffer against the Barre family.

"I'll purchase a special license so that we can dispense with the reading of the banns," he went on. "And we must take the time to buy you a new wardrobe."

"You needn't—" she began, a little embarrassed.

"Nonsense. Of course I must. A bride must have a trousseau, mustn't she?"

"But it is too much. We are not even married yet."

"Must I wait until after the ceremony?" he asked, his eyes twinkling. "Must we marry here and then purchase your clothes before we go to the estate?"

She grimaced. "Don't be absurd. There is no need to—"

"There is every need. Have you looked into a glass? I'll not have my wife going about dressed like a governess. I want the world to see how lovely you are. Do you want everyone gossiping about what a skinflint I am, making my wife wear old and dreary clothes?"

"Of course not," Juliana demurred, feeling foolish. It seemed somehow mercenary on her part to accept such a gift, as if she were marrying him solely for his wealth. *Which she was not! She was marrying him because—well, that probably did not bear thinking of.*

"Very well," she told him, putting on a smile. "We shall buy my trousseau."

They told Eleanor the news first. She was delighted to hear it, and almost as delighted to hear that Juliana was about to receive a new set of clothes.

"Wonderful! We should start with Madame Fourcey. She is all the rage among the modistes this year. It is rumored that she is the daughter of French aristocratic émigrés who fled the Revolution."

"Really?"

Eleanor shrugged. "As to that, I have no idea.

Indeed, I have my suspicions that she is more likely an adept actress from Ipswich. However, one thing I am certain of is that she is an artist at creating gowns."

"We shall rely on your expertise, my lady," Nicholas assured her.

The three of them visited the woman's store the next morning, and Juliana was immediately transfixed by a gown on display upon a mannequin. It was a ball gown of rich cream-colored satin, embroidered around the hem and on the small train in a floral pattern of pale gold thread. The embroidery was repeated in a line around the low scoop neck.

"Mademoiselle likes it?" Madame Fourcey asked in a heavy—too heavy?—accent, bustling up. She cast a gracious smile at Juliana, and then at Nicholas and Eleanor, recognizing money when she saw it. "It will be perfect with your hair and eyes. Do you wish to try it on?" She was already turning, signaling to an associate to remove the dress from the mannequin.

"Oh, I don't—" Juliana began, a little surprised by the deep, instant hunger she felt to wear the gown.

"Yes, she would," Nicholas answered. He turned toward Juliana. "That *is* what we are here for." His dark eyes twinkled down at her.

"Yes, I know." She had the grace to blush. She

knew she was being silly. But a lifetime habit of pinching pennies was difficult to break.

She let the dressmaker lead her away to the dressing room in the rear as Eleanor settled down on the green velvet sofa with a fashion book. The dressmaker and her helper whisked Juliana out of her plain dark dress, Madame Fourcey shaking her head sadly as she examined the gown, then tossed it aside.

"No, no, no, not for you, this color," she said emphatically. She tilted her head and added, with a spark of amusement in her eyes, "Not for anyone."

She and her assistant lifted the cream satin dress and slid it on carefully over Juliana's head. As the helper hooked it up the back, Madame Fourcey busied herself shaking out the skirt and straightening it until every fold fell to her satisfaction.

"Oh, yes," she said, beaming. "It is perfect. Well, a little short, but that is easily taken care of. A small ruffle, sewn beneath the skirt, so." She picked up the hem of the dress, illustrating for Juliana. "That way, there is no handwork hidden. Back to here, and then the train starts."

Juliana looked at herself in the mirror and was swept with a fierce desire to own this dress. Even with her hair knotted back in its usual plain fashion, she had never looked as beautiful. The cream and gold of the dress warmed her skin and were a perfect foil for her dark hair. She had never thought of herself as a vain person, but she could not help but love the way she looked in this dress.

The dressmaker smiled at her knowingly. "You see. Come, we show your…"

"Fiancé," Juliana supplied, aware of an upswell of pride.

Madame Fourcey whisked her out into the store, where Nicholas and Eleanor sat waiting. Nicholas rose to his feet at her entrance, and his dark eyes gleamed.

"Ah," he said with satisfaction. "That is how you should look."

Juliana warmed beneath his gaze. She felt the same tingling awareness she felt so often now in Nicholas's presence, and she wondered what, if anything, he felt when they stood close to one another.

"It is rather expensive," she hedged, though she already knew that she had not the strength of will to turn down this dress.

"Do not think about such things," Nicholas told her, coming closer. "I want you to have it. You will be my wife."

He looked into her eyes, and suddenly it struck Juliana that it was important to him that he provide her with an array of lovely clothes. It was more than a kind impulse on his part. It satisfied something in him, gave him pleasure, and that settled the issue for her.

"Thank you," she said simply.

JULIANA SPENT the next week in a veritable orgy of shopping. Nicholas, after the first day, left the matter in Eleanor's capable hands. As she had exquisite taste and a great deal of money, Eleanor was quite familiar with all the best modistes and milliners, and they went from shop to shop, purchasing so many things that it made Juliana's head whirl.

They purchased morning dresses of plain and sprig muslin, as well as afternoon dresses of a finer quality muslin, lawn and silk, trimmed with satin bands or embroidery about the hem and on the sleeves. They bought walking dresses to wear while out paying calls, and carriage dresses made of heavier materials for traveling.

When Juliana protested at the expense of a military-coated riding habit in deep blue velvet, saying, "But I don't even own a horse," her friend gave her a level look and replied, "You will."

There were numerous evening gowns, as well, though none could compare in Juliana's mind to the first ball gown she had tried on. These were of the most elegant silk satins and light taffetas, some with small trains, and all showing a good deal of bosom, with their wide square or scooped necklines.

But dresses, so many they made Juliana's head spin, were not enough. She must also have all new undergarments of softest cotton, from her chemise to her petticoats to the thin flesh-colored stockinet pantaloons that would cover her lower body beneath the thin dresses and petticoats that were the fashion. And she must also have new night shifts, trimmed with lace and embroidery, and dressing gowns of brocade and velvet.

Then there were the various forms of outerwear deemed sufficient for a lady of means—short spencer jackets and fur-trimmed pelisses, as well as mantles to wear with her evening dresses, and full-length redingotes. Of course, a number of shoes were also necessary: riding boots of gleaming leather, walking shoes, evening slippers in soft colored kid or embroidered satin. Nor could one forget silk parasols in a variety of colors to match her outfits, as well as gloves in differing lengths, materials and colors. Ribbons. Fans. Reticules. The list of necessary items, it seemed, went on and on.

And no wardrobe could be considered complete without the addition of hats. There were deep-brimmed, scoop-shaped bonnets, some tied with a scarf in the "gypsy" style, and others with wide colorful ribbons. There were close-fitting capotes that sweetly framed the face, and soft velvet turban-style hats. Some were flat-crowned and others were deep, still others following the newer style of a high crown. They were decorated, of course, with ostrich feathers or a cunning little cluster of painted wooden cherries, or flowers or ribbons.

It was an excess of riches, and though it was delightful, Juliana soon began to feel as if she had stuffed herself on sweets. After all, no one needed so many hats and shoes and accessories, and by the end of the week, she called a stop to it.

Of course, most of what she bought had to be made. A few dresses, such as the elegant evening gown she had first tried on, were already made up and required only a little altering, and the dressmakers agreed to rush the orders on several more dresses. But for the majority of the clothes, the modistes took measurements and would ship the clothes to Juliana at Lychwood Hall when they were done.

Given how busy the days were, she saw little of Nicholas until they left for Lychwood Hall a little over a week later. But that day seemed to arrive in a rush. Juliana could scarcely believe it when she found herself giving Eleanor a goodbye kiss on the cheek before she went to climb up into the waiting carriage.

She glanced at the vehicle, where Nicholas stood waiting to hand her up, and she turned back to Eleanor, fear suddenly clutching at her stomach.

"Oh, Eleanor," she murmured. "Am I doing the right thing?"

Eleanor smiled. "Of course you are. 'Tis just jitters at the actuality of getting married. Even I felt them, and you know that in general I am unflappable."

"But I scarcely know him, really," Juliana went on. "We have been strangers to each other these past fifteen years, and—"

Eleanor took her hand and squeezed it. "You know that you are welcome to stay here with me. If you feel it is too much of a rush—why, he will wait, I'm sure. You can come to Italy with Sir Edmund and me, and when you return, then you can marry him if you still feel so inclined."

Her friend's words were the perfect antidote to Juliana's sudden flash of nerves. Offered the option of not marrying Nicholas, she recoiled. She realized that whatever prewedding jitters she might be experiencing, marrying Nicholas was what she wanted.

She smiled, more in amusement at herself than anything, and squeezed Eleanor's hand in return.

"No. I don't want to wait. Truly. You're right—'tis only nerves at embarking on a new life. I am just as excited as I am frightened. I only wish that you were going to be there at the ceremony."

"I wish that, too," Eleanor assured her. "If we did not already have tickets for the ship…"

"I know. And you must not delay your trip." She did not mention, just as Eleanor did not, that the sound of her husband's cough grew worse daily.

With a final hug, Juliana parted from her friend and went down the steps to the street beyond. Nicholas took her hand to help her up into the carriage, then turned to bow to Eleanor before he swung up into the vehicle after Juliana.

He sat down on the seat across from her—it would, after all, have been considered improper for a gentleman to sit beside her in the carriage unless he was her husband or a relative, such as a father or brother. The carriage rolled off, and Juliana settled back against the luxurious seat. The squibs behind her back were well-padded, as was the seat, and the brown leather that covered them was as soft as butter.

"'Tis a beautiful carriage," she told him, a little uncomfortable now that they were alone together.

"I'm glad you like it. It's yours," he replied.

"It is?" Juliana looked at him, surprised.

He shrugged. "A curricle is fine for a bachelor. But a lady needs an enclosed carriage."

Juliana took another glance around the vehicle, a little amazed. He was right, she supposed; Lady Barre could scarcely be expected to pay her calls in his curricle or a pony trap. Yet she could not help but think that his purchase of the thing indicated more than just attention to what was necessary for his position. There had to be some degree of caring on his part for him to have picked out and purchased this carriage.

She smoothed a hand across the exquisitely soft leather. Was she only fooling herself, she wondered, to think that perhaps Nicholas cared for her more than he realized?

Juliana looked back at him. He was watching her, the strong lines of his face somehow softer, his eyes warm. Her eyes went to his lips, and she remembered how they had felt on hers the other day, firm yet pliant, warming her. The heat she had experienced then flooded back into her now, thinking of it. She glanced away, hoping he would have no idea what she was thinking.

She cleared her throat. "Thank you. You are very generous to me."

"I enjoy it," he told her simply. "There is a limit to how much one can buy for oneself."

Juliana looked back at him, her gray eyes twinkling as she said, "There are a number of people who do not realize that, you know."

"So I have noticed."

The carriage rolled slowly through the streets of London, but gradually the traffic grew less and the buildings fewer, and they were at last beyond the city. It was not a terribly long trip to Lychwood Hall, which lay in the green loveliness of Kent. To others, Juliana supposed, it would seem peculiar that Nicholas had not already visited his ancestral home. She, however, could well understand his reluctance. That understanding, she thought, was perhaps the main reason why he wished to marry her. In all the world, she was the only one who would know why it was so difficult for him to set foot again inside that cold mansion. She had seen the determined effort to break the will of the child Nicholas had been—the frequent punishments when he was locked in his room and denied his supper, the canings administered in Trenton Barre's study, and, perhaps worst of all, the simple cold lack of love for an orphaned boy.

As a child, she had been confused by the way the

Barres had treated Nicholas. She understood now that it had been jealousy that drove Trenton Barre, envy that this child would one day come into the estate and title he must have coveted. But she could not find it in herself to forgive him. Instead of the love he should have given his brother's son, he had offered him only loneliness and dislike. Nicholas had had only her, and the secret friendship of some of the servants and tenants on the estate. It made her a little sad to think that she was probably the only person on whom Nicholas was able to shower some of his fortune.

She looked over at him. He was gazing out at the passing countryside, his face unreadable. She wondered what he was thinking as he returned to his former home.

"It will be odd to see the Hall again," she commented. "I have not been there in over eight years."

Nicholas glanced at her. "I think it will be all too familiar."

"You are probably right," Juliana agreed. She paused, then went on. "What do you intend to do there?"

"Look over the books and the lands, I suppose. Deal with whatever problems have arisen. Crandall has been in charge since his father's death. I have grave doubts about his management, I must admit."

"Perhaps he has changed."

"Perhaps."

"Will you let them continue to live there?" she asked.

His smile was wicked. "I have to say that it would give me a certain amount of satisfaction to turn them all out." He shrugged. "However, it would serve little purpose. I have no real desire to live there myself, anyway. It's a grim, unpleasant place. I expect that I—that we—will spend most of our time in London or at my parents' house in Cornwall. It would be petty, would it not, to evict Aunt Lilith and Crandall?"

She smiled at him. "I am glad you are not petty. I have no liking for them, either, but…"

"But you have a kind heart," he finished.

"As do you."

"No. I simply see little purpose in creating uproar when it's unnecessary." His face turned grim. "However, I cannot say that my answer would be the same if Uncle Trenton were still there."

"He was a wicked man. I was always deathly scared of him. He had the coldest eyes. It was like looking into a pit. I never could have stood up to him as you did."

"My knees were often knocking, I assure you,"

Nicholas replied. "But I was not about to give him the satisfaction of seeing that he frightened me. It was sheer hardheadedness, not bravery."

"Well, I hope I have enough hardheadedness to go in the house again, then."

Nicholas looked at her in some concern. "Does it bother you so to return? I did not think—it was not necessary that we come."

"No, I think it *was* necessary—for you. Was it not?"

He took a moment to answer. "Yes. It was, somehow. But we did not have to marry there. You needn't have come."

"It is probably as necessary for me as for you. Anyway, my memories are surely not as bad as yours. But I must confess that I am glad you do not plan to reside there always. I think the house in Cornwall will be much preferable."

His face lightened. "Yes. It is a lovely house—or it was. It has fallen into disrepair in my absence. But I have already set the repairs in motion. It should be habitable in a few months. Until then, we'll be at Lychwood Hall."

"Cornwall is where you lived as a boy, right?"

Nicholas nodded. "Yes. It sits on a cliff overlooking the ocean. The view is glorious from the upper floors."

"I remember how you used to miss it," Juliana said softly.

"I think I missed the ocean most. We had a boat, and my father taught me to sail. It was my favorite thing."

"Is that where you went when you left Lychwood Hall?"

He nodded. "Not to the house. I was sure that was where Trenton would look first. But I went to Cornwall. I knew people there who would take me in. And I could work on the boats."

"Fishing?"

"Among other things," Nicholas replied. He looked out the window, then back to her. "Smuggling, too. The stories are right about that. It was good money, and a good way to hide from my uncle. Not that most of the people there would have given me up, anyway. But those who might have would have been scared to betray a smuggler."

"So you brought in goods from France."

"Aye, brandy and wine, mostly."

"And spying?" Juliana asked quietly.

"That too. Easy enough to add that to smuggling. By the time I was running my own ship, I was carrying spies back and forth to France, other times just bringing back information." He shrugged. "I didn't usually do any of the spying myself—'twould have been difficult to run my operation were I gone for months to France."

"Usually? Then you did sometimes stay in France? Gathering information?"

"A time or two. Once when communications had been disrupted and they needed to find out what had happened. They paid me enough for our losses. And again later, when I was ready to sell out anyway." He grinned at her. "So, you can see, the stories are true about that, as well. I'm not a very upright fellow. Perhaps you had better rethink your acceptance."

"You were spying for the British, though."

"Yes. I wasn't wicked enough to work for the other side."

"Then you were a patriot. And the smuggling was necessary for your cover, so it seems to me there was little harm."

"I would have smuggled anyway," he said flatly. "And they paid me very well for the rest of it. I did it for the gold, not out of patriotism."

"Say what you want," Juliana replied with a smile. "You are not going to convince me you are wicked."

An answering smile twitched at the corners of his mouth. "And I think that you are equal to me in stubbornness."

"I think perhaps I am."

"Just don't expect too much," he said in a more serious tone. "I do not want to see you feel disappointed."

"I won't." She did not elaborate whether her reply regarded her expecting too much or being disappointed. And Nicholas did not ask.

The rest of the day passed easily enough. They chatted at times, and the rest of the time were equally comfortable sitting quietly. It was remarkable, Juliana thought, how easy it was to be with Nicholas, even after the gap of all these years, and yet there were other moments when suddenly, out of the blue, she found herself noticing the sharp cut of his jaw, the dark curve of his brow or the way the sunlight fell across his crow-black hair, and then what she felt was not ease or comfort at all. It was the stirring, deep down, of quite another feeling, a sort of breathless excitement, a slow wave of yearning that made her stir restively in her seat and look away from him, a flush staining her cheeks.

It was at those times that she would remember the kiss he had given her, and she would wonder what he had meant by it. More than that, she would wonder if it would ever happen again.

They had a late lunch at an inn along the way, and as the afternoon wore on, Juliana napped in the corner, lulled by the monotonous rumbling of the carriage. When she awakened, it was late in the afternoon.

"We are almost there," Nicholas told her.

Juliana straightened and gazed out the window. The countryside looked familiar, and she realized that they were approaching the village. Lychwood Hall lay on the other side of the town.

She smoothed out her skirt a little nervously, then pulled back on the gloves and bonnet she had taken off during the carriage ride. She glanced at Nicholas, and he gave her a faint smile.

"Don't be nervous. If they offend you, they are gone."

She smiled back. "It is not them so much. It is— I don't know. It makes it seem so much more as if a whole new life is starting."

"It is."

They were through the village now and turning down another road. Hedges grew close beside the road, giving way after a time to a row of plane trees. And there, at the end, stood a large house, built in a simple rectangle, three stories tall, with an addition running back from it on one end. It was built of grayish stone, with narrow black flint running in alternate strips between the layers of stone. It presented a perfectly symmetrical front, with four gables, each set with mullioned windows, and had a three-story porch in the center, the Barre coat-of-arms carved at the top. It was a graceful and elegant house, but there was a certain cold look to its perfection.

They had arrived at Lychwood Hall.

CHAPTER EIGHT

THE DOOR WAS OPENED to them by no less a personage than the butler, Rundell. A rather stout individual, with a ring of hair that ran behind his head from ear to ear and a perfectly bald pate on top, he had been the butler since Juliana had arrived at Lychwood Hall almost twenty years earlier. His carriage remained as unbending as ever, though the ring of hair had grown noticeably whiter and thinner.

He bowed to Nicholas, saying, "Welcome home, my lord. Miss Holcott. Please accept my felicitations."

"Thank you, Rundell." Nicholas handed him his hat and gloves, and Rundell passed them to one of the footmen.

"I expect you will wish to see Mrs. Barre first, sir," Rundell went on. "Then, of course, if it pleases you, I would like to introduce the staff."

"Of course."

Juliana felt sure that there would be more joy in meeting the servants than the family, though she could not help but wonder if the others' demeanor toward Nicholas would have changed, given the circumstances.

Her hand hooked through Nicholas's arm, more for comfort than from polite behavior, Juliana walked with him in the butler's wake through the large square entry room and down the hall. Rundell opened the door to the formal drawing room, rarely used, and ushered Nicholas and Juliana inside.

There were four people in the room. One was a man whom Juliana had never seen before, a medium-sized individual with brown hair arranged in a care-fully windswept style made popular by Lord Byron some years earlier. His face was pleasant, if some-what nondescript, eyes a somewhat lighter shade of brown than his hair. He was standing by the window, looking out in a bored manner, when they arrived, and he turned toward them with interest.

The other three were women, two sitting on the sofa and one in a chair across from it. The oldest of the women was Lilith Barre, Nicholas's aunt, and the first thought Juliana had was how little the woman had changed since she had seen her last, almost nine years ago. Her pale blond hair, elegantly styled, was somewhat dimmed now by streaks of gray, but her face and hands were not badly wrinkled, a matter attributable to the woman's assiduous wearing of wide hats and gloves every time she ventured outdoors, as well as her equally disciplined applications of lotions and creams. Her figure was quite trim, as well, and that was due, Juliana was sure, to her devotion to riding. She loved horses, the one sign of any sort of affection Juliana had ever seen in her, and kept both a hunter and a mare for riding about the estate.

"Mrs. Barre." The butler bowed toward Lilith. "Lord Barre and Miss Holcott have arrived."

"Yes, I see. Come in." Lilith rose and came toward them, her voice calm and her manner regal. Not by a glance or movement did she display the slightest bit of either welcome or unease. "Lord Barre. Miss Holcott."

They might have been people she had never seen before, Juliana reflected.

"Please, sit down. You must be tired from your journey. And thirsty. Rundell, tea, please." She turned toward the other two women. "You know Lady Seraphina Lowell-Smythe, of course. Allow me to introduce to you to Mrs. Winifred Barre, my son Crandall's wife. Crandall, I fear, could not be here, as he is out of the house on estate matters."

Seraphina, Juliana noted as she stepped forward to greet her, had changed more than her mother. The years had taken away her slim figure, and she dressed fussily, perhaps in an attempt to distract the eye from her plumpness. A blue ribbon was wound through a riotous arrangement of golden curls on her head, matching the blue ribbons that sashed her white muslin dress. Blue and yellow flowers were embroidered on the hem and sleeves of her gown, as well as around the neck. A wide fluted band of stiff muslin sprang up from the neckline, and a gauzy shawl lay across her shoulders and arms. A coral cameo brooch was pinned to the center of the bosom of her dress, and matching coral earrings dangled from her ears. A golden chain and locket around her neck and several bangles of gold around her arms completed the ensemble.

"Juliana! Nicholas!" Seraphina trilled, smiling, and kissed Juliana on the cheek as if they were the best of friends, despite the fact that she had not laid eyes on Juliana for nine years and Nicholas for even longer—and had never been particularly fond of them even when they had all lived there as children. "How elegant you look, Juliana."

Her eyes swept with some envy down Juliana's slim, tall figure in her smart blue carriage dress. Then she half turned, pulling forward the woman standing a little behind and to the side of her. "Winnie, don't be shy."

The other woman smiled, and bobbed a curtsey to Juliana and Nicholas. "My lord. Miss Holcott."

Blond and blue-eyed like Seraphina, this woman was the opposite of her in dress and manner. Quiet, with a shy little smile, she wore a simple dress of spotted muslin, her only adornment the pearl studs in her ears and her wedding ring. Young and sweet-faced, she scarcely seemed to be the sort to be married to the Crandall Juliana remembered—or perhaps only such a girl would be able to stand the man, Juliana corrected herself.

"And this is Seraphina's husband," Aunt Lilith went on, gesturing toward the man by the window, who at last stepped forward to shake their hands. "Sir Herbert Lowell-Smythe. Seraphina and Sir Herbert are visiting us this summer."

It seemed to Juliana to be an odd time for the couple to be visiting, given that the Season in London was at its height. The Seraphina whom Juliana had known had dreamed of the day when she would be able to spend every Season going to soirees and balls in London. She had always found Lychwood Hall and its rural setting dreadfully dull. And since she was a married woman, her existence was not tied to the estate as Crandall's and his mother's were. All Juliana could think was that Seraphina's curiosity to see the new Lord Barre was great enough to lure her away from town.

Sir Herbert greeted Juliana and Nicholas in a friendly enough manner, inquiring as to their trip from the City. Everyone made a few general comments about the weather and the general sameness of the village, and then the limping conversation rolled to a halt.

"Well," Aunt Lilith said after a long moment of silence, "I imagine the two of you would like an opportunity to freshen up before dinner."

"Yes, thank you." Juliana seized upon the excuse gratefully.

"Very well. I'll ring for Rundell."

The butler answered her summons so promptly that Juliana suspected he must have been lurking outside the door. He escorted Nicholas and Juliana to the foot of the staircase, where they found a line of neatly uniformed servants waiting. Juliana remembered that he had asked Nicholas to meet the staff, and she groaned inwardly at this added duty before she could have a chance to be alone and lie down.

"Mrs. Pettibone, the housekeeper," the butler intoned, leading them to the head of the line, where a plump middle-aged woman in a starched white cap and apron over her severe black dress stood, the enormous ring of keys that were her sign of office hanging at her waist.

She curtseyed with great dignity, and the butler continued down the line, bringing to their notice first the cook, then the footmen, parlor maids, upstairs maids and so on, down to the last scullery maid and pot boy. It was a veritable army of servers. For the first time Juliana thought about the fact that she would soon be the one directing this veritable army, something completely beyond the scope of her experience. She only hoped that Nicholas's confidence in her abilities was justified. She would hate to come a cropper with Aunt Lilith there watching, and she was well aware of the fact that after many years of working for Lilith, the servants' loyalty would probably lie with the older woman. It was never an easy changeover when the reins of the household were passed from one mistress to the next, and this was certainly not the best of situations.

After the introductions, they were at last led to their bedchambers, and Juliana was finally alone. She flopped down on the bed and lay for a long moment staring up at the heavy brocade tester that hung several feet above her head. The bed was a massive Jacobean piece in dark walnut, upon which were carved a riot of animals, faces and scenes. The tester that was suspended from the tall, thick posts was patterned in rich dark green and gold, with matching draperies tied back at all four posts. Given the heavy magnificence of her bed, she could only imagine how large and ornate the master's bed must be. She wondered if this was always the bed of the current Lady Barre, or if Lilith had given it to her with the purpose of overwhelming her.

Well, it would take more than a bed to intimidate her, Juliana promised herself, her chin jutting out unconsciously. She sat up and looked around the room, taking in all the features she had been too tired to notice when she first came in.

It was a large bedchamber, with a row of pleasant south-facing windows, and it was furnished and decorated lavishly, even if somewhat overdone. A comfortable looking green velvet *chaise longue* with gold pillows arranged on it repeated the color scheme of the bed, and the heavy draperies beside each window were green velvet, as well. A large wardrobe and high, narrow lingerie chest with shallow drawers, as well as a dresser and another tall highboy, all in the same dark walnut, provided more than enough storage for her clothes. There were also a vanity with mirror and chair, a small writing desk, and a little round table beside the bed, and still the room had ample space. It was a place of luxury that was almost overwhelming for a woman brought up to save each and every penny, and again Juliana could not help but wonder if that was precisely the reaction Aunt Lilith had hoped to evoke in her.

There was a door set into one of the side walls of the room, and Juliana went over to it curiously. A key was inserted in the lock, and she turned it, opening the door to find herself looking into another room. Quickly, she eased the door shut. She could hear the sound of footsteps in the room beyond. Clearly her bedroom connected to another, which she supposed must be Nicholas's bedchamber. It was a common enough arrangement between spouses of the aristocracy.

She turned away, an involuntary flush staining her cheeks. She did not want to think about the possibilities that door raised.

A few minutes later there was a knock at the door, and two footmen carried in Juliana's trunks. They were followed by her new maid, a girl named Celia, who had been Eleanor's personal maid since she had been in England. The girl had balked at the prospect of accompanying Eleanor to Italy, so Eleanor had suggested that Juliana hire her, and Juliana had been quick to do so. Celia was a wizard with hairstyles, and it was clear that with her new wardrobe and lifestyle, Juliana was going to need a maid to keep up with everything.

Celia and Nicholas's valet, Roberts, had also come from London this morning, leaving earlier and arriving later, because they had ridden in a wagon hauling the luggage. Celia bustled about, unpacking Juliana's clothes, aided by one of the housemaids, and putting her things away. It was not long before the efficient woman had Juliana's possessions stored away and began busying herself with getting one of the elegant formal gowns, much-creased from its trip in a trunk, ready for dinner that evening.

Juliana chose her dress carefully. At this first dinner with Nicholas's family, she wanted there to be no room for criticism of her appearance. An unmarried girl had to wear a white dress, and even though Juliana felt that her age no longer put her in the category of young maiden, she felt it was best to adhere to the letter of the law. She donned a white silk evening dress, simple in design, yet elegant. Its only decoration was a wide ribbon in a deep blue hue that sashed it beneath her breasts, and Celia would wind a ribbon of the same color artfully through her curls. It had only the barest suggestion of a train and but one deep ruffle in front. Yet anyone who knew clothes would recognize it immediately as the work of a top modiste, and it showed Juliana's willowy figure off to advantage.

By the time Celia finished with Juliana's hair and handed her her fan, Juliana had the confidence of knowing she looked her best. She stepped out into the hall and glanced involuntarily toward the door of the next bedroom. At that very moment Nicholas stepped out, carrying a small flat box in his hands.

He looked up and saw Juliana, and a smile flickered across his face. "Juliana. I was just coming to see you." He stopped in front of her. "How lovely you look."

His eyes were warm as he gazed at her, and Juliana felt an answering warmth stealing through her. "Thank you," she replied softly. "I wanted to look worthy of—of being your wife."

"It is I who am not worthy of you, I assure you," he told her. "Nor are any of those vultures who wait for us downstairs."

Juliana let out a little giggle at his description of his relatives. "You are most unkind."

"I am honest, and you know it. And I hope you know, as well, how very beautiful you are." His voice was low and a little husky, and the sound of it sent a ripple of awareness across her skin, as if he had brushed his fingers over her arm.

Juliana scarcely knew where to look. She wondered if Nicholas had any idea of the effect he had upon her. *Did she cause any of the same sort of sensations in him?*

Nicholas extended the flat box to her. "I have brought you something."

"What is it?" Juliana reached out to take it, looking up into his face questioningly.

"Open it and see." He nodded toward the box.

Juliana turned up the lid. Inside lay a string of pearls, perfectly matched. Juliana drew in her breath.

"Nicholas! They are lovely."

"Then they will match you. Here, put them on." He took the necklace from its velvet display and opened the clasp.

"But such a gift… I cannot accept it."

"Of course you can. You are my fiancée. It's perfectly natural. And they are pearls. Eleanor assured me they were the proper gift. Pearls until you are a married lady. Then I think…um…sapphires would be in order, don't you? At least for this dress."

"Nicholas…" Juliana looked up into his face. He was right, of course. Pearls were proper for an unmarried woman, and a bridal gift was acceptable—indeed, expected from the groom to his bride. *Was she foolish for wishing that the gift had been prompted by something other than what was proper and expected?*

He held up the necklace, moving a half step nearer to her. His closeness stopped the breath in her throat. Juliana was tinglingly aware of him and only him. Nicholas reached out, around her, to fasten the clasp behind her neck. The pearls lay against her bare skin, cool and smooth. She felt the brush of his fingers against her neck as he worked, and she could not disguise the shiver that ran down her back at the contact.

The clasp closed with a snick, and Nicholas's hands slid away, his fingers lingering over her shoulders. His eyes were intent upon hers. Juliana felt as if she could lose herself in their dark depths, simply let go and…

She swayed a little toward him. He leaned down, his face looming closer. Her stomach tightened in anticipation, and her eyes closed.

There was a loud crack as a door opened down the hall, and Juliana jumped, her eyes flying open. Nicholas stepped back at the same moment, turning, as Juliana did, toward the noise. Sir Herbert stepped out into the hallway and turned down the hall. He nodded, giving them a smile.

"Hullo. Going down to dinner, are you?" he said jovially and stopped beside them. "Seraphina will be a while, I'm afraid." He gave Nicholas a smile of conspiratorial understanding and added, "You'll find out soon enough, old fellow."

Juliana mustered up a smile, even though her feelings toward the man were less than friendly at the moment. There was nothing for it now but to join Sir Herbert and walk with him down to the dining room.

The others were gathered in the small anteroom to the dining room. It was separated by sliding pocket doors from the larger room. The heavy walnut doors could be opened to make the formal dining room longer for large dinner parties, but most of the time the small room was used only for the predinner social hour.

Lilith was already there, along with Crandall and his wife. Lilith was sitting, stiff-backed, sipping a glass of sherry. Winifred was in a chair nearby, also with a glass of sherry in her hand, but she was clutching it so tightly that Juliana thought it was a wonder the fragile stem did not shatter. She was eyeing her husband nervously. Crandall was standing beside the liquor cabinet, and from the looks of him, his position there must have been constant this evening.

As the three of them entered the room, Crandall turned toward them, his movements unsteady, and regarded them belligerently. Juliana's hand tightened on Nicholas's arm.

"Well, well," Crandall said, bitterness scoring his voice. "If it isn't the prodigal son."

"Crandall," Nicholas replied evenly.

Crandall regarded him for a moment, his face stamped with its familiar arrogance. Then he turned toward Juliana.

"And little Juliana," he said, sweeping her a formal bow. The bow was somewhat spoiled by the fact that he staggered and had to brace his hand on the liquor cabinet. "Looks like you've gotten what you were after all these years."

"I can see that you have not changed, Crandall," Juliana remarked dryly.

Her statement was true as far as his personality went, but his looks had greatly declined in the nine years since she had last seen him. His personality had always shown in his face too much for Juliana ever to like his looks, but she knew that at one time Seraphina's friends had considered him quite handsome. He was lighter in coloring than Nicholas—his hair brown and his eyes a hazel color—but he was tall like both Nicholas and his father, and he had the same sort of angular face, with fierce black slashes of eyebrows. However, the years—and, if tonight was typical, much imbibing of alcohol—had added pounds to his frame and covered the sharp-boned face with doughy flesh. He was stuffed into a formal jacket and knee breeches, and his jowls and face puffed out, toadlike, above his ascot.

Looking at him, Juliana felt her skin crawl. She could not keep from remembering the last time she had been at Lychwood Hall. Crandall had trapped her in the library alone, backing her up against the shelves. She could still recall the hard shelves digging into her back as she pressed herself as far away from him as she could. He had been drinking then, too, and she remembered the smell of whiskey on his breath, hot against her skin. The weight of his body pressing into her, his hands gripping her arms to hold her still. She remembered, too, with more satisfaction, bringing her knee up hard in a most unladylike fashion, an action that had sent Crandall staggering back, clutching at the injured area and cursing her vividly. The next day she had pressed Lilith into writing her a letter of recommendation and had left for London.

"I cannot say the same for you, my dear," Crandall said, his eyes crawling down her body. "You look even more lovely."

Juliana felt Nicholas stiffen beside her, and she dug her fingers into his arm, casting a glance at Lilith for help. She was somewhat surprised to see the woman regarding her son with a glacial expression. She wondered if Lilith had finally begun to see Crandall for what he was.

When Lilith made no move in response to Juliana's look, Crandall's wife jumped up and went to him, laying her hand upon his arm. "Crandall, dear, why don't you come sit down with me?"

He looked at her scornfully. "And be bored out of my skull?"

Winifred ducked her head, a flush spreading painfully across her face. Juliana felt a surge of sympathy for the girl.

It was Sir Herbert who broke the awkward moment. He walked over to Crandall and Winifred, saying, "Don't be such a boor, Crandall. Pour me a whiskey, why don't you? Lord Barre?" He turned in question to Nicholas and Juliana. "Sherry, Miss Holcott?"

"Yes, thank you," Juliana replied, and went to Winifred. "Come, sit down with me, Mrs. Barre, and let us get acquainted."

The girl cast her a grateful glance. "Please, call me Winnie. 'Mrs. Barre' sounds so old. I mean…" She blushed again, casting a glance toward Lilith, realizing that her words were scarcely flattering to the other Mrs. Barre in the room.

"So adult," Juliana said smoothly. "I know just what you mean. Now, you must tell me how you and Crandall met. You are not from here, are you?"

"Oh, no. I'm from Yorkshire. Crandall came to visit at Brackenmore, you see. He was friends with one of the Earl's sons. I hadn't even come out, really. But my mother let me go to the ball at Brackenmore." She smiled, her eyes glowing a little with remembered excitement. "Crandall asked me to dance, and, well…"

She shrugged. Juliana could have told the rest of the story. Winifred, young and naive, had been dazzled by the ball and the attention of what she perceived as a fashionable London blade. She had tumbled head-over-heels in love with Crandall.

Now, a few years later, Juliana suspected that much of the glitter had worn off her vision of Crandall Barre. She felt sorry for the girl, coming as a bride to this cold house, with Crandall for a husband and the cold and disdainful Lilith for a mother-in-law. As the girl artlessly—and somewhat wistfully—described her family in Yorkshire, Juliana quickly got the picture of a girl from a respectable family, but not one of particular stature or great wealth. No doubt her parents had been as dazzled as she was by the match. And no doubt Lilith considered her a social inferior.

It was less clear to her why Crandall had wanted to marry such a sweet, naive girl. No doubt she had been quite pretty, and perhaps she had been livelier before four years of living with Crandall and Lilith had ground it out of her. But it was hard to picture Crandall falling madly in love, even if the girl was pretty. Perhaps he had responded instinctively to the opportunity to marry someone whom he could make miserable for years without any retaliation. Or, knowing Crandall's proclivities, probably the most likely reason had been that he had been discovered trying to seduce the girl and forced by a livid father or brother to marry her.

"Oh, dear!" Seraphina's voice at the doorway drew all eyes to her. She swept in, flashing them all a smile. "Am I the last to arrive again?"

"Of course you are," Crandall remarked.

"But well worth the wait, as always," Sir Herbert countered gallantly, stepping forward to take his wife's hand and raise it to his lips.

"Yes, you look quite nice," Lilith responded. "I shall tell Rundell that we are ready."

She rose and tugged at the bellpull. Crandall knocked back the rest of his drink in one gulp, apparently afraid to leave any of it behind as they went in to dinner. Lilith looked at her son, her lips tightening.

Crandall strolled over to his sister. "Nice earbobs, Ser," he commented, idly tapping one of the dangling rubies in question. "Are those new?"

There was a taunting quality to his voice, and his eyes danced as he looked at his sister, as if he were in on a joke that no one else knew.

Seraphina shot him a fulminating glance. "Of course not, Crandall, don't be a fool. They've been in Sir Herbert's family for years."

At that moment Rundell arrived in the doorway to announce that dinner was served, and they removed themselves to the dining room. Juliana hoped the food might sober Crandall up, but she soon saw that her hope was in vain. Crandall immediately gestured to one of the servants to fill his wineglass, and he continued to drink heavily all through the meal, so the food he consumed had little chance of counteracting the liquor.

He also continued to behave in the same obnoxious manner, making disagreeable comments to everyone at the table and cursing at the footman, who was not quick enough in refilling his wineglass.

Even his mother was moved to crisply tell him to mind his manners. When she did so, Crandall looked at her with a sneer.

"My manners? Oh, yes, that's all that matters to

you, isn't it? Appearances. We must pretend that we are polite and civilized, no matter what filth is lying beneath our feet, mustn't we?" He gave her a cold, hard smile.

"Crandall, really…"

"We all have to sit here and act as if we're just delighted that Nicholas has come home to take it all away from us." Crandall made a vague sweeping gesture that encompassed the room.

Juliana glanced around the table. Winnie, beside her husband, was looking down at her plate. Sir Herbert was regarding Crandall with an expression of disgust, and Seraphina was doing her best to avoid looking at her brother at all. Lilith's mouth was clamped into a thin line, and she, too, glanced away from her son. Nicholas's expression was one of resignation.

"Crandall…" Nicholas began in a warning tone. "I suggest you stop before you make a statement you will regret in the morning."

"Regret?" Crandall repeated, his voice thick with drink and fury. "The only thing I will regret is that you are here, taking the place that should be mine."

"Yours?" Nicholas responded, one eyebrow going up.

"Yes, mine!" Crandall thrust his head forward pugnaciously. "Who stayed here and took care of the land all these years? Not you. Not your father, who waltzed off to Cornwall to live so he could spend his years sailing. No, it was my father who stayed here and took care of the estate. It was he who managed it, and after him, me. I was the one who rode the land by his side. I was the one he taught to manage the estate. I should have inherited Lychwood Hall, not some upstart like you!"

Nicholas's expression did not change as he said calmly, "Clearly your father wronged you in raising you as if you would be the heir to the estate, when you obviously could not be as long as I was alive."

"It's just damnable luck that you *are* alive," Crandall growled.

"No." Nicholas smiled coldly. "'Twasn't luck that saved me, but good reflexes."

Crandall's face contorted, and he jumped to his feet, knocking his chair over with a crash. "Damn you! You should have died!"

He turned and slammed out of the room.

CHAPTER NINE

EVERYONE SAT FROZEN in their chairs, staring at Nicholas. Finally Sir Herbert cleared his throat, saying, "Really. Bad form, that."

Juliana ducked her head to hide a smile at the man's vast understatement. She glanced over at Nicholas and saw mirrored in his face the same appreciation of Sir Herbert's comment.

"I fear Crandall was somewhat the worse for drink," Nicholas replied, matching Sir Herbert's imperturbability.

One of the footmen hurried to set Crandall's overturned chair upright again, and they all turned their attention once more to their plates.

Conversation after that was stilted and sporadic. Two bright red spots burned on Winifred's cheeks, and Lilith's face was frozen into an expression of polite blankness. Sir Herbert commented with great frequency on the excellence of the food.

"You must tell us all the *on-dits* from London, Juliana," Seraphina told her brightly. "We have spent most of the Season here, and I have quite missed out on everything."

"I fear I don't know any gossip," Juliana replied. She wished very much that she did, just to carry them through this awkward meal. "I did not really move in the *ton* the last few years."

Seraphina, as it turned out, knew enough gossip for both of them. "Do you remember Anne Blaisebury? We went to school with her at Miss Blanton's," she began, and proceeded to chatter about the lives and fortunes of all the girls who had attended school with them.

Juliana had frankly forgotten most of them, but she was glad enough to let Seraphina talk about them to cover the uncomfortable silence. She only half listened, however, for her mind was busy going over the words that Nicholas and Crandall had exchanged.

Not surprisingly, there was no move to linger after the dinner was over, or to extend the evening by gathering in the drawing room afterward.

Nicholas turned to Juliana as the others scattered from the dining room, saying, "Allow me to escort you to your room."

"I want to talk to you," Juliana told him flatly, her tone brooking no dissent.

"All right. Well…" He cast a glance around. "As

I have an aversion to Uncle Trenton's study…" He gestured toward the room in which they had gathered before the meal. "Why don't we go back in here?"

Juliana nodded, and they walked next door to the small room, shutting the door behind them. Juliana dropped down into a chair with a sigh.

"That was ghastly."

"Yes. Crandall at his worst." Nicholas shrugged. "I'd almost forgotten how despicable he is." He strolled over to the liquor cabinet. "I think that after that performance, I need a drink…although I must say, seeing Crandall like that is enough to put one off alcohol altogether."

"He's a boor even when he has not been drinking."

"May I get you a sherry? Or perhaps something stronger would be in order."

Juliana shook her head. Nicholas poured himself a whiskey and came back to sit down in the chair closest to hers. He took a sip and sighed.

"I would say that at least the evening cannot get any worse, but I suspect that Crandall's capacity for trouble is greater than I can imagine," Nicholas remarked dryly. "I hope you did not allow him to upset you."

"I am used to Crandall," Juliana told him. "I expect rudeness from him, and I have never been disappointed. I must say, though, that he seems worse than ever."

Nicholas nodded. "No one at the table liked him. Did you notice? His sister kept glaring at him. His wife was obviously humiliated by his behavior and scared of him. Even Aunt Lilith seemed disgusted."

Juliana nodded. "He's a difficult man to like."

"I don't know what I'm going to do about him," Nicholas mused. "I will seem heartless if I turn him out of the only home he's ever known. And his wife will suffer, though she is not to blame for his actions. But I refuse to allow him to continue to disrupt everything."

"What did he mean, Nicholas?" Juliana asked.

"About what?"

"You know very well," she replied. "What you two were talking about—how you should have been dead, and damn your good luck, except it wasn't luck but your reflexes?"

Nicholas studied his drink for a moment, idly swirling the whiskey around in the glass. Then he sighed and raised his head to look her in the eyes. "I didn't just decide to run away when I was sixteen. I did so because Uncle Trenton had tried to kill me."

Juliana stared at him. She had suspected something of the sort from what had been said, but still the words shocked her. "How? What happened? Are you sure he tried to murder you?"

"It was unmistakable. It happened on the stairs. He shoved me, and I tumbled forward. Fortunately, I was quick enough to grab the rail and managed to do nothing more than get a few bruises and some strained muscles. But we were standing at the top, with the marble of the entry below. I could easily have broken my neck. Afterwards he tried to pretend that I had merely stumbled. But I know I felt a hand on my back, pushing me forward. There was no mistaking it. And I knew if I stayed here, I would never live long enough to inherit." He shrugged. "So I ran."

"Oh, Nicholas! How awful." Impulsively, Juliana reached out and placed her hand over his. His skin was warm beneath hers, and she was suddenly very aware of the feel of it beneath her fingers. Her heart picked up its beat, and she pulled her hand away, clasping it with her other and letting them lie in her lap. "Why didn't you tell anyone? Why didn't you say anything?"

Nicholas shrugged. "Who would have believed me? I was the one everyone considered wicked. My uncle was the most important man in the area, a fine upstanding citizen. Who would have believed his wild, wayward nephew? It was my word against his. We were the only ones there, besides Crandall—and I knew *he* would swear that his father had done nothing to me. How could I prove that he had shoved me?"

"Why didn't you tell *me?*" Juliana asked, a little surprised by the hurt she experienced over the fact that he had not. "Did you not trust me?"

"Of course I did. But what purpose would it have served to tell you? You were only a child, and you had to continue to live there. I could not put that burden on you. As long as you didn't know, you would be all right. Uncle Trenton would have no reason to harm you. Indeed, I presumed that your treatment would be better once I left, since you were usually in trouble only because you tried to help me. But if you knew what had happened, it was all too likely that you would have been brave, as always, and have spoken up. Then he might have felt he would have to shut you up. I could not do that."

Emotion welled up inside Juliana. She thought of the young man he had been—barely more than a boy, really—having to bear that burden all alone. It must have been horrible to know that his own flesh and blood had tried to murder him, and even worse to be unable to tell his only friend for fear of endangering her, as well.

"Nicholas...I am so sorry." Juliana looked up at

him, tears glistening in her eyes. She rose, her hands going out to him.

"Juliana…" Suddenly she was in his arms, his warmth all around her, and his lips were on hers.

Her arms went around his neck, and she clung to him. All her senses were abruptly, wildly, alive. His lips were hot, insistent, demanding her response. Juliana quivered, not sure what she wanted but certain of the need.

Nicholas's hands moved down her back, sweeping over her hips, then back up her side, coming to rest at last on the curves of her breasts. Her nipples tightened at his touch, her breasts swelling with desire. Juliana had never felt anything like this, indeed, had not even known such sensations existed. Unconsciously, her hands slipped upwards, gliding into his hair. The strands separated, sliding silkily around her fingers. She shivered, lost in his kiss.

His mouth left hers, and he kissed his way down her throat. Juliana let her head fall back, giving him access to the tender flesh. His breath was hot on her skin, his lips like velvet as they moved down onto the expanse of chest exposed by the low neckline of her gown. His lips reached the soft swell of her breast, and Juliana gasped at the touch, heat flowering deep in her abdomen.

Nicholas's hand curved gently around her breast, his thumb softly tracing the shape of the nipple. That small bud of flesh tightened, even as a pulse came to life between her legs. Juliana's breath rasped raggedly in her throat.

He breathed her name as his mouth moved over the supremely soft flesh of her breast. His tongue traced tiny patterns of desire over her skin, igniting a fierce hunger within her.

The neckline of her dress impeded his roving mouth, and Nicholas raised his head. Juliana let out a small moan of protest. But then he slipped his hand inside her dress, startling her, and cupped her breast, lifting it up and out of the dress.

He bent his head again, and this time his lips came down upon the nipple itself, sending a wave of heat through Juliana. He teased the small button of flesh with his tongue, first caressing, then whipping it into hardness. She choked back a sob of hunger, wanting more. His mouth closed over her nipple, pulling on it with strong, slow pulses, and passion slammed through her. Juliana moved helplessly, hungrily, thrumming with the force of her need.

Her skin was on fire, aching for his touch, and the tender ache between her legs swelled. Nicholas made a noise deep in his throat, and his hands went to her hips, digging in, pressing her against him so that she felt the hard length of his own desire against her abdomen.

Juliana let out a small sound of surprise, as much at her own body's leap of hunger as at the gesture itself. Nicholas raised his head, the sound penetrating the haze of his passion. He gazed down into her face for one stunned instant before he registered what he was doing and where.

He bit out an oath beneath his breath and released her, stepping back and turning away. Juliana stared at his back blankly, still dazed by the desire pulsing through her.

"Nicholas?" Her voice was soft and questioning.

It sliced through him like a knife. Juliana, the one person for whom he truly cared, had reached out to him in sympathy, and he—he had reacted like an animal, he thought savagely. Despite all his assurances, his promises, he had let himself be swept away by raw need. In another few minutes, he knew, he would have been lost to all reason, ready to pull her right down on the floor with him and take her.

"I am sorry," he said gruffly, not looking at her. "I should not have—this will not happen again. I swear it."

A shiver, not of desire this time, but of cold, shook

her. Juliana came back to earth with a thud. Nicholas did not want her. He regretted kissing her. She felt suddenly naked and ashamed. Her face flamed with red to her hairline, and she hastily adjusted her dress, covering her exposed breast, smoothing and straightening her dress. She hated to consider what he would think about her now.

"No. Pray, do not apologize," she replied stiffly, also turning away from him. "It was a—a momentary aberration. That is all."

She felt the treacherous burn of tears in her throat, and she swallowed hard. He had offered her one sort of marriage; she was not going to cry because it was not something else.

"It is forgotten," she went on quickly. "Good night, Nicholas."

She turned and hurried from the room.

It was a relief to find that her maid was not waiting for her when she reached her room. The last thing Juliana wanted was to have to put up a front for anyone just now.

She walked agitatedly over to the window and stood, looking out at the dark garden below her. She thought about the girlish dreams she had had as an adolescent. The sweet picture she had painted then was far different from reality. It had not involved desire that flamed up at Nicholas's touch or glance. There had been no kisses that pierced her to the heart, no caresses that left her panting and shaken, no fire roaring through her blood.

She put her hand on her chest, as though she could contain the thundering emotions that swirled there. The passion she had felt tonight had been so fierce, so elemental—and she knew that she far preferred it to the sweet, rather colorless love which she had imagined as a girl. It would be easy to succumb to her feelings, to fall into his bed like a wanton. It would be easier still to fall in love with him.

But she knew it would be mad for her to do so. Nicholas did not believe in love. Though she was convinced he was a far more emotional person, a kinder one, than he would ever let himself believe, she also knew how guarded he was, how separated from those emotions. She feared that Nicholas would never allow himself to really fall in love. He permitted affection such as he felt for her. He allowed a general kindness to temper his actions. But he kept his heart locked away, safe from the pain and loneliness he had endured as a child.

That much was clear from the kind of marriage he wanted. He had not fallen in love, had not given his heart to a woman. No, he had sought out a wife with whom he could be friends, a woman he thought of as a friend, a woman to whom he had no fears of losing his heart. He had offered to marry her out of kindness, of course, but Juliana was also sure that it was to protect himself, as well. He did not want love; he would not allow himself to love.

If she were to fall in love with him, it would be one-sided and would always remain so. Nicholas would never feel any more for her than affection, and she would be guaranteeing herself the pain of unrequited love.

Oh, he had felt passion, she knew. There had been no mistaking the fire that burned in him when he kissed her and caressed her. But he had not wanted to feel that passion. He had turned from her, reminding them both that desire was not intended to be a part of their marriage.

It was better by far, she knew, not to allow herself to be swept away again. It was better to accept the loveless marriage he had offered than to try to turn it into anything else. She had to put a guard on her own heart, as well. She must avoid similar situations with Nicholas. They could have a close, friendly marriage, a bond of affection, even love of a sort. But she could not allow it to turn into anything else. She could not let herself desire him, could not let that desire turn into passionate, romantic love.

Juliana turned away from the window. She felt achingly empty. She could not help but wonder if she had played the fool when she agreed to marry Nicholas Barre.

THINGS ALWAYS SEEMED better in the morning, Juliana thought, and the next day was no exception. When the maid pulled back the draperies to let the sun in, Juliana's spirits unaccountably lifted, and she smiled as she drank her morning tea and dressed, then hummed to herself as she went downstairs to breakfast.

Lilith and Nicholas were already seated at the table, eating their meal in silence, when Juliana walked in. When she saw Nicholas, she could not help but think of what had transpired between them the night before, and heat blossomed deep in her loins, just as it had then. She looked away, embarrassed at the memory and annoyed with herself for her seeming inability to control her desires around him.

Nicholas looked up and saw her, and immediately his face was stamped with a look of such relief that she could not help but forget her embarrassment in amusement. Obviously he had found it very uncomfortable being alone with his aunt.

"Good morning, my dear." Nicholas came around to take her hand and kiss it before he escorted her to her chair. A footman jumped to pull out the chair for her.

Juliana greeted Lilith, and the older woman nodded to her. It was the cool sort of greeting that Juliana expected from her mother's cousin. Juliana could not remember a time when Lilith had seemed pleased to see anyone—except, of course, for her horses. She had always been all smiles when she went out to ride. Juliana had often wondered how a woman could be so cold to people and so loving of animals.

"Am I the last again?" a voice trilled gaily, and Juliana turned to see Seraphina sweeping into the room.

Again there was a round of greetings. At least Lilith did manage to say hello to her daughter, though she did not unbend enough to offer her a smile.

"Sir Herbert and Crandall are not here," Nicholas pointed out.

"Oh, Sir Herbert never eats breakfast," Seraphina informed them. "He is something of a slugabed, I'm afraid. Even here in the country, where there is nothing to keep one up late. He likes to sit and read 'til all hours."

Her last words were spoken in a tone of wonderment that made Juliana smother a smile. She was sure Seraphina found such behavior decidedly bizarre. She could not remember ever seeing the woman open a book voluntarily.

Juliana noticed that Seraphina did not say anything about her brother. She suspected that, given the amount that Crandall had imbibed last night, he was nursing a severe headache this morning, and she doubted they would be cursed with his presence at breakfast. She wondered if heavy drinking were a nightly occurrence with him or a unique event brought about by Nicholas's arrival.

Juliana and Seraphina served themselves from the informal array of dishes on the sideboard, with Seraphina chattering all the while about the quantity of the food.

"If I ate all the time the way I do here in the country," she confided, "I fear I would be the size of a house."

"It is quite an array."

"I never have more than toast and tea in the morning in the City." Seraphina sighed. "But there is little to do here except eat, really."

"You could join me on my morning ride," her mother pointed out. "I have already been out. There's nothing like it for setting up one's day."

Seraphina gave an elaborate shudder. "I have no

desire to go throwing myself over fences at the crack of dawn."

"Scarcely dawn," Lilith pointed out. "As it is already past nine."

"I would be in bed another two hours if I were home," her daughter retorted, sitting down and digging into her food.

"I am surprised to find you here with the Season in full swing," Juliana commented.

Seraphina jabbed a piece of ham with her fork and said without looking up, "Sir Herbert desired a bit of peace and quiet in the country."

Juliana decided that this was a topic best dropped, so she cast about for something else to say.

"What do you have planned for the morning?" Nicholas asked helpfully, and Juliana cast him a grateful smile.

"Why, nothing, really," Juliana told him. "I scarcely know where to begin, I'm afraid. I must meet the vicar, of course, and speak to him about the ceremony. And then, of course, there is much to be done about the celebration after the wedding." She turned toward Lilith. "I do hope that you will guide me in what should be done, Aunt Lilith."

"Of course." The other woman looked as if nothing could please her less.

But apparently there *was* something that could do so, for the next moment, her expression grew even more sour when Nicholas said, "No doubt Aunt Lilith will want to show you about the place, Juliana. Teach you all the ins and outs…since you will soon be taking over the reins of the household."

"Naturally," Lilith murmured, turning toward Juliana. "No doubt it will take a little time for Juliana to learn what to do, since she was scarcely brought up to manage a grand house."

"I will do my best," Juliana replied stiffly.

"I am quite sure that Juliana is up to the task," Nicholas told his aunt, his face cold.

"You will be much better than I, I am sure," Seraphina remarked with a little laugh, somewhat dispelling the palpable tension in the air. "I am quite in awe of my housekeeper and hardly dare change anything she does. And when she drones on and on about the books, and the cost of this and the price of that, I vow, 'tis all I can do to keep from nodding off."

Juliana smiled at her cousin. Seraphina was still something of a fluffbrain, but at least she seemed to be trying to be friendly. "But perhaps you will help me with the wedding, Seraphina? It will be small, but I expect the celebration afterwards will be rather large. We will, after all, want to have something for the tenants and villagers, as well as the supper for family and friends."

Seraphina's face brightened at the prospect of any sort of party. "Oh, yes. There must be a ball, don't you think? And, of course, the meal before that. Perhaps some tables of cards, as well—for those who don't like to dance."

The idea of gaming tables at a wedding celebration sounded a trifle odd to Juliana, but, then, she was not up to date on the fashionable *ton* wedding.

"Don't be any sillier than you have to be," Lilith said bluntly, casting a disapproving look at her daughter. "One does not have card games at a wedding supper. I suppose we must have something for the tenants, of course. And a ball would be in order."

On that grudging note, another silence fell over the table. After a moment, Juliana tried to start a conversation again. "What shall you be doing this morning, Nicholas, while Aunt Lilith shows me around the house?"

"Going over the accounts with the estate manager and Crandall," he replied.

Juliana suspected that Crandall would feel little like going over any books this morning, but she said nothing. She wondered what Nicholas would find. It frankly would not surprise her to learn that Crandall had been cheating the estate during the years since his father's death—nor would it be remarkable to find that he had in fact done next to nothing at all concerning the place, leaving it all in the manager's hands. Crandall had never struck her as someone who was particularly industrious. Certainly he had made little effort in their school lessons.

As if sensing her thoughts, Lilith said, "Crandall has done an excellent job managing the estate. He has always been quite fond of the land."

There was a pinched look to her face, and Juliana suspected that she was thinking along the lines that Crandall had been last night—that the land should have gone to her son, not the interloper, Nicholas.

"I am sure I will find everything in order," Nicholas replied carefully. Juliana felt sure that he had the same sort of doubts as she did about Crandall's competence.

The meal continued in this joyless, stilted way, and it was a relief to Juliana when it was over and they were able to leave. Lilith turned to her as she rose.

"I shall take you to the housekeeper now, if you wish," she said with icy politeness.

Juliana suspected that Lilith hoped to intimidate her with her tone and manner, a reminder that Juliana was an orphan and a poor relation, whereas Lilith was the lady of the manor. Possibly she even hoped that Juliana would cave in and allow her to continue to run the house. Frankly, Juliana would not have minded letting the woman continue; keeping a house in order was not something she looked forward to with great joy. However, she was going to be Nicholas's wife now. It would be her duty and her responsibility. Besides, if she left the house in Lilith's hands, it would be a part of the estate that was being kept from Nicholas, and Juliana had no intention of allowing that to happen.

"Thank you," she replied with equal courtesy.

Lilith's lips thinned, but she said nothing further, just walked from the room and down the hall toward the kitchens. Juliana followed, determined not to let the older woman annoy her into rudeness.

When they reached the kitchen, the servants all turned toward them, bobbing curtseys as they watched them curiously. Juliana suspected that Lilith was not a common visitor in this area.

Rundell came out of the butler's pantry and hurried toward them. "Mrs. Barre. Miss Holcott. May I assist you?"

Lilith turned toward him. "I was showing Miss Holcott about, Rundell. Is Mrs. Pettibone here?"

"Of course." He turned as if to fetch the woman,

but the housekeeper was already bustling into the kitchen to join them, all smiles, greeting them even as she turned a fierce glare on the other servants, impelling them to return to work.

"Perhaps you would like to come into my sitting area," she suggested brightly. "Dorrie, bring us some tea."

Juliana would have liked to refuse, having just come from breakfast, but she knew that it would be taken badly if she refused to sit down to tea with the housekeeper, so she smiled and resigned herself to another cup.

Once they were all three seated in the housekeeper's small sitting room, waiting for Dorrie to bring their refreshment, Lilith turned to the housekeeper, saying, "Miss Holcott will be assuming control of the household when she marries Lord Barre, as you know. No doubt she will want to change the menu for the week and go over your schedule."

The housekeeper looked alarmed at this pronouncement, but quickly hid her reaction, saying, "Of course, ma'am. Just allow me to get the menu."

"Oh, no, Mrs. Pettibone. I shan't be changing the menu or your schedule. I am sure that you have laid out both quite well. No doubt Mrs. Barre misunderstood me." She shot a sharp look at Lilith. "I would merely like to look at your menu. And perhaps sometime in the future we might add a dish or two that are Lord Barre's favorites."

"Oh, of course, ma'am," Mrs. Pettibone agreed readily.

"I would not wish to disturb your work. However, sometime soon, I would appreciate it if you would show me about the house and familiarize me with the workings of your staff. If you would let me know when would be a convenient time for you…"

"Of course. Whenever you wish, ma'am. A little later this morning would suit me, if it pleases you. Give me time to make sure everyone is going about their business, if you know what I mean. Then I can get together the menu and such, and take you all about."

"That sounds fine. Shall we say…around eleven?"

"Lovely, ma'am. Lovely."

They endured a polite cup of tea and some more stilted conversation with the housekeeper, then left the kitchen. Juliana kept pace with Lilith, and when the woman would have started up the stairs, she moved in front of her, sweeping her arm toward the drawing room.

"I would like to speak to you, Aunt Lilith, if you please."

For an instant Juliana thought the older woman

was going to refuse, but then, with a twitch of her lips, she turned and walked past Juliana into the drawing room. She sat down on a chair and turned to face Juliana, her brows lifted inquiringly.

"I presume you will wish Rundell and Mrs. Pettibone to come to you with their questions from now on?" Lilith said.

"Aunt Lilith, I have no desire to wrest your authority away from you," Juliana told her calmly. "I am sure that right now, with the wedding approaching, there will be plenty to occupy us both. It would be nice if we could work together, instead of opposing each other. You know the house, the servants, everything, far better than I do. I am simply asking for your help. I would like you to teach me the ropes, to show me how you run the household and help prepare me to run the house myself. You are the expert here, and I would appreciate it if you could teach me."

"So that you may take over my authority?" A half smile played at Lilith's lips.

"Neither of us can do anything to change the fact that Nicholas is Lord Barre. However much you think fate has dealt you a poor hand in that regard, it is simply the way things are. And I am going to marry him. I will be Lady Barre. However, I have no desire to push you out of the way."

"Yet you are doing it nonetheless," Lilith responded sourly. "Do you think I don't know how much pleasure it will give you to displace me?" The older woman's eyes flashed. "I am sure it would be most gratifying to your mother to know that you are taking my place."

Juliana gaped at the other woman, taken aback by the venom that permeated Lilith's voice. She knew Lilith had never liked her or her mother, but she had never realized the depths of the other woman's dislike. Nor could she imagine the reason for it.

Lilith took advantage of Juliana's stunned state to rise. "If you are quite done humiliating me now, I am going up to my room."

She swept past Juliana and out the door, her back ramrod straight, her head high. Juliana followed her to the door, puzzled. There she found Crandall, leaning against the opposite wall of the corridor. He grinned when he saw her.

"Not so easy taking over, is it?" he asked.

"Do you make it a habit of lurking about listening to other people's conversations?" Juliana snapped, her exasperation heightened by the sight of Crandall.

"One hears such interesting things that way," he replied, still smirking.

"Your idea of interesting and mine must differ,

then," Juliana told him coldly, adding, "Aren't you supposed to be going over the books with Nicholas?"

"I'm sure that Nicholas can take over just fine without my presence." He scowled. "I'm sure he's happy to reap the benefits of my years of work. I was a damned fool to slave away all these years just so that bloody bastard could take over."

Juliana stiffened. "I will thank you to keep a civil tongue in your head."

"Oh, I'm sorry. Did I offend your ladylike sensibilities? You can't have too much pride if you're willing to marry that snake just to get a title."

"You know as well as I that the snake in this situation was not Nicholas."

"I've been here working while he was out trotting all over the globe, haven't I? I know all the tenants, all their children's names. I know what every crop has been like every year and what profit we've made on them, what profit we can expect this year. But none of it's mine. He'll snatch it away from me like that." He snapped his fingers for emphasis.

Juliana could see the real pain on Crandall's face. She could almost feel sorry for him…except for the fact that he was so filled with unreasonable hatred for Nicholas.

"You have known all these years that Nicholas

would inherit," Juliana pointed out. "Yet you stayed on. Why?"

"What else was I to do?" he asked, thrusting his chin forward pugnaciously. "This is my land! It's all I know. Where else would I go? What else would I do?" He levered himself away from the wall. "The truth is, I hoped he would never come back. There are lots of opportunities for death out there in the world. With any luck, Nicholas would have met one of them."

He looked at her, his eyes so cold that they made Juliana shiver. She thought about what Nicholas had said to her last night about his uncle trying to kill him. She could not help but wonder if Crandall might not decide to follow his father's example. Even though Nicholas had already come into the estate, if he were to die, the land and title would go to the next male in line, which was Crandall. What if Crandall intended to make sure he got what he had worked for all this time?

CHAPTER TEN

JULIANA SPENT the rest of the morning touring the house with Mrs. Pettibone. The housekeeper seemed intent on showing her every nook and cranny, from the cellars below the house to each and every room in the servants' quarters. She also brought along her planned menu for the week and went over it in great detail. Juliana was not sure if such meticulous attention to detail was because Lilith had convinced Mrs. Pettibone that Juliana would be a strict taskmaster or because Lilith herself had maintained such a tight rein on household matters. Whatever the reason, by luncheon Juliana's head was crammed with more information than she could possibly assimilate.

"I fear it will be some time before I have everything straight, Mrs. Pettibone," she told the housekeeper, smiling. "But until that day, I know I can rely on you to keep everything running smoothly. The house is obviously very well cared for."

Mrs. Pettibone beamed with pride. "Thank you, miss. You can count on me."

"Don't worry about the menu. I am sure it is just the thing, and I certainly don't want to disrupt anything. Especially with all the extra work the wedding will create."

"Don't you fret about that, miss," the housekeeper told her, with a decisive nod of her head. "The whole house is looking forward to that. If I may just say…welcome home, miss. We're that glad to have you here again."

Juliana smiled. The kitchen staff had always been kind to her when she lived here, often sneaking her bits of food to take up to Nicholas when he had been locked in his room without supper, or sending her home with a cake for her mother.

"Thank you, Mrs. Pettibone. I am glad to be here, as well."

Juliana decided that a good walk would be the thing to clear her head after all the information she had received this morning, so after luncheon, she set off for a walk to the village. She had just stepped off the front steps when she heard herself hailed, and she turned toward the voice, shading her eyes against the sun. Nicholas was striding across the stableyard, and she realized that he must have come from the estate manager's house.

"Nicholas!" She felt the now-familiar tug in her chest as she watched him striding toward her, his long, lean legs eating up the distance between them. His black hair glinted in the sunlight.

"Escaping already?" he asked with a smile as he drew close enough to speak.

"I was tempted," Juliana responded. "Mrs. Pettibone has been showing me the house today, and I fear she must have found me a poor pupil."

"I feel sure that is not true," he told her, coming to a halt in front of her. "Where are you off to?"

"I thought I would visit Mrs. Cooper. She was our housekeeper, you remember, when I was young. She would be quite hurt if I did not call on her soon after we came back. She was most devoted to my mother."

He nodded. "I'll come with you, shall I?"

Juliana smiled. "I should like that very much. But do you not have to work?"

He made a careless gesture. "I am through for the day. Blandings wants to take me around to introduce me to the tenants, but that will take the entire day, so we put it off until tomorrow. Perhaps Crandall will even deign to join us for it."

"He did not join you today?"

Nicholas shook his head. "No. He was noticeably absent. Poor Blandings was most distressed, as though he thought I would blame him for Crandall's poor manners."

"I saw him this morning."

"Who? Crandall?"

Juliana nodded. "Yes. He was lurking about in the hallway while I was talking to Aunt Lilith. He is a very bitter man."

"I know." He shrugged. "He has reason to be. He's overseen the estate all these years—and as best I could tell from the state of the books and from talking to Blandings, he hasn't done a bad job of it."

"I have to admit that that surprises me."

"It surprised me, as well," Nicholas agreed. "I think he has a true love for the place…much more so than I, certainly. Still, there is nothing that either one of us can do about the inheritance. I can't change the fact that it's entailed or that I am heir to the title. I don't want to displace him. I would not rip him from his home." He paused, then added in an exasperated tone, "If only the damn fellow were not so disagreeable."

"Crandall makes it difficult to like him."

"I know. I thought that I would lay aside our past differences when I came back. He was, after all, only a boy then, and he had the poor example of his father to follow. Perhaps, as an adult, I thought, he might have changed, and if I ignored our past, then he might, also." Nicholas shrugged. "But I can barely stand to be in the same room with him. And obviously he feels the same."

"I think he feels more than that."

Nicholas glanced at her curiously. "What do you mean?"

Juliana hesitated, then went on. "Crandall worries me."

"Worries you?" He frowned, puzzled. "Why?"

"I fear what he might do to you," Juliana continued in a rush.

Nicholas let out a short laugh. "Crandall? What could Crandall do to me? If you think that I could be bested by that drunken lout, I hate to imagine what you think of my fighting skills."

"It isn't fighting I'm worried about," Juliana retorted tartly. "I don't doubt that you would win in a fair fight. But I see no reason to believe that Crandall would ever worry about fairness. He isn't going to challenge you to a fight. But he could very easily shoot at you from a distance. He could arrange for an 'accident' to happen to you when you are out riding. Or—"

"You think he wants to kill me?" Nicholas asked, startled.

"Is that so unlikely?" Juliana countered. "His father tried it, after all. And Crandall was most emphatic about wishing that Trenton had succeeded in getting rid of you. If you were to die, Crandall would inherit this land, wouldn't he? Would he not become Lord Barre?"

"Well, yes…he is next in line. But that is all he would inherit. My own fortune would go by will to you, as my wife."

"I don't think Crandall cares about your fortune. What he wants is the land and the title."

"Crandall wouldn't have the courage. He has always been a weakling—the sort who hurt those who were smaller than he or in his power. At heart, he is a coward."

"How much courage does it take to shove a man down the stairs, as his father did?" Juliana countered. "You did not see the way he looked today, Nicholas. Crandall is filled with such bitterness and hatred for you."

In her concern, she reached out and took his arm in both her hands, looking up at him intently. He laid his hand over hers. "All right. I will watch out for him."

When she continued to look at him doubtfully, Nicholas smiled and added, "I promise. Don't worry. I won't let Crandall harm me. Now…let us talk of something more pleasant. How lovely you look in that dress, for instance."

Juliana chuckled, her heart lightening, and she allowed her concerns to slide to the back of her mind. "Complimenting me on my dress, sir, is merely complimenting your own good taste. 'Tis one of the ones that you picked out."

"It was not the dress I was complimenting," he responded, his eyes twinkling back at her. "It was the way you look in it. The dress is little by itself. It only allows your beauty to be shown."

"Flatterer." Juliana looped her arm through his, and they continued on their way down the path.

It felt so good, so right, she thought, to be with Nicholas like this. She was determined not to let the sensations that ran through her when she was with him lead her into ruining the wonderful companionship they could have. They were friends, first and foremost, and she would see to it that they remained so.

MRS. COOPER LIVED in a cottage just outside the village. It was a very small thing and quite overgrown with ivy, with a garden of riotously blooming flowers in front of it. The housekeeper came to the door at Nicholas's knock, and she peered out for a moment at Juliana before her face cleared and she beamed.

"Miss Juliana! And Mr. Nicholas—Lord Barre, I should say now. I had heard you were coming back to Lychwood, and I was hoping I might see you."

"Of course I came to see you," Juliana told her, stepping forward and hugging the short, stout woman.

Mrs. Cooper stepped back, patting at her hair as though it might have somehow escaped the large white cap into which it was neatly tucked. "Come in, please, and sit. Let me get you some tea. You must be thirsty. Have you walked all the way from the Hall?"

She bustled into the small kitchen, and they could hear her pumping water and putting the kettle on to boil, then rattling among the dishes. A few minutes later, she returned to the room, carrying a tray that contained not only a white china teapot and cups and saucers, but also a plate piled with small sweet cakes.

"It's good to see you again, Miss Julie," she told Juliana, reaching over to pat her hand. "It's been so long."

"I know. I have missed you," Juliana told her. She had conscientiously written to the woman over the years, letting her know where she was and what she was doing, but she felt a trifle guilty that she had not visited her. "But once I left here…"

"No need to explain, my dear," the older woman assured her kindly as she poured the tea out into their cups. "I know what I know. It was clear to me that you wouldn't be coming to visit at the Hall after you left."

She smiled as she handed them their tea. "But now here you are, returning to Lychwood Hall as the mistress. Your mother would have been so proud."

Juliana returned her smile, not sure what to say to that statement. But Mrs. Cooper did not seem to need any reply. She simply plowed on, talking about Juliana's mother. It was clear that Mrs. Holcott held a revered place in the woman's heart.

"She was a saint, your mother, a saint. Sad, always sad, but did ever a word of complaint escape her lips?" Mrs. Cooper shook her head in answer to her own question. "No. Never. She'd been given a poor lot in life, but she accepted it and carried on."

"She missed my father terribly," Juliana agreed. She remembered her mother looking wan and sad, moving through the days like a ghost, the stark black of her widow's weeds making her appear even smaller and paler than she was.

"Her heart was in the grave with him." Mrs. Cooper nodded. "I cried something fierce when she died, but I knew it was for me, not her. She was glad, I know, to be reunited with Mr. Holcott. She was at peace at last. And she didn't suffer much. It took her quick-like, her heart."

Juliana nodded. "Yes. The doctor told me it would not have been slow and painful."

"Like *he* went," Mrs. Cooper went on, nodding vaguely toward the wall.

Juliana was not sure about whom the woman was speaking, but then the housekeeper added, her voice dripping with scorn, "Trenton Barre, I mean."

There was no need to ask how Mrs. Cooper felt about Nicholas's uncle, Juliana thought. The look on her face went beyond dislike.

"I do not know how he died," Juliana said. "I was no longer living here at the time."

"Dropsy," the housekeeper said. "Painful. He was swollen up like a toad. They said it was his liver— no wonder, given the way he drank. He lingered for months." She shrugged. "Just a taste of what he was going to get hereafter."

Juliana blinked, somewhat taken aback by the venom in the woman's voice. She suspected that Mrs. Cooper was right in her prediction of the sort of afterlife Nicholas's uncle had faced, but it was not common for anyone to speak ill of the dead, even when what one spoke was the truth.

Fortunately, once again no reply was required of them, for Mrs. Cooper went back to the subject of her beloved Mrs. Holcott and the years she had spent working at her house. It wasn't difficult to maintain a conversation with her. Juliana needed to do no more than nod or shake her head, or make an appropriate comment whenever the talkative woman paused for a breath or cast a look of inquiry at her.

Sometime later, after they had finished their tea and Juliana had recalled every fond memory she had of the time she had spent in the cottage on the Barre estate, she and Nicholas took their leave of Mrs. Cooper and started home once again.

They walked along companionably, enjoying the fresh summer air and the quiet of the afternoon after the small confines of Mrs. Cooper's cottage. It was a moment before Juliana even realized that Nicholas had taken her hand as they walked. When she did, a treacherous heat stole up from that hand and spread through her body. She cast a sideways glance at him, wondering if he had been as unconscious of his action as she.

His hand was warm around hers, the palm slightly roughened, and Juliana's skin tingled at the contact. Whereas a moment before she had been pleasantly comfortable in his presence, now she was supremely aware of everything about him—how close his arm lay to hers, the texture of the cloth upon it, the thick brush of the dark lashes that framed his eyes, the clear-cut line of his jaw, faintly shadowed now. She wondered how it would feel to touch his cheek, if the skin was smooth or already roughened with incipient stubble.

He glanced down at her, and Juliana's cheeks warmed. Quickly she cast about for some topic of conversation other than the one on which her thoughts had dwelled. They had emerged from a copse of trees and were standing on a ridge. Across a meadow, they could see Lychwood Hall, standing on another rise in the land. The sun was low in the sky, and it bathed the gray stone house in a golden light.

"Look." Juliana pointed across at the house. "It's beautiful, isn't it?"

"Mm," Nicholas replied noncommittally. "If one doesn't know it."

Unconsciously, they both sighed. Nicholas looked down at her, smiling a little. "Are you ready for another supper?"

"Not if it is like last night's. Perhaps Crandall won't be there."

"I am afraid that's a vain hope." He looked back at the house. "It seems a shame that one cannot choose one's relations."

"What are you going to do?" Juliana asked softly.

"About Crandall?" Nicholas shook his head. "I wish I knew. He seems to want to force my hand. As if he will somehow win something if he drives me to tossing him out of the house. I can't imagine what he thinks it will get him."

"Perhaps what he wants is confirmation of what he has always believed about you," Juliana answered. "To justify the way he treated you. What his father did, what he tried to do, to you. Perhaps so you will give him that last little push he needs to get the courage to eliminate you."

"You won't let that go, will you?" He shook his head.

"I can't. Crandall is a dangerous man."

"He is too petty to take seriously," Nicholas retorted, but at Juliana's look, he added, "But I will take care around him. I will be quite cautious."

"I don't want anything to happen to you."

"I know." Nicholas looked down into her eyes for a long moment, and Juliana saw something change and darken in his gaze.

She tensed. *He was going to kiss her.*

But then he relaxed, moving back just a fraction. "Well?" he asked, a sardonic smile curving his lips. "Shall we go face the dragons once again?"

Juliana nodded, and they started forward.

THE DAYS THAT FOLLOWED moved quickly. There was little time to make preparations for the wedding, and the servants added to the burden by continually consulting with Juliana on even minor details of running the household, a situation that Juliana suspected was engineered by Lilith. At other times Lilith threw everything into disarray by issuing conflicting orders to the servants.

Juliana was determined to keep everything running smoothly, however, so she swallowed her irritation with Nicholas's aunt and simply coped with the problems as best she could. Seraphina was at least friendly enough and did not do anything to obstruct Juliana, but she was little help, for she was still determinedly lazy, spending most of her energies on thinking of ways to avoid doing anything.

Crandall's wife Winifred was at least helpful. She offered in her rather shy manner to help Juliana in whatever way she could. Juliana set her to addressing the invitations, and she was pleased to see that the girl had a beautiful copperplate hand. Juliana, who had always felt that her own handwriting fell short of beauty, was happy to turn the matter over to her.

Juliana sat beside her, blotting, folding and sealing the invitations as Winifred finished them, then marking them off the list. She glanced over and saw that Winifred's long sleeve had fallen back almost to her elbow as she wrote. Her forearm was circled with several small purplish bruises, dark against the girl's white skin. She opened her mouth to ask what had happened, and in that instant, she realized that the bruises lay in a ring, with a row of fingertip-size spots, and she knew at once that they must have come from someone strong grabbing the girl around the arm and squeezing hard.

She must have made some noise of astonishment, for Winifred looked up and saw where Juliana's eyes were directed. She flushed and quickly whipped her sleeve back into place, covering the bruises, then turned her eyes back to her task.

Juliana looked away, anger rising in her. She was certain that the bruises must have come from Winifred's husband. Crandall had obviously been impatient and irritable with the girl the times that Juliana had been around them, and it would not surprise her at all to learn that he had grabbed Winifred roughly or even hit her. She felt a fierce desire to help the girl, to protect her in some way.

But what was she to do? Clearly it was a matter between a husband and wife, and Juliana knew well that in marital situations, the husband had all the rights. Winifred was obviously embarrassed about Juliana's having seen the bruises, and Juliana hated to add to her humiliation by quizzing her about them. But neither could she just stand by.

"Winnie," she said softly. "Are you all right? Can I do anything to help you?"

Winifred glanced at her, her cheeks still flaming. "What? Why, I am fine."

"But your bruises…"

"Oh, those…" Winifred let out a forced chuckle. "That's nothing. I fear I am terribly clumsy. I am forever tripping over something or stumbling…."

"But those look like—"

"Oh, yes!" Again the nervous laughter came. "I almost fell, and Crandall had to grab me around the arm to keep me from tumbling. I bruise so easily— it is quite horrid-looking, isn't it?"

"Yes, it is," Juliana agreed, certain the girl was lying, but uncertain what she could do, with Winifred maintaining that Crandall had been helping her rather than hurting her. "You know, if you are, um, if you need help, you could talk to me about it. Nicholas would—"

"Oh, no!" Winifred looked alarmed. "Pray do not tell Lord Barre about it. I am just…often very foolish. But—there is no reason to disturb Lord Barre."

Juliana saw a very good reason to tell him. However, Winifred's anxious, pleading look kept her from acting on her suspicions. It was clear that Winifred would only repeat her patently false story to Nicholas, denying that Crandall had meant to hurt her, and while she felt certain that Nicholas would believe her no more than she herself had, there was no way they could prove that Winifred had not gotten the bruises as she had said.

Nicholas, however, would feel compelled to speak to Crandall about it, and, given the bad blood that already lay between them, Juliana had no desire to add any more reason for animosity. Besides, if Nicholas remonstrated with Crandall about his roughness with his wife, Juliana felt sure that Crandall would take his resulting anger out on the very woman whom she was trying to protect. And if Crandall and Nicholas got into such a fight that Nicholas threw him out of the house, then Winifred would be homeless and, worse, all alone with the man, who would doubtless blame her for his problems.

So, with a sigh, Juliana found herself, against her better judgment, nodding and saying, "All right. I won't tell Nicholas…for now."

She kept an eye on Winifred thereafter, however, looking for any further signs that Crandall might have hit her.

Crandall continued, of course, to behave in an obnoxious manner. He was rude to everyone, including his mother, and more than once Juliana saw Lilith's mouth tighten with annoyance or disgust at his behavior, something she had not been accustomed to seeing when she had lived with the Barres years ago.

There was clearly tension between Crandall and his sister, as well. He often made comments to Seraphina in a sly manner, his eyes alight with mischief. Juliana did not understand what he meant by them, but it was clear that Seraphina did, for her eyes would flash, and she would cast him a disgusted look or turn away without speaking.

Nor were his relations any better with Seraphina's husband. Sir Herbert seemed to avoid Crandall whenever possible, and when he was forced to be around him, as during a meal, Juliana noticed that he rarely spoke to him. Bizarrely enough, Sir Herbert was the only person to whom Crandall ever seemed to act in a civil manner.

Juliana understood both men's behavior better one day when she overheard them talking. She had stolen a few minutes away from the wedding preparations, and, eager to be alone for a little while, she had gone to a recessed window seat in the long gallery. There, armed with a book and an apple, she had settled down with her legs curled up under her, hidden from sight.

After a few minutes, she heard the sounds of

voices and, afraid that they might belong to someone looking for her, had scooted back and pulled one side of the draperies a little farther forward so that she was completely hidden.

But as the voices grew closer, she realized that they belonged to two men conversing in hushed but intense tones.

"I would pay it back, I swear," were the first words she was able to make out, followed by a deeper voice whose words she could not quite distinguish.

"But you don't understand," the first voice went on, and she was able to recognize it now as Crandall's. "Sir Herbert, I must have the money. I'm in desperate straits."

"No, *you* don't understand," came Sir Herbert's unbending reply. "It doesn't matter to me how desperate your straits are. I am through lending you money."

"I will pay it back. Charge me whatever interest you wish."

"I'm not a demmed moneylender," Sir Herbert protested. "I don't want your interest."

The two men seemed to have come to a stop only a few feet from where Juliana sat hidden. She squeezed as tightly into the corner behind the curtain as she could, wishing she could simply disappear. She could not pop out from the window seat now;

they would know she had overheard at least part of what they had said, and it would be an embarrassing situation. But it would be even worse if they glanced in and saw her hiding there. She closed her eyes, silently urging them to pass on by.

"I owe so much money. I cannot repay even a third of it."

"You would not be in this situation if you did not throw your money away in gambling hells," Sir Herbert responded. "I have lent you money time and again, and every time you say the same thing. You will pay me back. You will stop gambling. You will change. But you never do."

"I will this time." Desperation turned Crandall's voice into a whine. "You'll see. But you have to give me a chance. It isn't just the moneylenders. I've given my chit to several gentlemen. If I don't repay them, my name will be ruined."

"Your name is already ruined, as far as I'm concerned," his brother-in-law snapped.

"But we are family! How can you allow your wife's brother to be ostracized by the entire *ton?* I will be, you know, when it gets around that I don't honor my vouchers. I gave my word as a gentleman!"

"You don't know the meaning of the word 'gentleman,'" Sir Herbert said. "Good God, man, how can you have the gall to ask anything of me? To hold up your relationship to my wife as the reason I should help you? You are the reason she is in the trouble she's in. Why do you think we are rusticating here at the height of the Season? Because Seraphina has run up so much debt all over town that I had to dip into my principal to pay it! She spent all her allowance, and the household money, as well. She owed moneylenders and gaming companions. I have never been so embarrassed in my life as when Lord Carlton took me aside one day and told me that Seraphina owed him two hundred pounds."

"Well you paid it, didn't you?" Crandall asked sulkily. "Why didn't you just stay in the City? She doesn't have to avoid the *ton*."

"Of course she does! I cannot let her loose in London as long as she cannot control herself. I will not let her ruin her life as you have ruined yours. As if that was not enough for you, you had to lead Seraphina into destroying hers, too."

"I didn't!"

"How can you deny it? It was you introduced her to that crowd you run with. You took her to that Tomlinson woman's house to play cards. Then you encouraged her to keep going back, telling her that her luck would change, feeding her your idiotic notions that the only way for her to pay back her debts was to gamble more, hoping to win back her money. If I didn't know you for a fool who operates his own finances the same way, I would think you were receiving money from that sharp!"

There was a long moment of silence. Juliana waited, wondering what was happening outside in the hallway.

Apparently Sir Herbert had seen something in Crandall's face, for he burst out, "Good God! That is it, isn't it? You received money to bring in unsuspecting victims, didn't you? You led the lambs to the slaughter."

"It isn't as if I intended them any harm," Crandall replied feebly. "They wanted to play cards. I just introduced them to some of the more genial clubs. Seraphina *asked* me to take her to a gaming club."

"You are her brother! You should have protected her, not turned her over to be fleeced!" Seraphina's husband roared with justifiable indignation. "You bloody Judas. I ought to give you a thrashing."

"I'd like to see you try it," Crandall retorted rudely.

There was a thud as something hit the wall beside Juliana's seat, and then there was the sound of footsteps going back the way they had come.

"Stay out of my sight, Barre!" Sir Herbert shouted, only inches away from her. Juliana could only surmise that Crandall had shoved his brother-in-law against the wall and stalked off.

After a moment, Sir Herbert sighed and walked off, too.

Juliana let out a breath and relaxed against the wall of the embrasure.

So Crandall had introduced his sister to gaming. It was clear now why Sir Herbert despised the man. And doubtless it was because of that that Seraphina showed such dislike of her brother. The sly comments he made to her that earned him such black looks from her were probably hints about her gambling problem. Juliana was astounded at the extent of Crandall's villainy—to lure his own sister into gambling herself into debt…and then to jest about it.

Crandall was not at supper that evening, which was a relief not only to Juliana but to everyone else at the table. The conversation over the meal was almost normal. Lilith, of course, was as controlled and icy as ever, but at least Winifred, Seraphina and Sir Herbert joined Juliana and Nicholas in talking without everyone acting as if they were treading on eggshells.

There was no sign of Crandall throughout the evening or at breakfast the next morning—which was usually the case—nor did Juliana see him during the morning, so the relative peace of the household continued until luncheon.

The family, except for Crandall, had seated themselves around the table at the usual time, and the
servants had started around the table with their dishes
of food. At that moment Crandall walked into the
room. Juliana looked up at the sound of his entrance,
and her jaw dropped. Down the table, Winifred gasped.

Crandall's face was bruised, and his lip was
swollen, the skin beside his mouth raw and red. His
right eye was black and nearly swollen shut.

Involuntarily, Juliana glanced at Nicholas.

CHAPTER ELEVEN

LILITH ROSE to her feet, her hand going to her throat. "Crandall! What happened to you? Are you all right?"

Crandall ignored her as he jerked out his chair and sank down on it. Winifred reached over to place her hand on his arm, but he jerked it away, growling, "Leave it!"

Lilith swung to face Nicholas, exclaiming, "What is the meaning of this?"

Nicholas looked at her levelly. "I don't think I am the one to ask. Try your son."

"Crandall…" Lilith's voice was commanding.

He lifted one shoulder in a shrug. "It's nothing, Mother. Leave it alone."

"Nothing? Your face is black and blue, and you expect me to accept that it is nothing? Did Nicholas do this to you?"

Crandall grimaced. "A fellow in the village attacked me. That's it. Now, may we please eat?"

"No, we cannot," Lilith snapped. "You tell me you

were attacked and expect us just to go on as if nothing had happened? Who was it? Was the man arrested?"

"Aunt Lilith, I think that the less fuss we make about this matter, the better," Nicholas told her in a calm tone, and he cast Crandall a significant look.

"Fuss?" Lilith stared at Nicholas coldly. "My son was attacked by some ruffian, and you think we should not make a 'fuss'? I want to know if the man who did this to Crandall is in gaol."

"No," Nicholas replied shortly. "And this is hardly a fit discussion for luncheon. I suggest we postpone it until after the meal."

Lilith glared at him, fairly quivering with fury. "You may have swept in here and taken over, *Lord* Barre, but you will not dictate to me about what I can or cannot say regarding a vicious attack on my son. I want to know what happened. I want to know why this man is not in gaol!"

With a sigh, Nicholas set down his fork and turned toward the butler. "Rundell…"

"Yes, my lord." The butler turned to the footmen, making a gesture, and the servants filed out of the room. Rundell closed the door softly behind him.

"All right. We will discuss it." Nicholas turned first to Winifred, saying, "I am sorry that you have to hear this."

Winifred turned to look at her husband, her face pale and uneasy. "Crandall?"

Crandall ignored her, crossing his arms and sitting back in his chair sulkily. "Go on, Nick. I'm sure you can hardly wait to tell everyone."

"Believe me, I find little pleasure in talking about your indiscretions, and even less in dealing with their aftermath." Nicholas turned to look at Lilith. "I met with the man in question this morning, Aunt Lilith. He called upon me to warn me that I had better keep Crandall under better control. It seems that your son was making unwanted and even forceful advances to the man's wife. He walked in on them and, not unreasonably, objected to Crandall's behavior. That is why Crandall's face is in the condition it is this afternoon."

"What nonsense!" Lilith exclaimed. "Obviously the little tart lied to her husband. Doubtless she was acting in a forward manner, leading Crandall on, and then, when her husband found out about it, she pretended it was Crandall's fault to keep her husband from getting angry."

Clearly, Juliana thought, even though Lilith did not dote on Crandall as she once had, she was still completely deluded as to his relationships with women.

"The man walked in on them, Aunt Lilith," Nicholas repeated flatly. "His wife was struggling with Crandall, trying to push him away. I think there was little chance either that she tried to seduce Crandall or that Farrow was mistaken about what was happening."

"He's lying," Crandall protested and turned toward his mother. "They're both lying."

"Of course they are," his mother agreed. "Who is this Farrow? I am sure he is simply after money."

Across the table, Seraphina rolled her eyes, clearly unconvinced by her brother's words. Winifred stared down at the table, her cheeks flushed with embarrassment. Juliana was swept by sympathy for the girl. It must be very humiliating to have to sit there, listening to the tale of her husband's pursuit of another woman. No wonder Nicholas had tried to avoid discussing the topic at the table.

"I don't think money had anything to do with his presence in our house this morning," Nicholas replied, his voice crisp with irritation. "The man is furious, and with good reason. Farrow is the village blacksmith, and, frankly, given his size, I'd say that Crandall is lucky to have come away with no worse than a black eye and a few bruises."

"He came at me from behind!" Crandall exclaimed. "I didn't even know he was there."

"No doubt you were too preoccupied," Nicholas put in dryly.

"I've half a mind to go back there and—"

"Don't be absurd," Nicholas snapped. "You aren't going to challenge him to a fight, and we both know it. You are and always have been a coward, Crandall. You limit yourself to bullying women and those smaller than you. You would never take on a man like Farrow. I'm amazed that you were so foolish as to think you could have your way with his wife without his destroying you. If you thought your name would scare him off, then you are sadly mistaken. He is not interested in money, and even if he were willing to be bought off, you haven't the cash to pay him. And I can guarantee you that I will never spend one shilling to get you out of a predicament such as that."

"I never expected you to take my side," Crandall sneered.

"Very wise of you," Nicholas shot back. "I think I calmed the man down. I reassured him that such incidents will not happen again." Nicholas leaned closer, bracing his hands on the table. His eyes were cold and hard as marble as he stared into Crandall's face. "From now on, you will cease behaving in this manner. Do I make myself clear? Should I hear of Mrs. Farrow—or, indeed, any other woman hereabouts—being bothered by you, you will have to answer to me."

Crandall shot Nicholas a resentful look and slid lower in his chair, turning his gaze to the table, his jaw setting in rebellious lines.

"Sulk all you want, Crandall, you will adhere to my rules if you wish to continue to reside here," Nicholas said bluntly.

"How dare you!" Lilith exclaimed, her eyes flashing. "You think you can give my son orders?"

"If he wishes to continue to live off me, yes, I will expect him to live a certain way," Nicholas responded calmly.

"You know none of this is true," Lilith said, two bright spots of color staining her cheeks. "You are aiding that man in making up lies about Crandall. You're spreading vicious rumors about him. You hate him. You've always been jealous of him. He is so much better than you, so bright and clever—you've never been able to stand it. You've always attacked him, ever since you were a boy. The devil is in you. You cannot stand to see someone like Crandall succeed. You were wicked then, and you—"

"Stop it!" Juliana cried out, jumping to her feet. She quivered with rage as she faced the older woman. "Shut up! Just shut up!"

Lilith blinked, silenced by Juliana's outburst.

"You are the one who is wicked," Juliana went on,

past caring about courtesy or diplomacy. "You were a terrible mother and an even worse aunt. You are cold and self-centered, and the way you and your husband treated Nicholas was a crime. He came to you an orphan, a boy whose parents had been tragically killed. Yet you made no effort to love him, to care for him. You treated him with contempt and cruelty. Crandall was never worth half of Nicholas, but you were too blind to see that. You ruined Crandall by spoiling him and forgiving him all his misdeeds. And you tried to ruin Nicholas. But you could not succeed there. He escaped your clutches. He withstood all your attempts to grind him into dust."

Lilith rose to face Juliana, her pale eyes bright with fury. "How dare you speak to me this way? You pompous little upstart! You are as bad as your mother."

"My mother has nothing to do with this. I am talking about you and your neglect and abuse of a child who was in your care. Listen to me well. Your reign here is over. You are here on that very same boy's sufferance. He supports you. He gives you a roof over your head. So if I were you, I would take more care with what I say. Nicholas may be reluctant to cast his aunt out of the house, but I can tell you that I am not. I will send you and all the rest of your family packing if you ever again treat Nicholas with such disrespect."

Lilith stared at Juliana, her face white, her lips compressed into a thin line.

"Moreover," Juliana went on relentlessly, "I would suggest you think about this: In a few days' time I will be Lady Barre, and as such, I will have the power not only to cast you out of here, but to ruin you in Society. I can make sure that everyone around here and in London knows exactly what kind of woman you are. I will tell them how you treated Nicholas when he was a child, an orphan living under your care. How well do you think everyone will think of you then?"

Lilith's jaw tightened, and her eyes glowed with hatred. For a moment, Juliana thought that she was about to lash out at her in response. But she only said tightly, "Of course I meant no disrespect to Lord Barre." Not looking at Nicholas, she went on. "Pray forgive me, Nicholas, if anything I said offended you."

"Of course, Aunt Lilith."

"Now, if you will excuse me, I find I am not very interested in eating," Lilith told them and left the room.

Juliana stood looking after her for a moment, then sank back down into her chair, her knees suddenly too weak to support her. She felt faintly sick in the aftermath of her fury, and she was shaking so much that she had to clasp her hands tightly together to control them. She could feel the gazes of everyone else at the table on her.

No doubt they were all shocked at her loss of control. She supposed she should feel embarrassed about it, but she did not. Instead, she lifted her chin defiantly and looked first at Crandall, then at Seraphina.

"You know it's true."

Crandall, predictably, sneered, though he directed his look more at the table than at Juliana. To her credit, Seraphina blushed and nodded slightly, pressing her fingers to her mouth. Winifred, Juliana noted, simply looked astounded.

Juliana cast an uncertain glance over at Nicholas. He was watching her, his eyes warm and dancing with amusement. "Sir Herbert," he said calmly. "Would you be so good as to ring for Rundell? I think we are ready to finish our meal now."

The butler and footmen quickly returned, bearing the next course, their faces carefully wiped blank of the curiosity that Juliana felt sure they must be feeling. Everyone ate quickly, not venturing to make even a stab at polite conversation. And at the first opportunity, the other diners made a swift exit, leaving Juliana and Nicholas alone at the table.

Juliana looked over at Nicholas again, waiting a moment for the footmen to leave before saying, "I am sorry for causing such a scene. Normally I am quite calm." She smiled a little. "Though I realize that you may have trouble believing that now."

Nicholas grinned and reached across the corner of the table to take her hand. "I had not realized what a termagant you could be. I can tell that I will have to mind my manners with you."

Juliana let out a shaky little laugh. "I do not think that you will have to worry."

Nicholas brought her hand up to his lips. "Thank you for defending me."

The touch of his lips on her skin warmed Juliana all over. He turned his chair, tugging at her hand, and she stood, letting him pull her over and into his lap. She let out a breathless little laugh as he caught her, his arm curving around her back. It was amazing how natural it seemed, how easily she fit there, snuggled against his chest.

Nicholas bent his head, his lips pressing gently against her neck, then making his way up, nuzzling her hair and caressing her ears with a feather's touch. A shiver ran through her, igniting a fire deep within her loins. His other hand lay flat upon her stomach for a moment before sliding its way up to cup her breast. Desire pulsed through her, swift and hot. She wanted to feel his touch all over her, she realized. She wanted to lean back like a wanton in his arms, inviting him to explore her body, to caress and arouse her until she burned as she had the other night.

Juliana moved a little in his lap, and a low groan escaped his lips. He nipped at her ear, murmuring, "Wench. Do you mean to unman me?"

Emboldened, she moved again, turning into him and sliding her hand across his chest. He sucked in his breath, and when she looked up into his face, she saw that his eyes were blazing. His hand moved over her breasts, circling her nipples through the thin muslin so that they pointed, thrusting eagerly against the material.

His thumb teased her nipple as he continued to gaze down into her eyes. A ripple ran down through Juliana, as though a cord connected the bud of her nipple to some well of fire deep within her loins, loosing it to flood her body. She caught her lower lip with her teeth, closing her eyes at the exquisite pleasure of his fingers on her breast.

His hand left her breast, sliding down to the V between her legs, as though seeking the source of the heat. His fingers pressed against her, and even through the material of her dress and petticoats, the touch sent pleasure exploding through her. Her fingers dug into his shirt, and she leaned her head against his chest, luxuriating in the sensations he was creating.

She could feel his heart pounding beneath her ear, could hear the rasp of his breath. She felt as though she could drown in him, consume and be consumed by him.

There was a sound of steps at the door, and then a strangled gasp. Juliana's eyes flew open to catch a glimpse of a footman's back as he hastily exited the room.

Nicholas cursed beneath his breath, his hands falling away from her, and Juliana, blushing beet-red, jumped to her feet. Her hands went up to her flaming cheeks, and she gazed at him for a moment in an agony of embarrassment.

Then she whirled and flew from the room.

NICHOLAS LEANED FORWARD, propping his elbows on the table and dropping his head to his hands. Silently he cursed himself. He was acting like a randy adolescent. He had made Juliana a promise, and it seemed that he was breaking it at every turn. She had every right to be furious at him.

He knew he was not doing the right thing, not acting the part of a gentleman. Although he had never pretended to be a real gentleman, not in the truest sense of the word, the one person to whom he had believed he would never act with dishonor was

Juliana. Yet here he was, letting his desire for her lead him into breaking his promise to her. He had sworn to her that theirs would be a platonic marriage, and it was on that basis that she had agreed to marry him. His actions the last few days must make her wonder if he was capable of sticking to the bargain they had made. He was afraid she would even suspect that he had deceived her, offering her a marriage in name only with no intention of keeping to the pact.

In general, he was not a man who feared much. He had made his way alone in the world and had been more successful than most. Such success did not come to the timorous. But he found himself pierced by fear now. One thing he did not want to face was the possibility of losing Juliana's trust.

She was the one person in the world who was dear to him. She had been his companion, his friend, when he had felt most alone in the world. He trusted her, and he did not think there was another person in the world about whom he could say that. And for that reason, he could not allow anything to shatter the bond between them...no matter how much he lusted after her.

It had not occurred to him that he would feel this way. The Juliana of his memory had been a child, and he had loved her as a child. She had been like a sister to him. And though he had realized how beautifully she had grown up, how desirable a woman she was now, he had not guessed that desirability would beckon him so strongly that he would be in danger of losing all self-control.

He had offered to marry her without any ulterior motive, he told himself. He had simply wanted to help her. He had hated to see Juliana at the beck and call of people who were clearly her inferiors. She should have all the best in the world, and he had wanted to give her that.

But somehow, knowing her these last few weeks, she had become no longer merely a dear friend from the past but a woman…a very desirable woman. And the marriage that he had offered her no longer suited him at all. He wanted to seduce her, to take her to bed. He found himself looking forward to their wedding night with all the eagerness that was expected of a bridegroom.

But that desire, he knew, was unfair to Juliana. She had, after all, agreed to be his wife on the promise that it would be a marriage in name only. She had, in all likelihood, married him primarily because of her deep sense of loyalty to the boy who had been her childhood friend. She did not love him, had, indeed, been loath to marry him precisely because she did not feel love for him. And for a woman like Juliana, he knew, love and desire were inextricably entangled. She was not the sort of person he was, incapable of deep emotions.

Nicholas knew that Juliana believed he could feel as deeply as she did. But he was well aware that the truth was that she saw only her own reflection in him. It was simply the goodness of her own soul that caused her to see his every act in the best light, to pardon his sins and excuse each mistake. He was to her as she wanted him to be, and when he was with her, he could not help but act the role. But he knew how much it was only a role. He knew the anger that dwelled within him, the cold man he was who had heard of his uncle's death without a single twinge of sympathy or regret. He still clung to the hatred that had bubbled with every lash of the ferule his uncle had wielded against the backs of his legs. And he was aware of the laws he had broken and the others he had merely skirted, the rules of truth and even honor that he had ignored in his quest for riches.

He was not a good man. Only Juliana believed otherwise.

But he was not about to let the vision she held of him be tarnished. While he did not care what most people thought of him, what she thought was essential to him.

It was not that he thought she would struggle against him if he came to her on their wedding night. He knew she would give in to his wishes, his desire. She would, after all, believe it her duty as his wife. If nothing else, she would doubtless feel that she owed him whatever he asked for in return for giving her the better life she would have as Lady Barre. Nor was he modest enough to think that he could not make her feel desire, as well. He had felt her pliancy in his hands, had heard the catch in her breath, felt the racing of her pulse in her throat. His kisses and caresses aroused her.

But despite her desire, she did not love him, and that fact would tear at her. He did not want her obligation, her capitulation to his wishes. He did not want her to feel divided in herself, a slave to lust where she did not feel love.

Most of all, he could not bear to let her realize that he was not the man she believed him to be. It would be the worst stab of pain to have her look at him in disillusion, to know that she saw him for the man he was: one who would break the sacred promise he had made to her simply for the gratification of his animal lust.

He would not allow that to happen. Whatever it took, he would stick to his vow of celibacy in their marriage. It should not be so hard, he told himself. After a decent time spent here with her, he could avail himself of the services of some lightskirt in London.

Of course, he had to admit, the thought held little appeal. Quite frankly, the thought of any other woman paled beside Juliana. Even the most appealing of his mistresses from the past now seemed dull and undesirable compared to Juliana. He had no desire to turn to another woman to ease his lust, and that thought made the prospect of married life even grimmer.

He swore to himself that he would not bed Juliana when they married. The only problem was that he had no idea how he was going to make himself obey that vow.

CHAPTER TWELVE

THE DAY of the wedding dawned bright and clear. As the last two days had brought a dreary rain, the sunshine seemed a good omen to Juliana. She was too nervous to eat much breakfast, gulping down a cup of tea and a bit of toast.

She wished that Eleanor were there to support her through the day. Winifred came in to help her maid with the dress and hair, but though the girl was goodhearted, it was not the same as having someone who had been Juliana's close friend since school. Eleanor would have taken over in her brisk way, eliminating any problem that arose and sending everyone scurrying about their business. She would have reassured Juliana and kept her calm.

As it was, Juliana vacillated all morning between moments of terror that she was doing the wrong thing and moments of anticipation in which she felt that she could not wait to get to the ceremony. She was certain she was doing what she wanted to do, but she was far less sure whether it was the right thing for her.

Adding to her uncertainty was the fact that for the past few days she had been thinking about whether, when her wedding night came, Nicholas would take her to bed. He had said that their marriage would be platonic, of course, but the way he had kissed her only recently made her wonder if he had changed his mind. What would she do if he came to her bedroom tonight? She knew how she had responded to him; he would have every reason to think she wanted him.

The problem, of course, was that she *did* want him, but she feared that if he took her to bed, it would lead to eventual heartbreak for her. She would consider herself a real wife, but she suspected that Nicholas would not feel the same way. He had declared himself immune to love, and while Juliana did not believe that he could not love, she knew that his statement showed he had not fallen in love yet—which meant, therefore, that he did not love *her.* To fall in love with a man who did not love her, to grow deeper and deeper in love while he perhaps tired of her, would be a disaster. She would end up lonely and heartsore.

It would be far better, she thought, simply to remain friends with Nicholas, to refrain from venturing into deeper waters. If he wanted to sleep with her and she refused, she was certain that he would not insist on his rights as a husband. But she was far less certain that she would be able to resist the desire she felt for him. *Would she have the strength to turn him down?*

She was plagued by such thoughts, and Winifred's idle chatter did little to take her mind off them. It was a relief when the time finally arrived for the ceremony, and she could shove her thoughts aside and simply go forward.

They were married that afternoon in the church in the village, an old gray structure with a square Norman tower. The guests were small in number, mostly the local gentry and a few far-flung family members. Neither Nicholas nor Juliana knew many people, given their time out of the *ton*, and none of the Barres had shown much interest in inviting their friends. Indeed, Juliana had been rather surprised when one of Crandall's friends had arrived from London the day before, a young man by the name of Peter Hakebourne. Crandall, too, had looked stunned when he came into the room, and the two of them had gone off immediately to talk. Juliana wondered if, perhaps, Crandall's visitor was one of the gentlemen to whom Crandall owed money.

Still, the sparseness of the crowd did not bother Juliana. The simple ceremony moved her, and when she turned to face Nicholas, their hands linked, and they said their vows, her heart swelled within her. She smiled up at him, her eyes filling with moisture, and she knew that whatever came, she had made the right decision. Her life was intertwined with his, and their future lay together.

After the ceremony they returned to the house and received their well-wishers. Inside would be the wedding supper and ball for the bride and groom and their friends and family, but first they had to receive the congratulations of the tenants and villagers, all invited to a hearty feast outdoors under the trees. Juliana smiled and greeted the people, some of them remembered from her life here years ago and others strangers to her. Mrs. Cooper had come, brought in the pony cart that Juliana had sent for her. She beamed, taking Juliana's hands and assuring her that her life would be blessed. The tenants and their wives passed in dizzying numbers.

Even the blacksmith from the village was there, a blond giant of a man, taller even than Nicholas, and with the broad chest and thickly muscled arms that went with his profession. He said very little, nodding his head to them in a way that showed respect but no servility, and introducing the pretty young woman beside him as his wife.

As they moved on toward the table of refreshments, Juliana leaned closer to Nicholas and whispered, "Is he not the man who gave Crandall his black eye? I am surprised he would come to this house."

Nicholas nodded. "Yes. But he is a fair man, I think. I liked him. He knows that Crandall and what he does are a very different thing from my character and actions."

Juliana looked at the couple as they strolled along, the wife's arm curled through her husband's and his head bent down protectively toward her as he listened to her. "She is quite lovely."

"Yes. It's easy to see why Crandall was attracted to her." He grimaced.

"Do you know Crandall's friend?" Juliana asked curiously.

"The chap from London?" Nicholas responded. "What's his name? Something fishlike, wasn't it?"

Juliana chuckled. "Hakebourne. Peter Hakebourne."

"Ah, yes. No, I don't know him. But I find it somewhat curious that someone we don't know and did not invite should show up for our wedding," Nicholas commented.

"I don't think Crandall knew he was coming, either," Juliana commented.

Nicholas frowned. "Knowing Crandall, I can't think his friend is here for any legitimate purpose. I'll ask a few questions, see if I can discover what's behind his visit." He glanced at Juliana, a faint smile on his lips. "Do you think it's unkind of me to find it difficult to believe that anyone would visit Crandall out of sheer friendship?"

"I'd call it intelligent, rather," Juliana retorted.

There was a great deal of food and drink, both inside and out, and later there was dancing. Nicholas led Juliana out onto the dance floor for their first waltz as husband and wife, and when he took her into his arms, she could not help but remember the night, only a month ago, when she had seen him again for the first time in fifteen years.

She remembered how it had felt to have his arms around her, to look up into his face. It had not been long, yet it seemed almost a lifetime. She would never have dreamed then that only a month later, she would be Nicholas's wife.

And tonight…tonight, would she be his wife in

truth, not just in name? It was a question she still could not answer.

After their dance, there were obligatory dances with the other guests. These, Juliana thought with an inward sigh, were not nearly as enjoyable. She was piloted around the floor by Sir Herbert and later by Peter Hakebourne. Sir Herbert danced as if struggling to remember his lessons from years before; she could almost hear him counting as they twirled through the steps. When the song ended, the smile he gave her spoke more of relief that the dance was over than of any enjoyment of it. Hakebourne, on the other hand, was a passable dancer, but very poor as a conversationalist. By the time the song ended, despite her gently probing questions, she knew little more about him than she had when they started. Juliana was unsure whether the man was adept at avoiding questions or simply shy.

He bowed and left her when the dance was over, and Juliana watched as he wended his way across the room to where Crandall stood, a glass in his hand, moodily watching the festivities.

It took little imagination to see that Crandall was less than happy to see his friend. He scowled at Hakebourne when he arrived and cast a quick look around the room as though seeking escape. Hakebourne, however, planted himself before Crandall and began to talk with all the volubility he had lacked during his dance with Juliana.

At that moment Mr. Bolton, the middle-aged gentleman bachelor of the village, asked for her hand for the next quadrille, and she was too busy remembering all the steps to spare a glance for Crandall and his friend. However, when Mr. Bolton, who had turned out to be an accomplished and graceful dancer, led her back to a chair after the music ended, Juliana saw that Crandall and Peter Hakebourne were still talking.

They were, in fact, arguing, their voices rising. Surprised, the guests were turning toward the noise. At a gesture from Lilith, the string quartet quickly started up the next number, masking the noise of the men's argument.

Lilith crossed the room to Crandall, stopping in front of him and issuing a few short words. Hakebourne looked abashed and fell silent, nodding to Lilith in acquiescence. With a last look at Crandall, he moved off through the crowd. Crandall cast a sullen look at his mother and swallowed the last of his drink with a defiant air.

Juliana watched with dismay as he then turned and strode through the crowd straight toward her. He bumped against one of the dancers, stumbled, and pressed on without an apology. Juliana would have liked to turn and flee, but she knew it would be too obvious that she was avoiding Crandall. Heaven only knew what he might do in his inebriated state—shout across the room at her, perhaps.

Since the last thing she wanted was a scene on her wedding day, she stood her ground and watched his approach with a falsely pleasant look on her face.

"Ju-Julanna," he mumbled, sweeping her an extravagant bow that nearly toppled him over.

"Crandall, please…" Juliana whispered. "You're drunk. Go up to your room and lie down."

He leered at her. "'S that an invitation, m'dear?"

Juliana gritted her teeth. "Don't be any more of a fool than you've already proved yourself. Please think of your family, your wife—just think of yourself, for pity's sake. Do you want to humiliate yourself in front of all these people?"

"I want to dance with the bride," he told her, his words slurring together so that had she not already perceived his intent, she was not sure she would have been able to understand him. "Don't I get a dance with the bride on her wedding day?"

His voice had risen in volume during his last sentence, and Juliana could see heads turning toward them. Hastily she said, "All right, Crandall, I will dance with you. But only if you promise that you will leave right afterwards."

"'Course I will. Day's complete then, isn't it? Dance with the bride. Beautiful bride."

Crandall wrapped his hand around her wrist and pulled her onto the dance floor. Juliana suppressed her irritation and turned to face him. It would be a trial to dance with Crandall at any time, but especially when he was drunk. He took her hand and put his other hand on her waist. She could smell the alcohol on his breath, even though she was standing as far away from him as she could.

The music began, and Juliana did her best to follow Crandall. His hand was heavy on her side, and it seemed to her that he was pressing his fingers into her flesh far more tightly than was necessary.

"Beautiful bride," he said again.

"Thank you," she replied shortly.

He leered down at her. "Always wanted you, you know."

"Crandall…this is hardly an appropriate conversation." The man was incorrigible.

"'S the truth," he continued, as if she had argued

the point. "Ever'time I came home from school, there you were…teasing me."

"Don't be absurd," Juliana retorted indignantly. She knew it was useless to argue with a drunk, but she could not let his statement go unchallenged. "I never—"

"Oh, you may think you didn't," Crandall allowed, winking at her. "But I saw you. I know."

"You don't know anything." Her eyes flashed. "But at least you could refrain from showing your ignorance quite so openly."

He laughed and tugged at her waist so that she stumbled forward, barely catching herself before she landed against his chest.

"Crandall! Stop it before you create another scene," Juliana hissed.

At that moment a hand descended on Crandall's shoulder, and Nicholas's cool voice said, "Sorry, Crandall. I'm sure you won't mind if the groom steals his bride from you."

"Nicholas!" Juliana turned toward him in relief.

He looked at her face, taking in the color in her cheeks and the fire blazing in her gray eyes, then turned back to Crandall. "Don't you think that you have had enough to drink now? It's time you took yourself off to bed."

"I don't care what you think." Crandall glared at Nicholas. "We're dancing. Move. You're in the way."

"I'll do more than get in your way if you don't unhand my wife this instant," Nicholas replied in a level tone that was belied by the set of his jaw and the cold glitter of his dark eyes.

Crandall sneered. "Your wife…You looking forward to your wedding night? You actually think that you're going to be the first? I was there long before—"

Whatever else he planned to say was lost because Nicholas's fist flashed out, landing squarely on Crandall's jaw and sending him crashing backward to the floor.

A woman screamed. Crandall scrambled to his feet and launched himself at Nicholas. Nicholas stepped aside neatly, and Crandall staggered past him. Nicholas turned, grabbing him by the arm and swinging him around. Crandall lashed out wildly, again missing Nicholas, who sent a jab to his stomach and a quick uppercut to his jaw. Crandall went down with a thud.

"Nicholas!" Juliana grabbed Nicholas's arm. "Please! No!"

Nicholas's face was high with color, and his hands were knotted into fists. He waited, balanced on the balls of his feet, his fists ready, as he glared at Crandall, who lay on the floor.

Crandall cursed and rolled to his side, struggling to his feet.

"Nicholas," Juliana said urgently. "Don't. Please don't spoil our wedding day."

Nicholas glanced down at her, and she could feel his taut muscles relaxing. "I'm sorry, my dear."

He looked back at Crandall. "Go up to bed and sleep it off."

Crandall's lip curled, his defiant look somewhat spoiled by the swelling red spot on his cheekbone and the trickle of blood coming from his lip. "I ought to kill you."

"I wouldn't try it if I were you," Nicholas replied calmly.

"Don't be a fool, Crandall," Peter Hakebourne told him, slipping between the spectators and taking his friend by the elbow. "Come on."

He tugged at Crandall's arm, and after a moment's hesitation, Crandall went with him, staggering a little as Hakebourne led him from the room. The other guests parted to let them through, then turned to each other, buzzing with conversation about the scene they had just witnessed. Juliana thought with an inward groan that her wedding would now provide the gossips with food for weeks.

Nicholas turned to Juliana, saying stiffly, "I am sorry. I fear I have ruined the celebration."

"It doesn't matter," she assured him.

She looked at him. He seemed remote, suddenly a stranger to her, and she wondered, with a stab of fear, if Nicholas had actually believed what Crandall had said.

"Nicholas!" She gave him a stricken look. "You can't believe that Crandall—"

"What? Of course not." Nicholas's face went even stiffer, if that was possible. "The man's a liar and always has been. But I—I am sorry that you should have had to see this."

It had been years, he thought, since he had gotten into a fight. God knows, in his early years, fights had been regular occurrences, springing out of a deep wellspring of anger inside him, brought up by any slight or challenge. It had, indeed, been the only way he knew how to survive. Defiance and aggression had been his watchwords.

It had taken years to bring that side of himself under control. He had thought he had conquered his baser nature, and it surprised and unsettled him to find that it had swept up out of him so fiercely. He hated for Juliana to see him this way, to know that the animal still lived inside him, snarling and ever ready to flare into life. It was hard for him to even look at her, lest he see fear in her face.

It was a relief when Seraphina swept up to them and put one hand on his arm and the other on Juliana's. She smiled as gaily as if the past few minutes had not taken place. "It's time, don't you think? I know the two of you have been impatiently waiting, wishing all of us at the devil."

There was a little ribald laughter behind Seraphina. Juliana looked at her gratefully. Seraphina was trying to distract everyone by sending the bride and groom on their way.

"I wouldn't be hanging about down here if I were you, young man," joked an elderly guest, a retired general who lived in the area.

"Oh, no, you'd be leading the charge, General," retorted the squire's wife, a tall, iron-jawed woman who was one of Lilith's horsey set. It was hard to imagine the blunt woman as a friend of the pristine Lilith, but Juliana had long ago learned that the love of the hunt and horses made for odd attachments.

Juliana's cheeks colored at the woman's statement, and Seraphina said lightly, "There now, Mrs.

Cargill, you've made Lady Barre blush. Come, you two, it's time we got you out of here."

Juliana was happy to escape the ballroom and the other guests, although her heart beat a little faster as she thought about what lay ahead. She and Nicholas allowed Seraphina to whisk them out of the room, saying their farewells and receiving the cheerful good wishes of their guests.

They climbed the stairs, leaving everyone else at the foot of the staircase. Juliana's hand was tucked into the crook of Nicholas's arm; his muscles felt hard as iron beneath the material of his jacket. She was a jumble of nerves inside—excited, anxious, not at all sure what she wanted to happen. The time was upon them.

Nicholas opened the door to Juliana's room, and she stepped inside. He came in after her. She could not look at him for fear everything she felt would show on her face. She wanted him. She wanted him to take her into his arms and smother her face with kisses. She wanted to be his wife in every sense of the word. But she had no idea what *he* wanted, and because of that, she was afraid.

She glanced at the bed and quickly looked away again. It seemed as if everywhere she turned there was something to remind her of the possibilities ahead of her.

Behind her, Nicholas cleared his throat. Juliana turned to face him, lifting her eyes at last to his face.

She saw little there to encourage her or ease her fears. He looked suddenly like a stranger to her. His face was set; his dark eyes, which could be so full of warmth or laughter or deviltry, were flat and black, showing nothing of how he felt.

He glanced around the room, linking his hands behind his back. He looked, she thought, like a stern schoolmaster, deciding a student's punishment. She cast about frantically for something to say to ease the moment, to put them back into their usual position of easy friendship. Her first thought was of Crandall and the scene below, but those topics would do little to put them at ease.

"It was a lovely ceremony," she said at last.

"Yes. And the wedding supper was…um, lovely."

Nicholas looked at her, feeling foolish and stiff. She was beautiful, and he wanted her with a force so fierce it was almost painful. He had tried over and over again to think of some way that he could take her into his arms and make love to her without breaking his promise to her, but, of course, there was none. Seduction was gentler than demanding his rights to bed her, but it was nonetheless doing the very thing he had vowed he would not do.

And tonight he had made everything worse by demonstrating what a brute he was. Though he knew that Juliana had little liking for Crandall, she could not enjoy seeing her wedding celebration spoiled by fisticuffs—and how much worse it was that her husband was one of the men involved! She must have been repulsed by his behavior. He could not further prove his animalistic nature by taking her to bed, breaking his promise to her. One thing he did not think he could bear was to see Juliana's eyes show her disillusion and disappointment in him.

"Well…um…" He gestured toward the connecting door between their room. "I will just go to my room now. I wish you a good night's sleep."

Juliana nodded numbly. There was some relief in not having to make the decision of whether or not to sleep with Nicholas, but she realized that her primary feeling was one of disappointment. Had she been wrong about the signs of desire in him? Did he not even want to bed her? Was she silly to have even been worrying about what she would do when he kissed her?

"Yes. Of course. Good night," she replied, her throat tight.

She watched as he walked across the room and opened the door. With a nod to her, he stepped into his bedroom, closing the door behind him. Juliana sat down on her chair with a thump.

This was it, she realized, tears welling in her. This was what her married life would be like—Nicholas distant and removed from her, their relationship only friendship, never hoping to have the love and closeness of a true marriage. He had offered to give her children if she wanted, but she knew that she could never ask that of him. She did not think she could bear to have him come to her in such a cold and loveless way. Soon he would seek his pleasure elsewhere, and she would be left to grow old and dry alone, never having children, never knowing the passion of the marriage bed.

It seemed suddenly that, whatever the comfort and security she had gained in her life, she had made a very poor bargain indeed.

Listlessly, she got up and tugged on the bellpull for her maid. The elegant satin gown she had worn for her wedding was buttoned with a host of tiny buttons down the back, impossible to take off by herself. If she were like other brides, no doubt her husband would have acted as her personal maid, undoing the line of buttons himself.

Celia came into her room a few minutes later, smiling, and proceeded to lay out her mistress's nightgown, a delicate lace-and-satin affair appropriate for a wedding night. She chattered excitedly as she helped Juliana out of her clothes, casting meaningful glances at the connecting door to Nicholas's bedroom.

"Oh, miss—I should say, my lady—aren't you excited? Such a handsome man his lordship is. And so tall and strong."

Juliana gave her a perfunctory smile. The girl's chattering was getting on her nerves. She was very aware of the sounds that came now and then from Nicholas's room. She wondered what he was doing in there, if he was undressing, too. She thought of his long supple fingers working on his buttons, of the way he would shrug off his shirt, perhaps raising his hand to brush back the hair that always fell across his forehead. Juliana's fingers itched to reach up and brush that stray lock of hair back; she knew how it would slide silkenly through her fingers, how he would cast her an amused glance from the corner of his eye.

She curled her fingers in tightly. She reminded herself that she must stop thinking this way; she must accept her life as it was. *But was this what her entire future held for her*? The thought seemed too painful.

Juliana sat down to let Celia remove the pins from

her hair and brush it out. She blocked out the girl's chatter from her mind and gazed at her own reflection in the mirror. Was it that she was not pretty enough? she wondered. *Was her brown hair too straight, too thick, too ordinary? Or was it that her face was unexceptional, the eyebrows too straight, her nose and mouth pretty but not eye-catching? If she had possessed the high, sharp cheekbones and huge eyes, the wide generous mouth and firm jaw, that Eleanor did, would he have been more attracted to her? Would he have stayed in her room then?*

She told herself to stop thinking this way. Nicholas had promised to keep their marriage platonic because he had wanted only to help her. He had been thinking of her and had wanted the marriage to be easy for her. It was wrong of her to turn his generosity, his kindness, into an indication that he did not want her.

And yet, some little niggling doubt remained in her brain—even if he had offered her this sort of arrangement out of consideration for her, if he truly desired her, surely he would not be able to so easily step away.

Her maid stepped back and gave her a look up and down, beaming. "It's lovely you look, my lady. His lordship will be a happy man tonight."

She giggled at her own audacity and bobbed a little curtsey to Juliana before hurrying out the door. Juliana turned and looked around the empty room, wondering what she was going to do with herself now. She certainly did not feel like sleeping.

Belting the sash of her dressing gown a little tighter, she walked over to the chair and small table where the book she had been reading lay. She sat down and picked it up, but it remained neglected in her lap as she leaned her head back against the chair and stared at the wall opposite her.

She heard steps in Nicholas's room, and for an instant her heart lifted in hope, thinking that he was walking back to the connecting door. But then the footsteps moved away, and a moment later she heard the click that was the sound of his door into the hall closing. He was leaving his bedroom.

Juliana listened to his footsteps, muffled by the runner of carpet, as he walked down the hall past her door. Tears pooled in her eyes, and she blinked them away.

Sitting up straight, she forced herself to turn her attention to her book. She tried to read, but she could not keep her attention on it. She heard people going down the hall now and then, and she found herself listening, straining to hear, waiting for the sound of Nicholas's door opening and closing again.

It was some time later that she finally heard the sound she had been waiting for. She listened, trying to identify the noises as he moved about his room. She told herself she was being foolish in the extreme.

With a sigh, she stood up and turned to go to bed, untying her dressing gown and sliding it from her shoulders. She tossed the gown across the foot of the bed and started to crawl beneath the covers.

Suddenly the connecting door opened with a crack that made her jump. She whirled to see Nicholas standing framed in the doorway. Her heart began to race, and her throat was too dry to speak. She simply stared at him.

There was no mistaking the desire stamped on his face—the sensual set of his mouth, the heavy-lidded look of his eyes. He strode across the room as she watched him, breathless, and when he reached her, he grasped her arms and pulled her closer. She could smell brandy on him, and she thought he must have been downstairs, locked in his study perhaps, drinking. His eyes glittered as they gazed down into hers, and his fingers bit into her arms. Juliana felt faintly frightened, but far more excited.

"I can't stop thinking about you," he muttered

thickly. "I kept picturing you here, so close to me, sleeping in your bed. I can't sleep. I can't think about anything but you."

"Nicholas..." she breathed, melting at his words.

"I don't want a bloodless marriage. I want you in my bed."

He pulled her against him, his mouth coming down to take hers. His hand sank into her hair, wrapping its silken length around his wrist, his fingertips gripping her skull, holding her head still as his mouth ravished hers.

Juliana threw her arms around his neck, stretching up on tiptoe, fitting her body against his all the way up and down. Hunger swept through her, carrying her wildly forward, her mouth meeting his, kiss for kiss. Her breasts were full and swollen, aching for his touch, and she pressed herself more tightly against his chest. Only the thin material of her nightgown and his shirt separated their skin, and when she moved, her nipples tightened at the slight abrasion. She remembered his fingers on them, and the ache inside her grew.

Her hands went to the buttons of his shirt, her fingers trembling so that she could scarcely undo them. Nicholas released her in order to grasp her gown, and, bunching it up in his hands, he pulled it up and over her head. She stood naked before him, and she found to her surprise that she felt not the embarrassment she would have expected, but a flood of heat. She relished having his eyes on her, delighted at the fire that sprang into them at the sight of her bare flesh.

Nicholas jerked his shirt back from his shoulders, cursing when it caught at the cuffs on his wrist, still fastened by cuff links. He left it hanging, too eager to touch her to take the time to remove it fully. His hands went to her waist, and he pulled her forward a little, his head going down to the soft white orbs of her breasts. He kissed the quivering tops of them, his mouth working its way over the white flesh. His lips felt like velvet on her skin, sending shivers through Juliana, and when his tongue found her nipple, she let out a small sob of passion.

Nothing had prepared her for this—the heat, the sizzling excitement, the hunger that clawed at her, demanding release even as her body ached for these sensations to go on and on. His tongue encircled the small bud, making it hard and tight, supremely sensitive, and when his mouth moved on to her other nipple, just the touch of air against the wet button of flesh aroused her still more.

Moisture flooded between her legs, startling her,

and the ache there was hot and heavy, throbbing with the pulse of life. His hands slid down from her waist and curved over the fleshy mounds of her buttocks, his fingertips digging in, lifting her into him. Gently he pulled her nipple into his mouth, sucking and teasing at it with his tongue.

Juliana moaned, helplessly lost in her desire. Her hands slid into his hair, tightening against his scalp. She breathed his name, feeling herself sliding into a dark tunnel of passion.

Then, somewhere in the house, a woman screamed.

CHAPTER THIRTEEN

NICHOLAS AND Juliana froze. He lifted his head and looked at her dazedly. The scream came again and again.

He released her abruptly and hurried toward the door, pulling his shirt back up onto his shoulders and starting to rebutton it. Juliana pounced on her nightgown, lying discarded on the floor, and hastily threw it back on over her head, too distracted to notice that it was turned inside out. Nicholas charged out into the corridor, and Juliana, grabbing her dressing gown, ran out the door after him.

All up and down the hall, other people were coming out of their rooms, looking about and asking questions. Nicholas ran down the stairs, Juliana right behind him, everyone else following, as well. Downstairs, in the main corridor, they found a small knot of servants, with other servants running toward them from the back of the house.

The butler was gripping one of the maids by the

arms, and she was babbling hysterically, two other maids standing staring, eyes wide, at them.

"What is it? What's happened?" Nicholas demanded.

Rundell turned toward him with relief. "My lord! Mary Louise found—there's been a great tragedy."

"What?"

For answer, the butler led him down the corridor to one of the smaller reception rooms toward the back of the house. Juliana followed on Nicholas's heels, with the rest of the household bringing up the rear.

The room was richly paneled in walnut and very dark, with a kerosene lamp on one of the tables providing a circle of light. A sofa faced the fireplace, the space behind the couch leading toward the windows, which faced the side garden.

Behind the couch lay Crandall, sprawled facedown, his hair matted with blood.

Juliana sucked in her breath sharply, and Nicholas let out a sharp oath. He swung back, reaching out to stop the others, but it was too late. Lilith stood behind them, staring at the still form on the floor, her face bleached white and her eyes dark.

"Crandall…" she breathed. She looked at Nicholas. "What happened? Is he—"

"Juliana…" Nicholas said, and Juliana quickly

went to Lilith, taking her arm and turning her, leading her from the room.

It was doubtless a sign of the woman's shock that she went with Juliana without resistance. Seraphina was standing just behind her husband in the doorway, and Winifred hovered behind them. Juliana guided Lilith to the other two women, saying, "Seraphina, why don't you and Winifred take your mother and go, um, to the sitting room?"

"What happened?" Seraphina asked, looked scared.

"Why? What's in there?" Winifred asked, looking confused. "Did she say Crandall?"

"Crandall's been hurt."

"What?" Winifred started forward, but Juliana caught her.

"No. Don't go in there. You don't want to see."

"See what?" Winifred looked more and more frantic. "What happened to him?"

"I don't know," Juliana replied. "Nicholas will look into it. Right now, we don't know anything." Juliana glanced around, and, spotting the cluster of servants, she gestured toward her own maid. Celia, at least, having worked for Eleanor, would be both competent and not given to hysteria. "Celia, would you see to the ladies? You might get them a glass of brandy."

Celia nodded, proving Juliana's estimation of her by not asking questions but simply stepping forward to do as Juliana bade her. After the women had left, Juliana turned back, slipping past Peter Hakebourne and Sir Herbert.

Nicholas was kneeling beside Crandall, and he rose to his feet again when Juliana came back into the room. "He's dead."

"What happened?" Sir Herbert demanded.

"It looks like someone hit him in the back of the head. The fireplace poker is lying beside him, and there's blood on it."

"Good God." Sir Herbert looked shaken.

Mr. Hakebourne blinked and glanced nervously over at the body on the floor. "What are you going to do?"

"Send for the magistrate, I suppose. Judge Carstairs was just here." He turned to the butler, who hovered nearby, waiting. "Rundell, send one of the grooms to fetch him."

"Yes, my lord."

"But first, tell me what you know about this."

"Very little, I fear," the butler said. Though calm-spoken, Juliana noticed that he was a good deal paler than normal. "We had finished cleaning up and were about to go up to bed. One of the maids saw the light on in here and came to turn it off. That's when she saw Master Crandall...."

"She's the one who screamed?"

"Yes, my lord."

"Did you see anyone coming into or going out of this room?"

Rundell shook his head. "No. It was not really being used this evening. All the guests were in the main ballroom, and, of course, there were the people outside in the yard. Anyone could have come in here, but I did not see anyone."

"Including Crandall?"

"No. Yes. I mean, I did not see him, either."

"When was the last time you saw him?" Nicholas asked.

"I'm not sure, my lord. We were rather busy, in and out."

Nicholas turned toward the other two men. "Sir Herbert? Mr. Hakebourne?"

Seraphina's husband shifted uneasily. "Well, I suppose it was when he, um, when there was that altercation, um, between you and him. He left the room right afterwards."

"I took him out of the ballroom," Hakebourne offered. "We walked back upstairs to his room. Crandall was going to wash his face. I suggested that he stay and lie down, but…" He shrugged. "I'm not sure what he did. I returned to the party. I didn't see him again."

"I want to talk to all the servants," Nicholas told the butler. "Gather them in the kitchen after you send for the magistrate."

"Very good, my lord." Rundell bowed and exited the room.

The men looked at each other. Juliana could almost see the thoughts running behind Hakebourne's and Sir Herbert's eyes. Crandall and Nicholas despised each other. They had fought, verbally and physically, only this evening. Who was more likely to have taken a poker to Crandall's head than Lord Barre himself?

Anxiety twisted in Juliana. It wasn't Nicholas; it could not have been Nicholas. He had gone upstairs with her. They had been together when they heard the scream. But who knew how long Crandall had lain there before the maid had come into the room? It could have happened long before that…even during the time when Nicholas had left his room. No matter how certain she was that Nicholas had not killed him, she could not really prove it.

The men turned to look once again at Crandall. Juliana followed their eyes, and a shiver ran down her spine. She had thoroughly disliked Crandall—could not, frankly, remember any moment in her life when she had even thought kindly of him—but it was awful to see him lying there like that, lifeless and bloody. It was a horrible end to his life.

Nicholas crossed to the small table and picked up the lamp, bringing it over to hold above Crandall. The three men bent down, looking at him. The blood that matted the back of his hair gleamed dark and wet.

Juliana's stomach turned at the sight, and she quickly looked away. As she did so, she caught sight of a glimmer of something. She took a step forward, closer to the wall, and looked around the floor in front of the low set of shelves that lay there. At first she could not see anything, but then Nicholas shifted the lamp again, and its light caught something small and sparkly.

She bent down, seeing a small piece of glass. She picked it up between her fingers. It was red, and she could see now that it was not glass, as she had first thought, but a jewel. A ruby.

Juliana opened her mouth to point out to the others what she had found, but she quickly closed it and looked over at the men. None of them were watching her. Without a word, she pocketed the gem. It could have fallen from someone's jewelry at any time, she knew. But it also could have fallen from something on the murderer. It could very likely be a clue as to who had killed Crandall, and if that was the case, she did not want anyone to know what she had found. As long as the killer did not know that he—or she—had lost the gem, he would not get rid of whatever piece of jewelry it had come from.

It was possible that Hakebourne or Sir Herbert had been the killer. Juliana knew how much Sir Herbert disliked Crandall, and she had just seen Mr. Hakebourne arguing with him this evening. Even if neither one of them was the murderer, they were all too likely to tell someone else about her finding the jewel, and then news of the gem soon would be all over the house.

Nicholas turned and set the lamp back down on the table, and the men stepped back from the body. Juliana noticed that Hakebourne cast a frowning look at Nicholas, but he said nothing.

They left the room, closing the door behind them, and Nicholas posted one of the footmen outside in the hall with instructions to let no one in until the officials arrived. Nicholas went off to speak to the servants in the kitchen, and Juliana went in search of the other women. She found them in the informal sitting room. Celia had built a fire in the grate, and the room was excessively hot. Lilith, however, was sitting close to the fire, a shawl wrapped around her shoulders.

The older woman looked terrible. Her face was ashen, and her eyes were great pools of despair. Juliana felt a wrench of pity for her. Of all the people in the house, Juliana thought, Lilith was the only one who would truly mourn Crandall's death. Though she had clearly grown upset with his ways, in her heart she had never seen him as he really was but only as the fine upstanding son she had wanted him to be. She was responsible for many of his unattractive character traits, Juliana thought, spoiling him and filling him with the idea of his own importance, never believing any of the truth she heard about him, but accepting Crandall's own self-serving versions of what happened. But no one could deny that Lilith had loved Crandall, and Juliana knew that she must be devastated by his death.

Seraphina, who was sitting much farther away from the fire, on a couch with Winifred, fanning herself, looked up at Juliana's entrance and offered her a wan smile. Seraphina looked over at her mother, who was staring into the fire as if no one else were in the room. Juliana followed her gaze. She wasn't sure what to do. Comforting Lilith had never been something she had even thought of doing.

She walked over and sat down on a chair across from the older woman, doing her best to ignore the heat from the fireplace. "Aunt Lilith…"

Lilith looked at her vaguely, as if she was not quite certain who Juliana was.

"I am so sorry," Juliana told the other woman simply.

Lilith continued to look at her without saying anything.

"Perhaps you should go up to your room and lie down."

"I cannot sleep," Lilith replied.

"I can ask Cook to heat you a cup of milk," Juliana offered.

"I don't want to sleep," Lilith told her flatly.

Juliana could think of nothing else to offer. But she could not bring herself to leave the suffering woman. So she sat, as Seraphina and Winifred sat, waiting and saying nothing.

After a time, Sir Herbert and Mr. Hakebourne entered the room. It was as though none of them could bring themselves to simply go to bed, yet there was nothing to say, either. Sometime later there was the sound of a stir out in the hallway, and Juliana thought that the magistrate must have arrived. Her thought was confirmed when Judge Carstairs entered the room and bowed gravely toward Lilith, then the rest of them.

"Sad, sad thing," he commented generally.

"Judge Carstairs." Lilith rose and went over to him. "What have you found?"

He looked a little flustered at facing the murdered man's mother. "Well, um, Mrs. Barre…you know, you really should be lying down. This isn't a fit subject for a lady's ears."

"He is my son," Lilith replied with dignity. "I have a right to know."

"Well, um, certainly. It appears to be death by misadventure," the magistrate said. "Of course, we can't say for sure 'til the coroner's court, but I don't think the reason will change."

"Yes, but who did it?" Seraphina asked, her hands knotted into her skirts. "Do you have any idea who could have—"

The magistrate began to shake his head, but Lilith jumped in before he could speak. "That's obvious, isn't it? Who hated my son that much? Who came to blows with him this evening on the dance floor?"

The judge looked uncomfortable. He had been one of the wedding guests and, like all the others, had been witness to the fight between Nicholas and Crandall.

"Well, now, as to that, it doesn't mean that Lord Barre had anything to do with—"

"He couldn't have," Juliana said. "He was with me this evening after that fight."

"Well, there, you see." Judge Carstairs looked relieved. "Lord Barre has an alibi. Entire evening, you say?"

"This was our wedding night," Juliana pointed out.

"Harrumph, yes, well, of course." The judge looked more embarrassed than Juliana at the topic of conversation. He turned toward Lilith. "The coroner's court will conduct a full investigation, Mrs. Barre. Your son's murder will not go unpunished."

Lilith looked at the judge for a long moment; then her gaze went to Juliana consideringly. "I believe I will go up to bed now. Ladies, I suggest we leave the gentlemen to their work."

Juliana had no desire to leave, but when Lilith held out her hand to take Juliana's arm for support, she could do nothing else. The women went upstairs, saying little as they walked. Juliana presumed that, like herself, they were all too overwhelmed by the events of the evening to be able even to think clearly.

Once in her room, Juliana slipped her hand into the pocket of her dressing gown and took out the jewel. Going over to the lamp on the dresser, she bent down and examined the ruby in its light. She could tell nothing from it that she had not seen before, and finally she set it carefully in the top portion of her jewelry box. She pulled off her dressing gown and laid it aside, glancing over at the bed. She could not help but think about what she and Nicholas had been doing when they were interrupted by the scream. She looked down at herself and for the first time realized that she had put her night-gown on inside out. The front of it had clearly shown between the V of the neck of her dressing gown, she knew, and a blush stained her cheeks. It would have been obvious that she had dressed hastily, which would lead the mind to exactly what she had been engaged in.

At least, she thought as she climbed into bed and pulled the sheet up to her now-heated face, her appearance would have added verisimilitude to what she had told the magistrate about where Nicholas was.

Turning on her side, she tried to gather her thoughts. But she found that her mind was too scattered; she could settle on nothing for longer than a moment or two.

At last she heard the sound of steps coming up the stairs. They must have belonged to the other men, she thought, for no one entered the room next door. She continued to wait, thinking she would never go to sleep.

The next thing she knew, it was morning.

THE SUN WAS COMING through a crack between the draperies, and its light in her eyes had awakened her. She sat up groggily. She had not gotten enough sleep, but she knew she would not be able to slip back into slumber. She jackknifed her knees and laid her head against them, letting out a soft groan.

She would have liked to think that the events of the last night had been a dream, but she knew they had not. Crandall was dead. And someone had murdered him. Lilith obviously believed—or wanted to believe—that it was Nicholas.

The fact that he and Crandall had so publicly quarreled the night before would not look good, Juliana knew. And while she had given him an alibi, the word of one's wife was not the most reliable proof. It was imperative, therefore, that she and Nicholas find out who had actually committed the murder.

She got up and washed her face at the basin, then pulled out a morning dress that required no help for her to put on. She did not want to have to drag poor Celia out so early. After slipping on her shoes, she impulsively put the ruby in her pocket, then made her way downstairs.

Nicholas was the only one at breakfast. He looked up at her and smiled a little wearily as he stood up and came around to pull out her chair. "Could you not sleep, either?"

"I awoke early," Juliana told him. "I—my sleep was restless."

"'Tis no wonder."

As he sat down, one of the maids, a girl named Annie, came forward to pour tea for Juliana. Juliana noticed the poor girl's hand shook so badly that the teapot rattled against the cup. She looked up with concern into the girl's face. It was pale, her eyes huge.

"Annie, are you all right?" she asked.

The maid gulped and glanced over to where the footman was serving up Nicholas's eggs. "Yes, miss—my lady, I should say."

The girl looked so nervous that Juliana could not bring herself to press her. And there was no need to, really. There was little wonder that someone would be afraid in a house where murder had been done the night before.

The maid topped off Nicholas's cup, as well, and returned the pot to its place on the sideboard. She picked up a platter of breakfast meats and started toward the table, her back to the door. At that moment the butler entered the room as noiselessly as he always did, coming up to the sideboard behind Annie. She started to turn back, almost running into Rundell, and she let out a shriek and dropped the platter with a crash.

"Clumsy girl!" Rundell exclaimed. "Get back to the kitchen. At once."

"I—I'm sorry, sir," the girl got out, then burst into tears and rushed from the room.

The footman hurried to clean up the mess, and Rundell turned toward Nicholas and Juliana. "I beg your pardon, my lord. My lady. I'm afraid the girl is frightened out of what little wits she has."

"It's quite understandable," Nicholas replied quickly. "Don't worry about it."

"I shall bring in another plate right away."

The mess was soon picked up, and Rundell left the room, returning shortly with another full plate of meat. He sent the footman on his way and finished serving the remainder of the breakfast himself.

Nicholas soon dismissed the butler, as well, saying he was certain that the servants were in a turmoil this morning and his presence was needed to reassure them. Rundell nodded and bowed out of the room, closing the door behind him.

Nicholas sighed, setting aside his fork and knife. "I find I have little appetite this morning."

"Were you up late dealing with…?" Juliana paused, unable to think of a delicate way to express her thought.

"The body?" Nicholas asked bluntly. "Yes. I stayed until they left. And I locked the door myself to keep anyone else out of there." He grimaced. "Of course, I am probably the likeliest suspect."

"Nicholas…no."

He looked at her consideringly. "You did not tell the magistrate the exact truth last night. You said that I was with you the entire evening after we left the ballroom. Yet there was a good hour, at least, when we were apart."

"I know," Juliana replied evenly. "I heard you leave your room."

"Why did you not tell him that?"

"I know you didn't kill Crandall. And I certainly wasn't about to let Lilith create any doubt that you might have done so."

"You have too much faith in me. I have done a great many wicked things in my life. And I hated Crandall. How can you be so sure that I didn't knock him over the head?"

"I know you," Juliana told him simply. "I realize that you may not have lived an exemplary life.

Perhaps you have done things that were...not exactly legal. But I know you are not an evil man. If you had killed Crandall, you would have had good cause, and it would have been in the heat of anger, in a face-to-face fight, just as it was last night on the dance floor. You never would have attacked him in that sly and sneaky way, coshing him from behind with a fireplace poker."

Juliana reached over impulsively and took his hand in both of hers, looking into his face. "Am I not right?"

Nicholas looked at her for a long moment, and she saw then a subtle shifting of his face, a relaxation and warming, and his hand curled around one of hers. He raised her hand to his lips and kissed it gently.

"I am so grateful that you did me the honor of becoming my wife," he told her.

Juliana smiled at him. "No more than I."

"You are right, of course." Nicholas released her hand and leaned back in his chair. "I didn't kill Crandall. Nor am I the magistrate's choice in the matter. He is inclined to believe that it is Farrow."

"The blacksmith?"

Nicholas nodded. "He clearly had a grudge against Crandall. He knocked him about a good bit last week. And he had opportunity. He was here last night."

"But that was at some remove. Why would he

kill him a week later? Why not do it at the time he discovered Crandall assaulting his wife?"

"I don't know. I'm not convinced that he did. But it is possible that Crandall, who could be more foolish than one would have supposed possible, might have approached Mrs. Farrow again last night. He did go outside. When I talked to the servants last night, a couple of the footmen had noticed him outside mingling with the tenants."

"But he was killed inside the house."

"It would have been easy enough for someone to follow him inside. That room is not far from the side door. I do not think we can rule Farrow out." He paused, then added, "That said, I am not inclined to think that Farrow is the killer. He is, I think, straightforward and honest—not the sort, as you said about me, to knock a man on the head from behind. But I fear that the coroner's court will focus their attention on him. It would be far easier for them to convict one of the townspeople than a gentleman of influence."

"Or a lady of influence."

"You are right." Nicholas inclined his head toward her in agreement. "I am sure that there are a number of women who would have liked to do away with Crandall."

"We cannot let them lay the blame on Farrow if he did not do it. And I cannot help but fear that Lilith will do her best to convince them that *you* are responsible. We should look into it ourselves."

"I do not intend to leave it solely to the magistrate and the coroner's court," Nicholas told her firmly. "I intend to investigate myself. However, I—"

"The problem—" Juliana interrupted. She strongly suspected that Nicholas was about to tell her to stay out of his investigation, and she did not intend to let him exclude her. "—is that there are so few people we can rule out. Crandall had made enemies everywhere."

"That's true enough," Nicholas agreed.

"His friend Mr. Hakebourne, for instance. I saw him arguing with Crandall just last night during the dance. I don't think he came here just to see a friend. Crandall was quite surprised—and not well pleased—to see him. I think Crandall may have owed him money. I overheard Crandall and Sir Herbert talking one day. Crandall was trying to borrow money from Sir Herbert, and Sir Herbert said that Crandall owed a number of gentlemen money."

"Of course, if Crandall owed him money, it would not make much sense for Hakebourne to kill him. He'd never get the money back then."

"That's true. But he was clearly angry with Crandall last night. Anger could have overridden his common sense," Juliana pointed out. "And then there is Sir Herbert."

"His brother-in-law?" Nicholas quirked an eyebrow. "He seemed to have little liking for him, but enough enmity to kill him?"

Juliana shrugged. "I don't know. When I heard Sir Herbert and Crandall arguing that day, Sir Herbert seemed quite upset with him. Apparently, Crandall already had borrowed a great deal from him and not paid him back."

"Doesn't seem like something you'd kill someone over. Just don't lend him anything else."

"He was angry at Crandall for something else, though. Sir Herbert seemed to hold him responsible for getting Seraphina involved with a gambling crowd. Apparently she has lost a great deal of money at cards. That is why they are here instead of in London for the Season."

"Ah. Tapped out, then." Nicholas nodded his head. "I had wondered. Seraphina doesn't seem the sort to rusticate when she could be going to balls every evening."

"No. I dare swear she dislikes being here, and she may very well blame Crandall, too."

"There was little love lost there," Nicholas added. "Crandall was always making little comments that seemed to rouse her ire."

"Yes. I thought it was odd. What he said always appeared innocuous enough, but she would shoot him an absolutely furious look."

"Of course," Nicholas speculated, "the person with the most reason to want to get rid of Crandall would be his wife."

"Winifred?" Juliana asked, surprised. "But she is so small and, well, timid."

"Sir Herbert and Seraphina do not have to be around Crandall. If he is all that bothersome to them, why not just leave? But Winifred is stuck with the man. I am sure she must have realized long ago what a mistake she made in accepting him."

Juliana pursed her lips thoughtfully. "Yes, she would have the most reason to do away with him. It would be awful having to live with Crandall." She paused, thinking of the marks she had seen on Winifred's arm the day the girl had helped her write out invitations. "I think he might have hurt her—physically, I mean. One day she had bruises around her arm, as if someone strong had grabbed her tightly. And she would have been faced continually with the news of his betrayal of their wedding vows—Crandall would not have left other women alone, I'm certain of it. And just the other day at lunch…"

"Yes. Clearly he was at least attempting to be unfaithful to her in that incident with the blacksmith's wife. There was no way she could ignore that," Nicholas said. "As for her being small and timid—well, he was struck from behind and with a poker, which would have evened out the physical disparity between them."

"We cannot discount the possibility that it could have been a woman," Juliana agreed. "Look at what I found on the floor in that room last night, only a few feet from Crandall's body."

She reached into the pocket of her skirt and pulled out the ruby, holding it out to Nicholas in the palm of her hand.

Nicholas's eyebrows soared upwards. "What is this?" He took the gem from her and held it toward the light coming in from the window. "A ruby?"

"Yes. I saw it when you held the lamp over Crandall's body. It glinted in the light. It was lying at the foot of the cabinet near Crandall's feet. What if it came from the killer?"

Nicholas studied the ruby thoughtfully. "It could have, of course. The room is used little, and it seems that if it had fallen from someone's person in the past, a servant would have seen it when cleaning and picked it up."

"Possibly. Unfortunately, it is not large. It could have been overlooked. I noticed it only because you moved the lamp."

Nicholas looked at her. "Have you told anyone else about this?"

"No. I said nothing when I found it. I was afraid that if I said anything, it would give the killer—"

"A chance to get rid of the ornament the ruby came from," Nicholas finished for her. "You're right. Good. It isn't conclusive proof, of course, but it might give us a better idea of who did it." He paused, then said, "Even if it does belong to the killer, it doesn't mean that it's necessarily a woman. This ruby could have come from a tie pin or shirt studs."

Juliana nodded. "I wish I could remember what everyone was wearing that evening."

"That's a hopeless effort as far as I'm concerned. I remember only how you looked." Nicholas stopped, and, to Juliana's amazement, color darkened his cheeks beneath his tan. He stood up quickly and walked away, going over to the sideboard and refilling his cup. He stood there for a moment, looking down at it, then swung back around.

"I must apologize," he said stiffly, still not looking

at her. "For my behavior last night. I—well, I have no other excuse than that I had been drinking."

It took her a moment to realize what he was talking about. When she caught on to the fact that the behavior in question must be the way he had taken her into his arms and kissed her wildly, her spirits plunged. What she had found so vastly pleasurable was an embarrassment to him.

"I see," she replied faintly. Nicholas regretted kissing her; he wished he had stayed in his room and not given in to his passion. *Had he truly not felt anything for her? Had it been only alcohol that had driven him to act as he did?* It made her want to cry to think so.

"I should never have imposed myself on you in that way," he went on.

"It wasn't—"

"No!" He shook his head sharply. "Don't excuse me. We set the boundaries of our marriage, and I overstepped them. I acted inappropriately. I hope you will forgive me. I promise you that it will not happen again."

Juliana looked down at her plate, feeling awkward. She wondered if it followed from what he said that Nicholas thought *she* had acted inappropriately, too, since she had responded to him with a passion equal to his own. Perhaps he did. Perhaps she was not acting in the way he wanted his wife to behave.

"Of course I accept your apology," she told him, tightly reining in her own emotions.

"That is very good of you."

He remained by the sideboard for a moment. Juliana could not bring herself to turn her head toward him for fear of what might show in her face. At last he moved, going over to the door and opening it.

At first she thought he intended to leave, but then he came back over to the table and sat down. Juliana pushed the food around a bit on her plate. She did not feel able to eat it anymore. She set down her fork and looked up, keeping her face as expressionless as she could.

Nicholas was watching her, his face a trifle uneasy. She wondered if he was afraid she was going to cause some sort of scene. She smiled at him brittlely, about to excuse herself from the meal.

At that moment there were footsteps outside in the hall and Peter Hakebourne stepped into the room. Nicholas glanced at Juliana, and she knew what he was thinking. The first of their suspects was here, and Nicholas intended to get whatever information out of him that he could.

She set aside all thoughts of leaving the dining

room now. She might not be a wife to Nicholas in the truest sense, but at least in this, she would be united with him: She intended to help him find Crandall's murderer.

"Ah, Mr. Hakebourne," Nicholas said genially, rising and getting the pot of tea to pour a cup for the other man. "We are serving ourselves this morning. I hope that is all right with you."

"Of course, of course," Hakebourne agreed pleasantly.

"Did you sleep well, Mr. Hakebourne?" Juliana asked.

"As well as could be expected, I suppose," Hakebourne replied as he sat down. He took a sip of his tea and set down the cup, then said, "Um, do you—have you heard anything about whom they suspect did it?"

"Not really," Nicholas answered. "Lady Barre and I were just discussing it. Do you have any thoughts on who the killer might be?"

Hakebourne shrugged. "I don't imagine it would be difficult to find someone who would have wanted Crandall dead." He looked back across the table at Nicholas, his expression challenging, as he went on. "The hard thing, doubtless, would be narrowing it down to just one person."

CHAPTER FOURTEEN

A SILENCE HUNG in the air for a moment after Hakebourne's provocative statement.

Then Nicholas asked disingenuously, "Had Crandall that many enemies, then?"

Mr. Hakebourne shrugged. "You knew the man. What would you guess?"

"Crandall could be very annoying," Nicholas conceded. "But enough for someone to kill him?"

"Perhaps for some, it doesn't take much," Hakebourne countered.

"What about you, Mr. Hakebourne?" Juliana asked quietly.

Hakebourne turned toward her, his eyes wide. "Do you mean, did I kill him?" Before she could answer, he went on. "The answer to that is no. But as for being quite put out with him, I certainly was that. Crandall cheated me."

"Cheated you? How?" Nicholas asked.

"Sold me a worthless piece of horseflesh. Oh, I

know—*caveat emptor*, as they say, especially when it comes to horses. But blast it! The man claimed he was my friend. Then he turned around and sold me a hunter when he knew it had been injured. Damned bad form that. 'Scuse me, my lady."

"So he sold you a crippled horse?" Nicholas asked.

"He wasn't when I looked at him here. I was visiting Crandall, and I admired the horse, offered to buy it from him, but he was not having any of it then. A few months later, in London, he told me he had decided he had to sell the horse. He was short of cash, you see. Naturally, I said yes—damned fine horse. But first time I rode him, I realized something had happened to him. 'Course, Crandall denied it all, said nothing had ever happened to him. Clearly untrue."

"Is that what you were arguing about last night?" Nicholas asked.

"Arguing?" Hakebourne looked surprised.

"I noticed you and Crandall exchanging words during the dance," Juliana explained. "It didn't look particularly friendly."

"Well, it wasn't. He was trying to tell me it was my fault. *My* fault!" He looked at them indignantly. "As if I was a green 'un. That's why I came here—didn't know about the wedding, you see." He smiled a little apologetically. "Didn't mean to intrude upon you. I thought if I talked to Crandall, he'd see the error of his ways. I mean, really, one doesn't cheat a friend."

Juliana thought it was probably not right to cheat *anyone*, but she refrained from pointing that out.

"I presume Crandall refused to give you back the money you'd paid him," Nicholas interjected.

"Flatly! And not just once."

"You must have been quite angry," Juliana sympathized.

"Indeed, I was. It isn't as if I'm flush in the pocket, either. I could have used that money. But all Crandall could say was that he didn't even have it any longer, that he'd used it to pay off some debt or other." Hakebourne made a noise of disbelief. "More likely he'd used it to place another bet. The man could not stop. He was obsessed."

It was a common enough problem among Crandall's peers, Juliana knew. Many a gentleman's fortune had disappeared into the pockets of gamblers.

"On what did he bet?" Nicholas asked.

"Anything," Hakebourne replied candidly. "Horse races, card games, boxing matches…whatever he could find. Once he bet on a race between mice with Everard Hornbaugh. 'Course, in the end, he lost it all. And he was in debt to a number of people—not only money lenders, but gentlemen, as well."

"Are you the only person he cheated?"

"I wouldn't think so. I should think he had done so to a number of other people before he tried it with an old friend. He borrowed like mad, as well."

"From whom?"

"Anyone who was foolish enough to lend him money. His sister's husband, for one. He would always turn to Sir Herbert first, because of the family connection, you know. Sir Herbert has lent him hundreds and hundreds of guineas over the years, and Crandall never paid him back a cent. But I think Sir Herbert had finally stopped giving it to him. He was furious over Lady Seraphina, you see."

"Because Crandall had introduced her to gambling?" Juliana asked.

Hakebourne nodded. "How did you know? He'd been doing it for a while, to pay off his debts to the gambling hells. He'd bring in flats for them to fleece, and they'd forgive some of his debt or give him credit."

"Flats?" Juliana asked.

"Inexperienced players," Nicholas informed her.

"So he was betraying his friends there, too?"

Hakebourne shrugged. "Well, most of them were new to town, if they were willing to believe Crandall would lead them to an honest game. But I suppose Lady Seraphina didn't think her own brother would do that to her. Or perhaps she had been too sheltered. Sir Herbert is a trifle stuffy. At first she won—that's the way they do it, you see. But then she started to lose. I hear she lost a fortune. That's why they're rusticating. That's what the gossips say, anyway."

Juliana and Nicholas exchanged glances. Hakebourne's words confirmed what she had overheard between Crandall and Sir Herbert. Hakebourne was silent for a moment as he ate his breakfast ham, looking thoughtful as he chewed. Finally he said, "I think he got money from Seraphina, too. Don't know where she came up with it, with all she'd lost."

"What do you mean?"

"Last time I saw him, when I purchased the hunter, Crandall was hinting that Seraphina was giving him money. I was surprised…after what he'd done to her, you know, but he said she knew she'd better pay him to keep him from telling Sir Herbert her secrets."

"What secrets were those?" Nicholas asked.

"Don't know, really. Crandall wouldn't say. He was like that—always finding things out about people, getting information that would embarrass them, then using it against them. Usually to get money."

"What a despicable excuse for a human being!" Juliana exclaimed.

Hakebourne turned his interested eyes on her. "He did it to you, too?"

"No. I'm sure he would not have hesitated to, though, if he had known anything he could use against me. I never liked him, but I hadn't realized he would stoop to extortion."

"Wasn't much Crandall would not stoop to," Mr. Hakebourne mused. "But I think he was worse lately. More desperate for money."

"Why is that?" Nicholas asked, leaning forward interestedly.

"Well, actually, I think it was because of you."

"Me?" Nicholas looked surprised. "Because he thought I would send him packing?"

"I'm not sure. Maybe. But I think it was more that people were calling in their debts. Until you came along, you see, a number of people just assumed that Crandall would inherit the family fortune when the old Lord Barre died. Not everyone, of course. Some people knew that the line came down through your father, my lord. The downy ones." He paused, then added, "Not me."

"Really," Juliana murmured. "You surprise me."

"Oh, well, I've got plenty of town bronze, you see. But I've never been much of one for the books or things like family trees and so on."

"Was Crandall telling everyone that he expected to inherit?" Nicholas asked.

"It wasn't so much that," Hakebourne said. "It was more the way he talked about Lychwood Hall and how he was always coming back here, taking care of matters. He acted as if it would be his someday. But then, when the old lord died and everyone found out that it wasn't Crandall who inherited the estate but somebody no one even knew...well, then there were plenty who got worried about their money. Didn't know whether they'd ever get any of it back. They started plaguing him, calling in his debts and so forth."

"Ah. I see."

Hakebourne took the last bite of food left on his plate and washed it down with a gulp or two of tea. "Well..." He patted his stomach in satisfaction. "You keep an excellent table, my lord."

"Thank you, Mr. Hakebourne. I hope you will continue to enjoy our hospitality for a while."

"Really?" Hakebourne looked surprised but pleased. "I was thinking...well, since you don't really know me and I was friends only with Crandall...well, that perhaps I should be on my way soon."

"Nonsense," Nicholas replied, favoring the man

with a smile. "I would be quite honored if you would stay on with us at Lychwood Hall."

"Well." Hakebourne beamed back at Nicholas. "Demmed decent of you, my lord. I wouldn't mind, I confess. After all, there's Crandall's funeral. Must pay my respects, you see. And, well, it's a bit uncomfortable for me in London right now. Hard to keep the creditors from the door…especially after Crandall wouldn't return my money."

Assured once more that Nicholas was happy to have him escape his creditors at Lychwood Hall for the time being, Mr. Hakebourne went happily on his way.

"He seems to be dealing admirably with his grief over Crandall," Nicholas commented dryly.

"Yes. I thought it was interesting that Mr. Hakebourne's indignation over Crandall's cheating ways evinced itself only as it affected himself."

"I think we can agree that Mr. Hakebourne is not a man of strong moral fiber," Nicholas went on. "But I wonder if he has it in him to murder Crandall, especially since it would not benefit him."

"He certainly seems to be one who does only what benefits him," Juliana agreed.

"Of course, he might not have been telling us the truth about why he pursued Crandall here—or at least not the full truth."

"That's true. And his eagerness to tell us all about

everyone else's reasons for disliking Crandall is a little suspicious. He doesn't seem like a killer, but I don't think we can cross him off the list just yet." She sighed and stood up. "Little as I like it, I must see to arrangements for Crandall's funeral. And doubtless there will a multitude of other things to do. I must check on Lilith and Winifred, and see what I can do to ease their pain. And, of course, we must find out who killed Crandall."

"Juliana..." Nicholas said, rising as she stood up. There was a note of warning in his voice. "Do not lose sight of the fact that someone in this house killed Crandall and may not look kindly upon your asking questions. Please don't go about questioning people without me along."

"I have to talk to everyone, anyway," Juliana pointed out reasonably. But as Nicholas's eyebrows knitted darkly, she added, "However, I promise I will be very careful to say nothing to alarm the killer."

From Nicholas's expression, she suspected that he had some doubts about her carrying through on that promise, so she slipped quickly out the door before he could bring up more objections.

She spent much of the rest of the day trying to keep the household running smoothly. The servants—like everyone else in the house—were somewhat on edge. Dishes were broken and things overturned. Juliana noticed that the maids seemed to work in pairs now, and it didn't take much guesswork to figure out that they were afraid to be by themselves in the large house.

It did not help matters any that the village constable spent most of the day interviewing all the members of the household. The man was quite deferential when he asked Juliana questions, and he accepted without question her statement that Nicholas had been with her the entire night after they left the party. But his very deference worried her, for she feared he would not look seriously at any of the Barre family or their guests, but would concentrate solely on the blacksmith, without making an effort to get to the truth.

Given the sort of person Crandall had been, it seemed likely to her that the killer had hated him and no one else would be in danger. Still, she understood the general air of uneasiness that pervaded the house now. What had once seemed secure and safe, protected from any of the evils of the outside world, had been invaded by evil. It was not hard to feel suddenly afraid.

The responsibilities of arranging the funeral fell largely to Juliana, as did dealing with the visitors who came to offer condolences, since both Crandall's wife and his mother kept to their rooms.

She went first to visit Winifred, whom she found sitting, still in her dressing gown, staring dully out the window. She turned as Juliana came into the room and tried to smile.

"I came to see if you wanted anything," Juliana told her, crossing the room and sitting down on the vanity bench near Winifred's chair.

Winifred shook her head. "They brought me something to eat, but I couldn't." She looked at Juliana, her face pale and older than her years this morning. "I'm a terrible person."

Juliana wondered wildly if the girl was about to confess to killing Crandall, but she said only, "I'm sure that's not true."

"But it is." Winifred nodded her head. "I can't cry about him. I want to. I have tried to. But I cannot." She leaned forward, looking at Juliana earnestly. "My husband is dead, and I—I feel relief."

She brought her hand up to her mouth, covering it as though to keep the feelings inside her. Juliana did not know what to say. She could understand quite easily how anyone married to Crandall would feel the way Winifred did.

"His mother is prostrate with grief," Winifred went

on in a low voice. "I know when the maid comes in, she expects to find me crying, too. You have come to try to comfort me. But I…" She sighed and looked out the window again. "When I met Crandall, I thought he was the most handsome man I'd ever seen—that dark hair and those splendid eyes. And so sophisticated. So witty. He had done so much, seen so many things."

Winifred's eyes sparkled a little at the memory, and she went on, her voice almost happy. "I couldn't believe that he singled me out among all the girls there. I was barely out of the schoolroom. And I had been nowhere, done nothing. But he paid me so much attention that my mother warned me to be careful of his intentions. He would have waltzed with me three times that evening if my mother had not strictly forbade me."

"It sounds very romantic," Juliana said, hoping her own dislike of Crandall did not show in her voice.

"It was." Winifred's mouth curled in fond reminiscence. "When he asked me to marry him, I was the happiest girl in England." Her smile faded. "But later he regretted marrying me."

"No, Winifred…" Juliana wasn't at all certain that she spoke the truth, but she could not keep from wanting to shield Winifred from sorrow.

Winifred shook her head, casting a grateful look

at Juliana. "You are very kind. But it is the truth. I know it. The other day…when Lord Barre said that about the blacksmith's wife—"

"I am so sorry you had to hear that," Juliana told her, reaching over to take one of the girl's hands.

"It was not the first time it had happened. I had heard things, whispers among the servants, Seraphina taking Crandall to task…. I knew. And I knew it was because he should not have married me. Mrs. Barre said as much."

Juliana gritted her teeth. "You must not mind what Lilith says. She is a—well, she can be quite cutting and mean. It has nothing to do with you. That is simply the way she is. And she would have thought no one good enough for her son. When we were young, she worshipped him."

"That is true," Winifred agreed. "Even now, I think, though sometimes he was not very nice to her. He would always ask her for money. I know many times she did not want to give it to him, and he would get quite sharp with her. He would talk about how she was concerned with the way things appeared, so she would not want her son to wind up in debtors' prison and be a blot on the family name. And he would look at her in this taunting way that made me surprised that she didn't just slap him down. But she never did. Eventually, she would give him the money, or some jewelry to sell."

"So, you see, you cannot take what Aunt Lilith said as the truth."

"But he thought so, too. I know it. I wasn't clever enough for him. I didn't know anybody or know how to do things. He never once took me to London with him, and when I asked…" Now the tears that Winifred had been unable to bring up before filled her eyes. "He told me that I would embarrass him. That his friends would dismiss me as a country simpleton."

Juliana felt an upswell of sympathy for the girl. Winifred was better off without Crandall, Juliana was sure of that. But her future would not necessarily be a happy one. From everything Juliana had heard the past weeks, Crandall had been penniless; he would leave his wife nothing. Of course, Nicholas would allow her to live here, and he would not make Winifred feel the sting of being a poor relation. But even so, she would know that was what she was.

Juliana got up and crossed over to the girl, kneeling down beside Winifred's chair to look her in the face. She laid her hand on top of Winifred's and said, "I have known Crandall since he was a boy, and I know that he was capable of being as cruel and unbending as his mother. Everyone frowns on saying ill of the dead, but the truth is that Crandall often played fast and loose with the truth. You must not put too much faith in what he said to you. He probably just did not want to have a wife in London." She looked at her significantly. "Crandall's faults were not your responsibility. And I—well, it seems quite understandable to me that you find it difficult to cry over him. Sad as it is to say, I don't think anyone in this house particularly mourns him, except for his mother."

Winifred looked at her sorrowfully. "I know. It *is* sad. But thank you for saying what you did. It makes me feel…a little better." She gave Juliana's hand a squeeze and offered her a small smile.

"Now…do you think you might eat a little something?" Juliana stood up. "I can send one of the maids up with a cold luncheon for you, if you wish."

"Yes, perhaps I can." Again Winifred smiled at her. "Thank you."

Juliana left the room, reflecting that she found it difficult to picture Winifred as the killer. While the girl clearly had ample reason to dislike her husband, she seemed to have been more sorrowful over the loss of their early love than angry with Crandall, and inclined to lay the blame on herself rather than where it belonged.

Of course, the girl could have been putting on an

act for her benefit, but if that were the case, why would Winifred not have pretended to be mourning her dead husband instead of candidly talking about the poor state of her marriage?

Juliana rang for a maid and ordered a light meal brought up to Winifred, adding, "See if you can get her to take a little nap, as well, will you?"

After the maid left, Juliana made her way to Lilith's room. Whatever the awkward state of their relationship, Juliana could not help but feel for the woman. She was probably the only person in the whole house who felt sorrow for Crandall's death.

Juliana knocked quietly at Lilith's door, half expecting Lilith to call to her to leave, but after a moment, she heard Lilith say, "Enter."

She stepped inside. Like Winifred, Lilith was sitting in a chair beside the window, gazing lifelessly out. Of course, nothing, not even extreme grief, could have made her appear so slovenly as to wear a dressing gown in the afternoon. She was dressed in a severe black dress with a high collar and long sleeves; not even a ruffle relieved the plainness of the dress. Her hair was done up in its usual elegant way, anchored with a black comb.

Lilith turned to look at Juliana sourly. "Have you come to gloat?"

"Aunt Lilith!" Juliana exclaimed, shocked by the animosity in the older woman's voice. "Of course not. How can you say that?"

"Why not? I'm not a fool, Juliana. I realize how much you dislike me."

"You have given me little reason over the years not to," Juliana pointed out quietly. "However, I cannot believe that even you would think I would take satisfaction in your grief. I am very sorry for your loss."

"I hope you do not expect me to believe that you feel grief for Crandall."

"No. I am not a hypocrite. But I know that you—"

"You know nothing," Lilith cried in a low voice. "Nothing about how I feel. I held him in my arms when he was a baby, and I knew no one would ever make me feel that way again. I loved him."

Juliana felt a stab of pity for the woman, despite Lilith's harsh dismissal of her sympathy. "I know you did."

Lilith turned and looked up at the portrait of her husband that hung on the wall. "Of course," she said with some bitterness, "I loved his father, too. For all the good it did me." She studied the portrait for a moment. "I thought he hung the moon and stars when I married him. We were perfectly matched in every way. A perfect couple…that's what I believed."

She frowned, seeming to come out of her reverie, and her mouth twisted as she turned back to Juliana, snarling, "It was all her fault!"

Juliana stared at her, taken aback by the hatred that shone in the older woman's eyes. "I—I beg your pardon?"

"Your mother! The ever-so delicate and lovely Diana. The Huntress. An apt name—though one would never know it from that butter-wouldn't-melt-in-her-mouth face. So sweet, so quiet, so 'in love' with her dead husband."

"She loved my father very much." Juliana felt compelled to defend her mother. "I don't understand what you're talking about. What was my mother's fault? I assure you that she never meant to do anything to upset you. She was very grateful to you for letting her live here."

"Grateful! Hah! Does one express one's gratitude by stealing another woman's husband?"

"What?" Juliana gaped at her. *Had Crandall's death unhinged his mother?*

"She was a huntress indeed, though she was sly about it. She never let anyone know as she went about working her wiles on him. She was so pitiful, so sorrowful—no doubt she needed his big strong shoulder to weep on. No doubt she needed him to explain this business matter or that to her. And all the while she flirted with him, teased him, encouraged him...."

"No! Aunt Lilith, I don't know why you think this, but you are wrong!" Juliana exclaimed.

"Wrong? I think not." Lilith stood up, facing her, the long-ago fury lighting her eyes once more. "I am not mistaken in the slightest. Why do you think you were allowed to live here for so long? Why do you think you were taken in and educated with my own children?"

"You're mistaken," Juliana repeated faintly. "It was because my mother was your cousin."

"You think *I* wanted her here?" Lilith scoffed. "I can guarantee you that if she had been here on my say-so, the two of you would have been tossed out of your house within weeks of your arrival. It was my husband who housed you and your mother in that cottage. It was my husband whom she thanked—in that very special way of hers."

"No." Juliana stared at her aunt, aghast. Her stomach knotted within her, and she turned away, unable to remain in Lilith's company a moment longer. "Please. Excuse me."

She hurried to the door and out into the hall, not stopping until she reached the safety of her own room. There, she sank down onto her chair and dropped her head into her hands.

It could not be true, she cried inside. Her mother could not have had an affair with Trenton Barre. She could not have given herself to that cold, wicked man. She could not have loved him.

Juliana let out a soft moan. She thought about her childhood. Looking back on it, she could see that even though she had suffered as the poor relation to the family, her circumstances could have been much worse. Their cottage had been large and nicely appointed. And if many of her clothes were hand-me-downs from her cousin Seraphina, at least they were plentiful and richly made. It was unusual for the Barres to have sent her to a finishing school, even if the flighty Seraphina had needed watching over. She had not, after all, been a great deal more of a handful than some of her friends, all of whom were sent there without a relative hanging on.

Most of all, as Lilith had made clear, the generosity Juliana and her mother had received had not been at her cousin's hands. Lilith had clearly despised her mother and would have gotten rid of her quickly. Obviously Trenton had been the one who had given them the house, who had provided for them, who had sent Juliana to school.

And just as clearly, Juliana knew that Trenton Barre would not have done such things simply out of kindness. Consider the way he had treated Nicholas, his own nephew. Trenton Barre had not been moved by charitable instincts; he had never been given to pity.

She wondered how she could not have seen that fact before.

She thought back to her childhood, to the visits that Trenton Barre had made to their household. For the first time, she considered how odd it was that it was always Trenton, never her mother's cousin Lilith, who came to call on them. She could count on her fingers the number of times Lilith had darkened the doorway of their cottage. but Trenton Barre's visits had been weekly.

Juliana remembered her mother's agitation, the way she would sit down, then stand up, going frequently to the window to look out when it was time for him to arrive. She recalled how her mother had always insisted that Juliana look her best for Mr. Barre, with a freshly tied bow in her hair and her best dress on. Her mother, too, had always been careful to look her best—her prettiest dress, her hair done up in attractive curls, color pinched into her lips and cheeks. It was not surprising, certainly; one would expect to put on one's best front for a benefactor. Still, she could not help but wonder about it now. Had her mother been dressing up because he was their benefactor…or because he was her lover?

Whenever Trenton came into the house, her mother would whisk Juliana into the parlor, where she was expected to smile and bob a polite curtsey. Juliana remembered those visits well. She had hated them. She had feared and hated Trenton, and it was agony to have to stand there, smiling and answering his questions politely. It had always been a vast relief when, after a few minutes, her mother would nod and tell her to go to her room. Juliana had always run to her room and closed the door, overjoyed to be out of the man's presence.

She had never questioned why Trenton had always stayed for so long after she left. Or why her mother told her to stay in her room until Mr. Barre had gone. She had simply been glad not to have to see him again.

Juliana pressed her hand against her stomach, feeling ill. She felt as if her life had been suddenly turned upside down. Was everything she had thought about her mother a lie? Had she not spent the rest of her life grieving after Juliana's father? Had she actually lain with so foul a man as Trenton Barre? Had she loved him? Had she been an adulteress, stealing the affections of her cousin's husband?

It seemed too horrible to contemplate. Surely Lilith was lying to her. Lilith had clearly been jealous of Diana—and little wonder, given her mother's sweet, gentle personality and the way it must have contrasted with Lilith's icy demeanor. Perhaps Lilith had simply been suspicious and jealous without any cause. Perhaps she believed what she had said about Diana and Trenton…but that didn't necessarily mean that what she thought was true.

There was one person who would know the truth, Juliana realized, and she fastened onto the thought like a lifeline. Mrs. Cooper, the woman who had kept house for Juliana's mother from the first day they moved here. She would know what had happened all those years ago. A child might not have realized what was going on when Trenton Barre came to visit, but there was no way a grown woman working in the small cottage, so close to the mistress of the house, would not have known if their frequent visitor was Diana's lover.

She would go to see Mrs. Cooper again. She knew, with a sick fluttering in her stomach, that what she learned from the woman might be devastating to her. But Juliana could not go on not knowing. However much it might hurt, she had to discover the truth.

CHAPTER FIFTEEN

CRANDALL'S FUNERAL WAS the following day. It was far too bright and sunny a day for a funeral, Juliana thought. The cemetery looked not at all gloomy, but a pleasant place of dappled sunlight and shade. Roses climbed against the iron fence at the edge of the church-yard, showering their sweet scent upon the gathering.

Juliana glanced at the people grouped around the freshly dug grave site. The women were all dressed in black, and the men wore black armbands of mourning. Juliana had made it a point both yester-day and today to check whatever jewelry each person was wearing. The problem, she quickly discovered, was that so soon after the death, no one was wearing anything as festive as rubies. Earrings were uni-formly of jet or onyx, and the men's cuff links and tie pins were of the same ebony shade, or a simple gold or silver. It would be difficult, she knew, to get a chance to look into the others' jewelry cases.

On one side of Juliana, Winifred stood, her hands

tightly clenched together, staring down at the casket. Across from them, Lilith was ramrod-straight, and, though very pale against the stark black of her dress and hat, her face was composed. Lilith, Juliana thought, would never allow her emotions to overcome her, even for her son.

The vicar finished his words and said a short prayer; then the casket was lowered into the ground. One by one the members of the family passed by, starting with Lilith, and continued on toward their waiting carriages. Juliana knew it would be the proper thing to do to go to Lilith, to support her as much as the woman would allow, but Juliana simply could not face it today.

She had slept little the night before, her mind running in the same tracks as it had been ever since Lilith had blurted out the news that Juliana's mother had had an affair with Lilith's husband.

Juliana turned and walked not toward the carriages, but toward the other family graves that lay nearby. Trenton Barre's grave was next to his son's, and after that were the other Barres. At the bottom of the family plot, separated from the Barres, was her mother's grave.

She stopped in front of the simple headstone and gazed at it for a long moment. She felt Nicholas come up beside her, and he slipped his hand around hers. Juliana glanced up at him, a faint smile touching her lips. Somehow the touch of his hand strengthened her.

"You are troubled," he said.

Juliana looked at him, startled. He smiled at her.

"I can see it in you. There is something besides Crandall's death that worries you."

Juliana nodded. "I—it—Lilith accused my mother of stealing Trenton from her. She told me they were having an affair."

Nicholas stared at her. "What? Do you believe her?"

"I don't know why she would lie about something like that. She loved Trenton, and she would not besmirch his name casually, just to upset me. I think that *she* believes it. But whether it is true…I don't know. I don't want to believe it of my mother."

She looked up into his face, her eyes filled with distress. Nicholas squeezed her hand.

"Aunt Lilith is a woman who likes to believe the worst of everyone," he told her. "She is filled with anger and disdain. The fact that she believes it does not make it so."

"I know. I keep telling myself that. But there are things…"

"What things?"

"Oddities…about our situation here at Lychwood Hall. My mother was Lilith's cousin, no relation to Trenton. Yet clearly it was not Lilith who allowed us to stay here, so it must have been Trenton. And when did you ever know him to act out of kindness?"

"He took me in although he hated me," Nicholas pointed out.

"Yes, but he had to. Your grandfather turned you over to him, made him your guardian. And clearly he hoped that you would die before your grandfather, and he would inherit the estate."

"Still, both of them were given to doing what *looked* good. They would not have wanted their peers to label them parsimonious or ungiving. Turning away Lilith's cousin and her daughter would have reflected badly on them."

"I just wish I could know. I—I thought that Mrs. Cooper might be able to confirm whether Lilith was telling me the truth."

"Perhaps she can. You should talk to her before you believe Lilith. I will go with you. Tomorrow afternoon."

Juliana smiled up at him, feeling better. Somehow, whatever she found out, it would not seem as bad if Nicholas was with her.

JULIANA WAS GOING down to supper that evening when she saw that Seraphina's door was standing open. She glanced in. Seraphina was standing at her dresser, a jewelry box in front of her. She was picking through her jewelry, frowning.

Juliana's heart began to beat faster. Quickly she stepped into the room, saying, "Are you going down to supper? I'll walk with you, shall I?"

"What?" Seraphina turned toward her distractedly. "Oh. Yes. Sorry, I feel so…strange. As if everything around me is going faster than I." She shook her head. "Silly, really. I have been standing here trying to find some earbobs I can wear. I own nothing jet, it seems."

Juliana walked over to her side, looking down into the jewelry box. "You have so many beautiful jewels."

She spotted a red glint among the jumbled-up jewelry, and she reached in to pick it up. It was an earring, a dangle of rubies, but none were missing. Trying not to be obvious, she scanned the box for its mate. Or perhaps a necklace that matched the earrings.

Seraphina practically snatched the earring from Juliana's hand. Juliana looked at her, intrigued by the other woman's reaction. There was a look of…yes, almost fear in Seraphina's eyes.

Juliana's heart thumped wildly in her chest. *Could it be that it was Seraphina who had killed her*

brother? Was that why she was sorting through her
jewels, trying to find the ruby that was missing?

"Those are lovely rubies," Juliana said, watching
Seraphina's face as she spoke. "Is there a necklace
that matches them?"

"Yes, of course." The alarm in Seraphina's eyes
intensified.

"I should love to see it." Juliana did her best to
keep her voice casual, despite the tension that was
rising in her.

"Why? Oh, God, you know, don't you?" Seraphina raised her hands to her mouth, her eyes
growing huge. "How could you know? Oh, please,
don't tell Herbert...."

"Seraphina...I am sure that there must have
been a reason for what you did," Juliana said,
keeping her voice calm as she reached out to lay
a hand on Seraphina's arm. "It won't go so hard
on you if you confess."

"No!" Seraphina jerked her arm away, backing
away. "I can't tell him. I can't! You don't understand!" Tears welled in her eyes. "How did you
know? Did Crandall tell you?"

"What?" Juliana gaped at her.

"He promised he would not tell anyone. That is
why I paid him!" Seraphina cried.

"Seraphina…what are you talking about?" Juliana asked, realizing that they were talking at cross purposes. "What did Crandall promise not to tell? Why were you paying him?"

"You mean you didn't know?" Seraphina stared at her. "But you—I must be going mad. I thought you realized that the rubies were glass." She let out a wild little laugh.

"Glass? You mean they aren't real?"

"No. That is the whole problem!" Seraphina wailed. "Sir Herbert will be furious if he finds out. I dread that one day he will look at them closely, that he will realize…"

"He doesn't know that they are glass?"

"Of course not! Oh, what a muddle." Seraphina plopped down on the chair in front of her vanity and propped her elbows on the table, leaning her head in her hands. "Why did I ever let myself lose so much money?"

"Gambling?" Juliana seized on the one thread of the conversation that she thought she understood.

Seraphina nodded. "Yes. At first I kept winning. It was so exciting!" She looked up at Juliana, her eyes sparkling at the memories. "And Crandall knew them. He introduced them to me. I thought they had to be proper people, even if *I* didn't know them. I mean, they were simply card games in Mrs. Battle's house. It wasn't as if I were going to a gambling hell."

"But then you lost money," Juliana supplied.

Seraphina sighed. "Yes. Barrels of it. I didn't see how I could lose so much after I had done so well at first. Sir Herbert says they tricked me—that they let me win in order to catch me in their web." She looked at Juliana. Tears sparkled on her eyelashes, and she reminded Juliana of a child learning the truth of Father Christmas. "Do you think he's right?"

Juliana felt an unexpected twinge of pity for Seraphina. "Yes, I'm afraid he probably is. Mr. Hakebourne was telling us that Crandall did that sort of thing, taking people to 'friends' who cheated them at cards."

Seraphina nodded, her expression sad. "I wouldn't have thought he could do that to his own sister. I—we weren't terribly close, and I know Crandall did things that weren't nice, but…"

"It was wicked of him," Juliana agreed. "He was desperate for money, I think."

Seraphina's expression hardened. "I know. He made me pay him to keep quiet."

"Keep quiet about what? Sir Herbert knows about your gambling losses, doesn't he?"

"He doesn't know about the jewels," Seraphina told her. "I sold them. I couldn't pay my IOUs, and they wouldn't allow me to continue to play if I didn't pay them. This was before Sir Herbert found out. I didn't know what to do—I had used all my allowance and more. I hadn't paid the dressmaker or the milliner, because I'd gambled the money for my clothes, too. I was at my wits' end. I had to keep on playing. It was the only way that I could get my money back, don't you see? Then Crandall—and it's so unfair because he is the one who suggested it to me!" Seraphina looked indignant.

"Suggested what to you? That you sell the jewels?"

Seraphina nodded. "Yes. Crandall said I could pawn them and use the money to play. And I thought I would win the money back, and then I could get the jewels back. And in the meantime, he said, I could have copies made. It seemed such an easy solution, so I gave them to him—the whole ruby parure. And my pearls. My rings. The sapphire bracelet Herbert gave me as an engagement present."

"You pawned all of those?" Juliana asked in awe.

"Not all at once. Bit by bit. They gave me so little money for them!" Seraphina looked outraged. "And then I could never win anything back. I just kept on losing and losing. Finally Herbert found out about the gambling, and he was so angry with me. He said…" She let out a sigh, looking devastated. "He said he was ashamed of me. I think he wishes he'd never married me. So I couldn't let him know I'd sold all my jewelry. I don't know what he would have done if he had known that."

"I see."

"And then—" Seraphina's eyes narrowed as she spat out, "Then Crandall started threatening to tell Herbert about my pawning the jewels. He said I had to give him money or he would tell him. It's so unfair, when he was the one who suggested that I do it in the first place!"

Juliana could think of nothing to say. *Was there nothing that Crandall would not have done?* It seemed as though every day she learned worse and worse things about him.

"He was always making comments—and that was even after I'd paid him. He would compliment me on my necklace, and I knew he was laughing at me, that he was reminding me of what he knew and how I'd have to pay him. I didn't have much. Herbert keeps me on a short allowance now, and I had to give Crandall almost all of it. It's awful, I know, but when we saw Crandall there on the floor, dead, I thought— well, I was glad! I was so relieved that he wouldn't be able to extort any more money from me."

Juliana let out a long sigh. She wondered if Seraphina had any idea how much she had revealed. Clearly Crandall's sister had good reason for wanting him dead. As long as he was alive, she would live in terror of his revealing the truth to her husband, giving him all her money. His death had released her from a great burden. It was not a long leap from that fact to the realization that perhaps Seraphina had been the one who killed him.

Still, Juliana could not help but feel sorry for her. Even though Crandall would no longer be able to extort money from her, she was still obviously afraid that her husband would find out what she had done with her jewelry.

"Seraphina…maybe it would be best if you simply told Sir Herbert what you did. He knows you were desperate for money."

"No!" Seraphina's eyes widened. "I couldn't. Sir Herbert mustn't know. The rubies were family heirlooms. So were some of the rings. And many of them were presents from him. He would be horribly angry."

"I know he might be angry right now, but don't you think it would be better in the long run? As it is, you are living in fear that he will discover the truth. And at least he might be able to recover some of the jewelry."

"But he would have to pay for it!"

"Well, yes, he'd have to pay back the money

you borrowed, but at least he would still have the family heirlooms. It would be much worse if he learned of it years from now and could no longer recover any of them."

However, Seraphina was insistent that she could not tell Sir Herbert the truth, so Juliana gave in and assured her that she would not reveal to him what Seraphina had told her. She did not add that she fully intended to tell Nicholas about her discovery. And if it turned out that it had indeed been Seraphina who murdered Crandall, then everyone would know all about the woman's troubles, in any case.

Juliana left Seraphina's room, thinking how horrible it would be to live in fear as the other woman did, lying to her husband, always worrying that he would find out. How could Seraphina be happy in her marriage when she always had to pretend? The two of them could not be close with such a secret between them.

But that night, as Juliana lay in bed alone, awake, waiting, hoping for the sound of Nicholas opening the door into her room, she had to wonder whether she was not living just as big a lie as Seraphina. She was pretending to be a wife, yet she spent her nights alone. She should never have agreed to this empty form of marriage. And she could not help but ask herself how she was going to get through the rest of her life this way.

Tears welled up in her eyes and seeped out the corners, trailing down the sides of her face. Juliana turned her face into her pillow. She had lied, she thought, not only to her husband but to herself, pretending that a friendship with Nicholas was all she wanted.

The truth was, she knew, that she loved Nicholas. She had loved him from the time she was a child. All through the years of his absence, that love had lain dormant inside her, and it had taken only his return to breathe life back into it. She had tried to deny it, to pretend that what she felt for him was the love of a friend, but with every day that passed, she realized that what she felt for him was the kind of love that bound a man and a woman together throughout life, founded on the bedrock of their past, and flowering into something rich and deep and vibrant.

In her heart she was his wife; he was the only man whom she would ever love. But she wanted more. She wanted to be the center of his life as he was the center of hers. She wanted to join herself to him in every way. She wanted to know his touch, his kiss, the passion that she knew could flare between them.

But like a dark cloud hovering over her marriage was the knowledge that Nicholas did not feel the same. He professed for her the affection of a friend; he talked of his gratitude to her, and his pledge long ago to come back and rescue her. But he did not talk of love and desire. The fact was that he did not believe he was capable of love.

Juliana was certain that he was. What chilled her heart was the insidious thought that perhaps he was simply not capable of love with *her.*

THE NEXT MORNING Juliana and Nicholas rode to the village to visit her mother's housekeeper. It was a glorious day, soft and warm, one of the last dying days of summer that made it seem as if autumn would never come. Juliana had awakened with a headache, a product, she knew, of having cried herself to sleep the night before, but outside in the sun and gentle breeze, with Nicholas by her side, she found that her headache vanished along with her cares.

They rode along in their companionable way. She wondered how it was possible to be so comfortable with him and yet to be in a low simmer of excitement all the while, just from being with him.

He smiled at her, and she felt almost giddy. His laugh filled her with happiness and sent her searching her brain for something else witty to say to bring that laugh again. And when he reached up and put his hand around her waist to help her down from her horse, a tingling ran all through her.

Mrs. Cooper greeted them at the door, all smiles, and invited them in, offering to get them tea.

"Oh, no, please, we cannot stay long today," Juliana told the woman. "I just—there was something I wanted to ask you about my mother."

"Why, of course, dear. Come in, come in." She directed them toward the grouping of chairs in her tiny parlor. "What is it you wish to know?"

Juliana hesitated, unsure how to begin the conversation, now that she was facing the woman.

The older woman looked at her with kindly expectation.

Juliana had the feeling that what she was about to ask would shatter this woman's calm. "Mrs. Barre, Lilith Barre, told me yesterday—well, she said that my mother and Trenton Barre, um…"

She did not have to finish the sentence, for Mrs. Cooper's eyes flashed, and she almost snarled, "Mrs. Barre! That woman! Your mother was always polite to her, no matter how wickedly that woman treated her."

Tears came into Mrs. Cooper's eyes, and she dabbed them away, saying, "No matter how Mrs. Barre acted, how she snubbed her and accused her, Mrs. Holcott never answered her in kind."

"Then Lilith talked to my mother about her suspicions?"

"If you can call it talking. She ranted and raved at her, as if any of it was Mrs. Holcott's fault. As if she was to blame for the abominable way that man treated her."

"Trenton?" Nicholas asked, speaking for the first time. "My uncle?"

"Yes!" Mrs. Cooper fairly spat out the word, and her face looked as if the taste of it was sour in her mouth. "He was evil. Evil. When I think of how he used Mrs. Holcott, how he took her sweetness and—"

"Mrs. Cooper," Juliana said, leaning forward and taking the woman's hand. "Are you saying that he…that Trenton forced my mother?"

The housekeeper's face hardened, and her eyes were bright and cold. "Not physically, mayhap, but he forced her nonetheless. Your mother didn't want anything to do with him, but she knew she had to…to accommodate him if she wanted to continue to live there. She had to do it to save you from a life of poverty."

"She did have an affair with Trenton?" Juliana asked.

Mrs. Cooper nodded, but she grasped Juliana's hand tightly, pleading with her, "Don't blame your mother, child. She was a good woman. She was only doing what she had to. She was scared of that man.

She dreaded his visits. She hated his touch. There was no other man for her but your father. But if she did not give in to Barre, she would have found herself out on the street, with no way to support you and herself. She was terrified of what would happen to you, you see. There was nothing she could do, especially with having a child, except to take in sewing or even laundry."

Juliana knew that what the woman was saying was the truth. Prospects would have been bleak for a penniless widow with a child. Such jobs as Juliana herself had held would not have been available to someone who would be bringing a child with her. Even any sort of servant's position would have been unattainable. Juliana remembered how frightened her mother had been in the weeks after her father died, how she had paced the floor and cried, how relieved she had been when Trenton Barre arrived.

She recalled the way her mother had cried and held her, telling her, "We've been saved, darling." Juliana wondered if her mother had known then the price that Trenton Barre would demand for offering them shelter…or if that was something she had found out only after they had moved into the cottage on the estate.

"Oh, my God," Juliana breathed, her hands coming up to her face.

"She did it all for you," Mrs. Cooper went on. "Don't think ill of her, child."

"Of course not," Nicholas assured Mrs. Cooper grimly. "It is my uncle who was at fault. We are well aware of that." He curled his arm around Juliana's shoulders, saying to Mrs. Cooper, "Thank you for telling us. Juliana needed to know. We must take our leave now."

The housekeeper was still frowning worriedly as Nicholas turned and swept Juliana from the room. She did not protest, only went with him numbly. He gave her a hand up onto her horse, then mounted as well, and they started back toward Lychwood Hall.

It seemed to Juliana that the day, which had started out so beautiful and bright, was now dull. Her head felt fuzzy, and it was difficult to think. She wanted to sob, but she swallowed hard and clamped down on her emotions, promising herself that she would not cry until she was alone again.

But as they neared the Hall, Nicholas urged his horse down a lesser-used path. Juliana followed listlessly, her mind still slowly trying to come to terms with what she had learned about her mother. It took her a moment to realize that Nicholas was heading now toward the cottage where she had lived as a child.

Juliana stiffened, about to cry out that she did not want to go there, but at that moment they passed through a copse of trees, and there before them was the small house where she had lived. It was achingly familiar. She had sat in that large tree with the low branches and read her books, and there, in the garden behind the cottage, she had played with her dolls. And there was the window to her bedroom, where she had stood innumerable times looking out.

She realized that far from being unable to bear to see it, this place was exactly where she wanted to be right now. They sat for a moment, looking around them. The bushes and trees had grown up around the small house, and its windows were shuttered against the elements. It looked closed and abandoned, and though Juliana had never thought she liked the place, it made her heart sad to see it looking so.

"I should have sent someone here to see about the cottage," Nicholas said quietly. "It should not look like this. I will have the yard trimmed and the house cleaned."

Juliana smiled at him faintly. "Thank you. It isn't, I suppose, very useful."

"There is no need for it to be useful," Nicholas replied quickly. "It is dear to me."

Juliana glanced at him, a little surprised.

He saw her gaze and said, "It is where I escaped to from that huge, cold house. It was where you were, and I would come here to see you. Mrs. Cooper always had a jar of cookies, and she would press a plate of them on me. And your mother was kind. She would smile and tell me I was growing taller every day. That is what my mother used to say."

"Oh, Nicholas!" Impulsively Juliana reached out and took Nicholas's hand. "I didn't know...."

He kept his hand around hers as he went on. "It sounds foolish, I suppose, but it seemed to me to be a refuge. A place of happiness."

"I wish it had been so for her," Juliana said quietly.

He turned to her. "I'm sorry."

Juliana shook her head. "You needn't apologize. It is not your fault. He tainted all our lives. Surely even Crandall would have turned out a better person if he had not had Trenton for a father."

They dismounted, and Nicholas tied their horses to one of the trees. The door stuck, and he had to put his shoulder to it to open it.

Inside, there was a faint smell of must. The furniture was covered with sheets, humped shapes in the dark room. Nicholas strode over and opened the curtains and windows, unlatching and pushing out the shutters to let in light and air.

They walked slowly through the house, opening a window here and there. Juliana trailed her fingers along the wallpaper in the hall, thinking about her childhood.

"I always thought she was unhappy because my father had died…that all those years she was mourning him."

"No doubt she did mourn him."

"Yes, but I realize now how unhappy her life must have been. I knew she disliked Trenton, even though she made me smile and be polite. I could feel the bite of her fingers on my shoulders when she would bring me in to curtsey to him. It must have been so awful for her…and I used to be mad at her because she wouldn't be happy!"

Tears gushed into her eyes, and Juliana could not hold them back now. She brought her hands up to her eyes, crying and struggling not to. "She did it all for me! She enslaved herself so that I could have a nice place to live, and pretty clothes and an education. And I resented the fact that she didn't laugh and play with me!"

"She loved you." Nicholas reached out and pulled her into his arms, cradling her against his chest. "She did the best she could for you. What she wanted was your happiness, and I know she wouldn't want you to blame yourself."

His hands stroked her back comfortingly, and Juliana buried her face in his chest, giving herself up to her tears. She cried for her mother and the sacrifices she had made, and she cried for the child she had been, always a little lonely and wishing for the mother Diana had been before her father died.

Gradually her tears subsided, but still she stayed in his arms, enjoying the warmth and safety of that strong circle. She felt Nicholas's lips brush against her hair; she felt the slow circling of his hand over her back.

And something stirred within her. A deep sensual longing, the ache that yearned for him. She flushed a little with embarrassment that she should feel the stirrings of desire when all Nicholas had done was offer her comfort, that she should want him even on the heels of her sorrow for her mother. But she could neither deny nor expel the heat that curled in her loins, tender and throbbing. And she knew that the ache was not only physical but an emptiness in her very heart, as well.

Without thinking, she rubbed her cheek against his chest, and his hand stopped its movement. For a moment they were frozen, suspended and uncertain. Juliana could hear the soft rasp of Nicholas's breath, feel the thud of his heart beneath her cheek.

Then, slowly, Juliana moved back a little, turning

her face up to look at him. The desire she saw in his face took her breath away. He hungered for her as she hungered for him. The only wrong thing, Juliana thought, would be to deny what they both felt.

Going up on the balls of her feet, she lifted her lips to his.

CHAPTER SIXTEEN

NICHOLAS'S ARMS WENT around her fiercely, pulling her up and into his hard body, and his lips sank onto hers. Juliana felt as if she were sliding down, down, into a dark abyss of pleasure, falling without fear. Her body surged with heat, enveloped by his answering warmth.

His hands fumbled at her hair, pulling the pins from it and sending it tumbling down in a shining mass. He plunged his fingers into the silken strands, holding her head as his mouth plundered hers. Juliana slid her arms around his neck, clinging to him fiercely, and kissed him back. Eagerly their bodies pressed against each other, seeking the release they both desired.

Caressing each other and tugging haphazardly at their clothes, they kissed, turning and twisting in a dance of desire. Her riding jacket wound up tossed on a chair, his coat on the floor. He pulled her mannishly-cut shirt from the skirt of her riding habit, but the small round buttons foiled his fingers, until finally she reached up and unfastened them for him.

He watched her with heavy-lidded eyes as she unbuttoned the shirt, and pulled it back and off her shoulders, letting it slide down her arms and off onto the floor. Her breasts swelled up above the top of her white chemise, barely restrained by the ribbon-tied neckline.

Nicholas took one end of the blue ribbon and pulled it gently, and the bow slid open, the sides of the cotton chemise falling apart. One by one he undid the bows the rest of the way down the front of the feminine undergarment, his eyes intently following the path of his fingers.

He looked back up into her eyes then, and Juliana saw the fierce glint of desire in their darkness, the hunger that burned hotter than any fire.

"I have lain awake every night thinking about this," he whispered hoarsely. "I have called myself ten times a fool for ever suggesting that we play this chaste charade."

Juliana let out a breathless little laugh. "So have I."

He chuckled then, and bent to kiss her hard and quick, before he pulled back and opened the sides of her chemise. Softly his hands slid across her chest as he pushed the material aside. He ran his hands down her arms, shoving the garment off and letting it join their other garments on the floor.

His eyes lingered caressingly on her breasts for a

moment before he lightly brushed his fingers over the soft white orbs. Her nipples tightened in response, growing harder with each delicate movement of his fingers. He cupped her breasts in his hands, his thumbs stroking over her nipples until her every fiber was thrumming with pleasure.

Juliana let out a sob of breath. She wanted more, wanted to feel everything it was possible to feel, need throbbing deep within her.

Bending down, he kissed the quivering top of each breast, his lips moving over her flesh with exquisite tenderness, tasting and arousing with every movement. Juliana's knees trembled so that she feared she might fall, but then his arm went around her back, hard as iron, holding her up, as he lifted her up and his mouth settled on her nipple.

A chord of sensation so bright with pleasure that it was almost pain vibrated through her, sending moisture pooling between her legs. A pulse throbbed there with every pull of his mouth, and Juliana dug her fingers into his shoulders, unable to hold back a moan.

She wanted him to go on forever, and at the same time she wanted him to pull the rest of her clothes from her and send them both racing to the bright pleasure at the end. She wanted everything at once, her feelings wildly chaotic.

Her fingers went to the buttons of his shirt, shakily making her way down the front, and she slid her hands beneath the cloth. She explored the skin of his chest, delighting in the varying textures, finding and caressing the flat masculine nipples, and smiling at the soft noise of pleasure he made when she did so.

Hastily he straightened and pulled his shirt off, and Juliana seized the opportunity to lean forward and place her lips against his chest. He went still, hardly daring to move as she made her tentative way across his skin, kissing, her tongue creeping out to taste or to flick across his nipple. Breathing her name, he clutched a fistsful of her hair, his fingers clenching in the silken mass as her mouth explored him.

At last, when he felt as if he might explode, he pulled away from her, jerking off his boots and skinning out of his breeches. As he did so, Juliana quickly undressed, too eager now to be embarrassed or shy. She looked at his long, lean body, so hard and masculine, and desire shivered through her. She had never seen a man naked before, but in Nicholas she saw a stark, raw beauty of muscle and bone.

"You are beautiful," he murmured, and pulled her into his arms again, kissing her as if he could never get enough of the taste of her.

Juliana melted against him, luxuriating in the feel

of his hands moving over her body, finding and exploring the soft, feminine secrets of her flesh. His hand slipped between her legs, separating and caressing, and she let out a groan, moving against him in response.

He pulled one of the covers from the furniture and laid it out on the floor, then pulled her down onto it with him. Stretched out beside her, he took his time kissing and caressing her, extending her pleasure until she thought she would shatter.

Then, at last, he moved between her legs and slowly entered her. She gasped at the flash of pain, and he paused, looking down at her. She smiled at him and pulled his head down to her so she could kiss him, and he slid into her welcoming body.

Slowly, carefully, he began to move within her. Juliana wrapped her arms around him, her hands digging into his bare back, as he thrust in and pulled back in a building rhythm. He drove them onward, passion rising with each movement, moving faster and faster, racing toward some elusive something that seemed to dangle just beyond their reach. Juliana's breath rasped in her throat, and her whole body was taut with tension—eager, waiting, wanting.

Then, at last, he cried out, shuddering, and desire exploded in Juliana, sending long waves of pleasure thrumming throughout her body. With a soft groan, Nicholas collapsed against her.

Juliana closed her eyes, savoring the moment. Her hand slid over his back, damp with sweat. He did not love her, she knew. A part of her was afraid he might never love her. She was well aware that what had happened between them had sprung from desire on his part, not love.

But, she thought as she held him, for right now, this was enough.

JULIANA WENT THROUGH the rest of the day in a haze of happiness, a happiness made even more complete that night when Nicholas opened the door between their rooms and took her in his arms. They made love, and she was delighted when he did not leave her afterwards but held her in his arms throughout the night, waking in the morning to make love again.

He left her sleeping, and, somewhat to her embarrassment, she slept until long past breakfast. She blushed when her maid entered the room, smiling happily and a little knowingly at Juliana, with a tray of tea and toast for her. But her inner joy was too much to be dented by a little embarrassment, and she hummed as she bathed in the slipper tub and dressed in the morning dress that Celia got out for her.

The dress was high-necked, she noticed, and covered up the red patch on her lower neck where Nicholas's morning stubble had scraped her delicate skin. Celia, she thought, was both sharp-eyed and discreet.

Later, bathed and dressed, she made her way downstairs to the drawing room, schooling her expression into one that was more suitably grave for a house in mourning. She found Seraphina and Lilith there before her. Lilith was stitching on something in her lap, Juliana saw, and Seraphina was staring out the window, looking bored.

She looked up with a smile when Juliana came in. "Oh, good. I was hoping for a distraction. Winnie has gone for a walk and left me here with nothing to do."

Lilith looked up at her daughter, sent a fleeting glance at Juliana and returned to her work. Clearly she was not interested in alleviating her daughter's boredom.

"What would you like to do?" Juliana asked amiably. She started to suggest that they play cards, then realized that was hardly an appropriate thing to offer Seraphina, given her predilection for gambling.

"Anything," Seraphina replied. "I was almost ready to go join Winnie in the garden."

Juliana knew that a number of letters of condolence had arrived, and needed to be read and answered, but she was equally sure that this task would not be one Seraphina wanted any part in.

"Perhaps we could go out to the garden, and cut some of the flowers and fill the vases."

Seraphina wrinkled her nose at that idea. "I will leave that to you and Winnie. Life in the country is so deadly dull. Even the entertainments are dull."

"Really, Seraphina," Lilith said sharply, raising her head to fix her daughter with a cold blue gaze. "I don't expect Juliana to mourn your brother. It doesn't surprise me that she should think it is all right to bedeck the house with flowers, even though he was buried only two days ago. But I would think that you, at least, could show some spark of respect."

"Sorry, Mother." Seraphina looked chastened at her mother's rebuke.

"So am I," Juliana said quickly. "I did not think. We won't put out any flowers."

"Do what you will," Lilith replied coolly. "It is, after all, your house now."

Juliana suppressed a sigh. Clearly grief had not made Lilith forget about her other grievances.

At that moment there was a crash in the hall outside, and Juliana jumped to her feet, hurrying over to the door. There she found a young woman on her knees, picking up the pieces of a vase. The girl glanced up over her shoulder at Juliana. Tears sparkled in her eyes.

"I'm sorry, miss…. I didn't mean to—it was an accident."

"You are speaking to Lady Barre," Lilith said crisply from behind Juliana. "You do not address her as 'miss.'"

The girl's face flamed with embarrassment, and she jumped to her feet, bobbing a curtsey to them. "I'm ever so sorry, m—my lady. I meant no disrespect. I'm new. I'll clean it up ever so quick." She turned a frightened, pleading look on Juliana.

Juliana felt sure that the girl was scared of losing her new job, and she said kindly, "It's all right. Just get a broom and sweep it up."

Lilith turned toward Juliana, one brow rising in a disapproving way. "You have taken on new staff, Juliana?"

"No. I mean, I assume the housekeeper must have. She didn't say anything to me about it."

Lilith's silent look was eloquent. She clearly found Juliana's control of the household lacking.

The maid, who had turned away, turned back, saying, "Mrs. Pettibone just took me on this morning. She had to get a maid fast-like, 'cause one of the others quit."

Surprised, Juliana asked, "Who?"

"I'm not sure, mi—my lady," the girl answered. "But it was real sudden, she said."

"Much as you might like to hang about in the hallway, gossiping with the servants, Juliana," Lilith said, "I think you ought to let the girl get about doing her job."

The maid turned and fled at Lilith's remarks. Color rose in Juliana's cheeks, and her fingers curled into her palms. She would have liked to snap back at Lilith that none of this was any of her business now, but she kept a tight rein on her irritation. The woman had, after all, just lost her son only a few days earlier. She could scarcely take her to task over her biting words.

"If you will excuse me," Juliana said with all the calm she could muster, "I will go to speak to Mrs. Pettibone."

"Why don't you?" Lilith replied sourly, turning and going back into the drawing room.

Seraphina, who had been standing behind them throughout the foregoing scene, gave Juliana a small, embarrassed smile and a shrug of her shoulders, then turned and followed her mother back into the drawing room.

Juliana strode off down the hallway toward the kitchen area. She trusted Mrs. Pettibone's competence and did not really care that the housekeeper had hired a new maid without talking it over with her, but she did not think she could go back into the drawing room and make polite chitchat any longer with Lilith, so she seized on the excuse to leave.

She found the housekeeper in the hallway outside the kitchens, scowling at the young maid who had knocked over the vase. When Mrs. Pettibone saw Juliana coming toward them, she looked chagrined and quickly dismissed the girl.

"My lady," Mrs. Pettibone said. "Please forgive me for not consulting you about hiring the new maid." She cast a critical look down the hall after the girl. "I fear she may not be experienced enough. But I had so little time."

"What happened?" Juliana asked. "The girl said that one of the maids left abruptly?"

Mrs. Pettibone nodded, leading Juliana back through the hallway into her small personal sitting room. "May I get you some tea, my lady?"

"Yes, thank you." Juliana realized that the prospect of sitting down for a cup of tea and a chat with the housekeeper was far more appealing than trying to talk to Lilith.

Mrs. Pettibone opened the door and cracked out an order for the tea, then returned, sitting down at Juliana's nod. "I must apologize, my lady. Everything's been at sixes and sevens this week, what with the constable coming and going, asking the servants all sorts of questions. And then Annie Sawyer left, the silly girl. Said she was frightened of being in this house and went back home."

"Oh, yes." Juliana remembered the maid who had appeared shaken and scared at breakfast the morning after Crandall's murder. "Well, a murder in the house is enough to upset anyone, I suppose."

Mrs. Pettibone sniffed, obviously unimpressed. "I don't know what she thought she had to be scared of. It isn't like there is a madman loose in the countryside, going about chopping up whoever he meets, is it?"

"No," Juliana agreed. "I would think that the killer was interested only in harming Crandall."

"And there was plenty as disliked him, Lord knows." The housekeeper stopped, looking aghast as she realized how much of her own feelings for the man she had just expressed. "I'm sorry, my lady. I shouldn't have said that."

"Why not?" Juliana replied. "It's certainly true.

There's little use in pretending that Crandall was a popular man."

Mrs. Pettibone sighed. "Sad to say. The constable keeps asking about the blacksmith." Her grimace revealed her opinion of that line of questioning. "As if Farrow would sneak up on a man like that. I told the constable, there's a good number of folks wished that man dead and he'd be better looking elsewhere." She shrugged. "Ah, well, I'm sure that's not what you came here for. It's about Cora's knocking over that vase this morning, isn't it? Don't worry, I'll see to it that she's punished. And it won't happen again. I've put Cora to cleaning floors, where she can't hurt anything."

"I'm sure Cora is just nervous," Juliana said reassuringly. "No doubt she will improve as she gets used to it."

"Aye, she will," Mrs. Pettibone agreed grimly, her expression promising little hope for poor Cora if she did not.

Juliana stayed for a while longer with the housekeeper, having a cup of tea and talking over a few household matters, making sure that Mrs. Pettibone's feathers were soothed over the matter of the new maid. Then she bade goodbye to the woman and started back to the main part of the house.

She thought with some reluctance that she should

return to the drawing room. As she was lady of the house, Lilith and Seraphina were, to some extent at least, her responsibility. There was little chance of lifting Lilith's mood, of course, but she might perhaps find something to relieve some of Seraphina's boredom.

However, as she turned the corner into the main hall, she met Nicholas walking toward her, and all thoughts of Seraphina and Lilith fled. He smiled, and she felt her heart lifting inside her chest as if it might take flight.

"Nicholas."

"Juliana." He came to her, reaching out to take both her hands, smiling down into her face in such a way that she felt almost giddy with happiness. "I was looking for you."

"I have been talking to Mrs. Pettibone about one of the servants."

"I wanted to ask you to go for a ride with me." He leaned in a little closer, his voice lowering as he continued. "I want to be alone with you."

Juliana could not keep from smiling back at him with just a hint of flirtatiousness, her eyes sparkling. "Indeed?"

"Indeed." His eyes returned her dancing look. "I

have sent word to the stables to saddle our horses. And to Cook to pack a picnic luncheon for us."

The idea sounded perfectly delightful, Juliana thought, and she agreed readily, saying, "I shall go upstairs and change."

"All right." However, he did not let go of her hands, but pulled her even a little closer, bending down to murmur, "Perhaps I should help you."

His eyes darkened, the meaning in them clear, and Juliana's breath hitched a little. "My lord, I think 'twould take much too long if you did that."

He grinned. "Perhaps you are right. We might wind up not leaving your room at all."

He pressed his lips to the top of her head, then to her forehead, lowering them finally to brush across her lips. Juliana's heart fluttered wildly in her chest, and she wanted to throw her arms around him and kiss him wantonly right there in the central hall. Had he taken her into his arms right then, she rather suspected that she would have.

But he moved back, raising her hand to his mouth to kiss it, and then let her go. He nodded toward the stairs. "You had better go now, or we shall never get started."

Juliana nodded, not trusting herself to speak, and hurried up the staircase to her room.

A HALF HOUR LATER, she and Nicholas were riding out across the estate, heading this time not toward the village but away from it, crossing the meadow beyond the gardens and orchards. The air smelled of new-mown hay, and the sun lay warm on her shoulders.

"Where are we going?" she asked, although she really did not care, as long as she was with Nicholas.

"There is an abandoned mill not far from here," he replied. "It's in ruins, but a very scenic spot. I thought it would be a nice place to sit and watch the river."

Juliana smiled at him. It sounded perfect. "I think I remember it now. We used to explore around there. It seemed very exotic and exciting."

She had not gone there after Nicholas had left, and it had gradually faded into the back of her memory. But she could remember now the moss-covered gray stone walls and the high water wheel.

They passed several of their tenants' farms, and children came out to wave at them. At one or two houses, the wife of the tenant also emerged. Nicholas, she noted, had come prepared for their greetings, for he reached into his pocket and withdrew wrapped pieces of candy, which he tossed to the children. They stopped and talked to the adults, and Nicholas introduced her to the women, who beamed and curtseyed to her.

"I remember you when you were this high," one of them told her, a sturdy woman with dark hair liberally streaked with gray. She held up her hand about the level of her own waist. "The two of you, running down to the river to fish."

Juliana smiled. She had not cared whether they fished. She had been happy just to be with Nicholas then, too. "Yes, I remember."

Beyond that farm, the lane narrowed into a track as they entered the woods. They emerged from the trees and stopped, looking down at the scene before them. The river lay below them, narrowing here, the gray-green water that had moved so lazily upriver tumbling faster here. The old mill was there, shrubbery having grown up around much of it. Juliana looked at the tall wooden water wheel; then her gaze moved on to the gray stone walls of the mill.

Nicholas dismounted and came round to help her down. The path down to the mill was twisting and rocky, and it was easier to walk their horses down it. As they turned to start down the path, Juliana caught a flash of movement at the door of the mill, and she stopped, her hand going out to catch Nicholas's arm.

He turned to look in the direction in which she was staring. A person was coming out of the mill, turning back to talk to someone. It was a woman in a dark riding habit, and she carried a hat in her hand. Even in the shade cast by the mill, her hair was a light golden-blond.

It was Winifred. She stepped away from the door, and the person to whom she was talking emerged from the mill. It was a man, his dark-blond head bent to listen to what she said.

Juliana sucked in a surprised breath, and Nicholas stiffened. Quickly he stepped back into the shade of the trees, taking Juliana and their horses with him. They stood, hidden by the overhanging trees, watching the scene before them unfold.

Winifred and the man paused, talking to one another. Winifred's pale face was turned up to him. Finally he bent and kissed her, a long, slow kiss that left little doubt as to the relationship between them. Then they turned and walked around the corner of the building, heading toward the trees behind it.

Juliana looked at Nicholas, not knowing what to say.

"I think it would be best if we picnicked elsewhere," he said mildly, taking her hand and walking through the trees, heading upriver.

They said nothing as they went, emerging finally

some distance upriver. The river had curved a little, and trees grew down to the rocks beside it, so the mill was hidden from their sight. Nicholas found a cozy little nook beside the water, a small bit of land sheltered by trees and shrubs and two large rocks.

He spread out the blanket across the dirt, and they sat down on it with their picnic basket. For a moment they said nothing, just looking at the peacefully flowing river.

Finally Juliana turned to Nicholas. "Do you know that man?"

He nodded. "It looked like Sam Morely. He's one of my tenants…a hardworking, honest sort, as far as I have heard."

"I don't suppose there is any way that what we saw was not a…"

"Tryst?" Nicholas finished. "I don't see how. It seemed fairly clear why they were there."

"I know it's wrong," Juliana said. "Still, I find it difficult to blame Winnie. Crandall was a dreadful husband, and he made her miserable."

"I'm sure he did. That seems to have been his main talent in life," Nicholas said dryly. "But we cannot ignore the possibilities that this opens up."

"It gives Winifred even more reason to want to get rid of Crandall," Juliana agreed.

"And it gives us another suspect," Nicholas pointed out. "I have a little trouble envisioning Winifred, however much she hated him, bashing in Crandall's head with a poker."

"But a man who loved Crandall's wife, who wanted to save her from him, wanted even to marry her, could have struck such a blow," Juliana said, finishing his thought. "Yes, you're right. Was he there that night? Did you see him?"

"Yes. He shook my hand and congratulated me. You saw him, but perhaps you don't remember."

"It was rather a blur of people," Juliana admitted. "But as you said, if he was in the gardens, it wouldn't have been difficult to come into the house and go to that room. Perhaps he even followed Crandall there."

Juliana unpacked the basket, and they ate as they talked, scarcely noticing the excellence of the meal Cook had prepared for them, so deep was their involvement in the subject.

"I have been thinking of something else," Juliana said, when they reached a lull in their discussion of Winifred and her lover. "One of the servants, Annie, left abruptly. Mrs. Pettibone had to hire a new maid."

Nicholas looked at her, one eyebrow raised.

"Annie was very scared, she said. She told Mrs. Pettibone she wanted to go home. She was the maid who dropped the plate that day at breakfast, after Crandall was found dead."

"What are you saying?" Nicholas asked. "Do you think she may have had something to do with the murder?"

"I don't know. I didn't think much about her fear at the time. It didn't seem unreasonable, given that a man had just been murdered in the house. Several of the servants were jumpy. Indeed, I have been more apt to start at shadows than before. But everyone else seems to have calmed down. As Mrs. Pettibone pointed out, surely it was not a random killing. The murderer would have no reason to harm anyone else."

"Unless they had seen something," Nicholas mused. He looked at Juliana. "Is that what you are suggesting?"

"I'm not sure," Juliana admitted. "Perhaps it means nothing other than that Annie is more nervous than the others, more easily scared. But what if she saw someone go into that room besides Crandall? Or what if she saw something that might somehow identify the killer—like that jewel I found?"

"Then she would have good reason to worry that the killer might have seen her, too. That he might decide she is too dangerous a loose end to leave hanging around."

Juliana nodded.

"Perhaps we should make a visit to the village tomorrow," Nicholas said. "Visit Annie and find out exactly why she is so frightened."

"I think that would be a good idea."

Nicholas set his plate aside and stretched out on his side, propped up on his elbow. "And now," he said, "I am tired of talking about murder and murderers. I came out here to be alone with my wife." He stretched out his hand to Juliana, and she took it.

He tugged her down onto the blanket with him, and she nestled against him, her head in the crook of his arm.

"I have been wanting to get you to myself all morning. Sitting there with the estate manager, all I could think about was you. I have no idea of half of what he said." Nicholas smiled down at her, his eyes warm as they traveled over her face.

His other hand rested on her stomach, palm flat against her, and as he spoke, it drifted, sliding up over her rib cage and onto the soft mounds of her breasts. Juliana felt the flood of pleasure in her loins at his touch, and she closed her eyes, luxuriating in the feelings he aroused.

Nicholas smiled at the stamp of desire on her face, and he bent to brush his lips against hers, murmuring, "You are so beautiful."

He kissed her mouth again, and his lips traveled across her face to nibble suggestively at her ear. Juliana shivered in response, aware of the throbbing that started between her legs, the ache that would grow and spread until she was completely caught up in it. Her throat tightened in anticipation.

"Is this what you brought me out here for?" she asked teasingly, opening her eyes and looking up into his face. His hair glinted black as a raven's wing in the sunlight, and his eyes were searing.

"Precisely," he replied, and bent to nuzzle her neck. "I meant to carry you away and ravish you."

Juliana let out a breathless little giggle. "My lord…you are quite scandalous."

"My lady…I am quite desperate," he replied, his hand roaming lower, curving over her abdomen and delving into the valley that lay between her legs.

Juliana found herself quite wantonly opening her thighs at his touch, and he stroked her through the material of her clothes, heightening the fire that already burned there. He bent and kissed her, his hand bunching up her dress, pulling it and her petticoat upward, until her legs were exposed. He slid his hand beneath the petticoats, caressing her stockinged calves and gliding up, seeking out the heated center of her desire.

He caressed her through the thin material of her pantalets, thoroughly dampened now, and Juliana arched up against his hand involuntarily.

"Nicholas…"

His own desire spiraled at the hunger in her voice, and he untied the drawstring of her undergarment, sliding his hand beneath it and down into the hot, slick folds of her femininity. Juliana's breath caught at the pleasure that shook her.

"What if…what if someone sees us?" she asked.

"No one will come by," he assured her. "But if you want me to stop…"

"No!" Juliana smiled at him, her eyes filled with promise, and she reached up, curling her hand around his neck, and pulled his head down.

Their kiss was slow and deep, and desire burgeoned within her. He caressed her intimately, pulling her pantalets down. She opened herself to him eagerly, and he moved between her legs, freeing himself from his own breeches.

And then he was inside her, filling and fulfilling her, and they were surging together, soaring to their shattering moment of completion.

CHAPTER SEVENTEEN

THE NEXT AFTERNOON Nicholas and Juliana went into the village to the home of Annie Sawyer's parents, where they were surprised to learn that Annie was not there.

Her mother, flustered by the arrival of such important visitors, could scarcely put two coherent words together at first. She flew about, whisking invisible dust from this chair and that, clucking about where they should sit, before she dashed off to prepare tea and biscuits for them. But finally, when the niceties had been observed, and Juliana had complimented her on her home and the quality of her biscuits, she was at last able to calm down and reveal that they had missed Annie by a day.

"Set off yesterday, she did," Mrs. Sawyer said, nodding and glancing toward her younger daughter for confirmation. "Went to her cousin's in Bridgewater."

"Bridgewater?" Juliana asked, turning toward Nicholas.

He nodded. "It's east of here, a two-hour ride or so."

"Yes," Mrs. Sawyer agreed. "She was so insistent about going. To tell you the truth, she's not been the same since Mr. Barre died. She was jittery and jumpy."

"Did she tell you why?" Nicholas asked.

"She said she was frightened because of him being killed, that's all. I told her there wasn't any reason to think anything would happen to her, but she wouldn't say anything else. I tried to get her to go back to Lychwood Hall. I said they'd give her her job back, they'd understand she got scared. But she wouldn't do it. Then when she got that money yesterday…well, she just up and left."

"Money?" Juliana sat up straighter. "She got some money?"

Her mother nodded emphatically. "Oh, yes, my lady. Such a lot of money it was, too."

"How? Who gave it to her?"

"I don't know. It was in a packet at our door when we went out yesterday. Annie's name was on it. She turned real pale, and I had to make her open it, but then when she did, there was fifty pounds sterling in it!"

"Was there a letter with it?" Nicholas asked.

"No, nothing, my lord. I didn't know what to make of it. I asked her who would be sending her such an amount of money, but she wouldn't tell me.

She just said it was better I didn't know, and after that she threw her things together and took the mail coach when it came through. I couldn't get a thing from her." She looked anxiously at Nicholas and Juliana. "She's not in trouble, is she? My Annie's a good girl—she really is."

"I don't think she's done anything wrong," Nicholas reassured her. "But it is possible she might know something about my cousin's murder."

"Annie? How could she know aught?" Her mother looked genuinely confused.

"I don't know. But I must speak with her. If she does know something about who killed Crandall, then she herself could be in danger."

Mrs. Sawyer sucked in her breath sharply. "My Annie? In danger? Bertram Gorton—he's a butcher in Bridgewater. That's where she's staying. My niece Ellen married him two years ago, and that is where Annie went, to stay with them," Mrs. Sawyer told him quickly. "Will you go see her, sir? Will you help her?"

"Yes," Nicholas promised. "I will do whatever I can to help her."

"DO YOU THINK Annie knows who killed Crandall?" Juliana asked a few minutes later, when the two of them were in their carriage rolling back to Lychwood Hall.

"I don't know. She obviously knows something that scared her," Nicholas replied. "Whatever she knows, the killer must have been afraid she might tell it. He must have been the one who sent her the money."

"The thing is, how can the murderer be certain that Annie won't tell what she knows? How can he know that in a few weeks or months—or years, even—she won't be consumed by guilt or fear, and reveal the killer's name?"

"He can't," Nicholas replied flatly. "That is why Annie is still in danger. And she will continue to be until she reveals what she knows. Once she has told, there will be no reason for the killer to go after her. But as long as she is silent, the killer will be safe—and he can ensure her permanent silence only by killing her, too."

"Then I suggest we go talk to her tomorrow," Juliana said.

Nicholas nodded thoughtfully. "But I think it's best that we tell no one where we are going or why."

"You think it's someone in the house, don't you?" Juliana asked quietly.

"I can't be sure. It could have been someone else. But Annie was terrified to stay in that house. That implies to me that she thought it was one of us who murdered Crandall, not someone from the village. If she had thought it was a villager, surely she would not have gone to her parents."

"There is the money, as well."

"Yes. It has to be someone who has that sort of resources. The blacksmith and Sam Morely do well enough, but I can't imagine either of them being able to lay his hands quickly on fifty pounds."

"I think it would be best to tell everyone at Lychwood Hall that she has left. That way, whoever it is will think that his bribe has succeeded," Juliana suggested.

Nicholas nodded. "Yes. And I would like to see everyone's expressions when they hear she's disappeared."

So that evening at supper, after the soup had been served, Juliana said casually, "We went to visit Annie Sawyer this afternoon."

She glanced around the table, trying to judge each person's reaction. Most of them gazed back at her blankly.

"Who?" Seraphina asked.

"One of the maids," Winifred explained. "The girl who left the other day."

"Oh." Seraphina returned to her soup, uninterested.

"Yes." Juliana could not tell whether Winifred's look was anxious or merely surprised.

"Is she going to come back to work here?" Winifred asked. "I think she was merely upset because, well, you know, because of what happened."

"Nonsense. I wouldn't have her back," Lilith said scornfully. "She's clearly unreliable."

"No, I don't believe she will return," Nicholas said. "She has left the town entirely."

"The devil, you say," Sir Herbert commented. "Where'd she run off to?"

"I have no idea," Juliana lied. "Her mother doesn't know. She just said that she caught the mail coach yesterday. She said she was scared, you see. Which makes one wonder what frightened her so."

"Why are we talking about one of the maids?" Seraphina asked, bored.

"The girl is silly," Lilith said. "Scared of ghosts or some such nonsense. A thrashing would drive that idiocy right out of her head."

"Yes, I know how fond you are of that sort of solution," Nicholas told her coolly, his eyes flat and hard.

Lilith raised her brows slightly, then turned back to her soup.

"I think she knows something," Juliana told them.

"Knows something?" Winifred asked, looking puzzled.

"About the murder, you mean?" Sir Herbert asked.

"What?" Lilith asked, looking surprised. "You think that Annie killed Crandall?"

"Well…" Sir Herbert glanced at Winifred, then away. He squirmed a little uncomfortably in his seat. "I wouldn't think it's impossible. Crandall, um, did have a certain reputation."

Seraphina seemed to have caught on to what the others were talking about at last, for she nodded at her husband's remark, adding, "Annie is a pretty girl."

"You mean you think Crandall made advances toward the chit?" Peter Hakebourne spoke up. "And she killed him?"

"What nonsense!" Lilith exclaimed, her eyes flashing. "How can you say such a thing? Do you think you can impugn Crandall's reputation that way simply because he is no longer here to dispute it? I won't have it!"

Hastily, Juliana said, "We are not trying to cast any aspersions on your son, I assure you. I don't think that Annie killed Crandall. But what if she saw something? Or found something?"

Juliana cast a quick glance around at her last words, hoping that something would show in one of the others' faces when she mentioned finding something. If she was right and the ruby had been lost by the murderer, he or she might have realized that the jewel was missing. But she detected no knowledge of anything in anyone's eyes.

"But if that were the case, if she saw something, why wouldn't she have spoken up?" Sir Herbert asked.

"I don't know. Obviously she was quite frightened. She might have thought the killer would go after her if she told what she had seen. Or perhaps she isn't quite sure who it is," Nicholas pointed out.

"But if she has taken off, how are we to find out what she knew?" Seraphina asked.

"I suppose we cannot," Juliana replied, frowning. It wasn't difficult to appear frustrated, she thought, for she found herself stymied by the others' lack of expression.

"Well," said Lilith firmly, "this is scarcely a fit conversation for the dinner table."

Juliana gave in meekly, taking up her spoon, and the discussion died.

THEY TOLD NO ONE of their plans to travel to Bridgewater the next morning. When they went down to breakfast, they found Lilith and Peter Hakebourne there, along with Sir Herbert. They talked casually of a number of things, primarily the weather and Sir Herbert's plans to buy a new pair of grays for his carriage.

Lilith inquired politely, with a notable lack of interest, into what Juliana planned to do that day.

"I thought I might go see Mrs. Cooper," Juliana lied. It was the best excuse she could think of for being gone most of the day.

Lilith nodded. "More tea?"

"Yes, thank you." Juliana handed her the cup.

Lilith, she noted, seemed in slightly better spirits today. There was a little more color in her cheeks, and she was participating in the conversation.

That conversation turned to the estate crop, with Sir Herbert evincing interest in it and Mr. Hakebourne looking thoroughly uninterested. Juliana wondered how long his lack of money would overcome his sheer boredom at being stuck in the country.

Juliana pushed her eggs around her plate. Her stomach was far too jittery for her to eat any more of them. She took a few sips of tea and another bite or two of toast, and cast a glance around her at the others' plates, hoping that they would soon finish. She was eager to be on their way, worried that Annie Sawyer might take it into her head to go someplace else before they got there.

At last the others began to finish, and Juliana said, "If you will excuse me…?"

"Of course, my dear." Nicholas jumped up to pull out her chair.

Juliana stood up quickly. Her head spun at the movement, and she swayed. Nicholas reached out and grabbed her arm.

"Are you all right?" he asked, frowning.

"I felt…a trifle dizzy…" Juliana said, surprised. She placed her hand against her stomach, which was now rolling uneasily.

"Perhaps you'd better lie down," Lilith suggested.

"Yes, perhaps, for just a moment," Juliana agreed.

They left the room, Juliana holding on to Nicholas's arm rather more tightly than she normally would have. The floor seemed somehow to move beneath her feet, to tilt and undulate.…

She stopped, pressing her hand to her mouth. She swallowed hard, concentrating on keeping her food down. It would be too humiliating to toss up her breakfast here in front of everyone, especially Nicholas.

"I'm sorry," she said quietly.

"There's nothing to apologize for," he said. "You look terribly pale. I'll carry you up the stairs."

"No, I can walk," Juliana protested, but he paid

no attention, sweeping her up in his arms and starting up the stairway.

Juliana closed her eyes and let her head rest upon his shoulder, putting all her efforts into trying to control her nausea. Had she eaten something bad? she wondered. Or could it possibly be…no, surely it was far too soon…. Even if by some chance she had gotten pregnant already, it seemed unlikely that morning sickness would start so quickly. Still, she could not quite douse a little flicker of pleasure. *A baby…Nicholas's baby…*

She swallowed again and realized that, oddly, her mouth seemed to be watering excessively.

They had barely reached the room, where Nicholas laid her down on her bed, when Juliana's maid came rushing into the room. "Mrs. Barre rang for me and said you was ill!" she exclaimed, hurrying around the side of the bed and reaching out to feel Juliana's forehead.

The room was spinning badly now, and Juliana gritted her teeth. "I feel sick…."

"I'll just fetch a pot for you," Celia said calmly and went to do so.

Juliana summoned the last of her strength. She knew that before long she was going to be thoroughly and violently ill. Her stomach was roiling now. She most desperately did not want to appear in such a state before Nicholas.

"You'd better go on," she told him, struggling to sound normal.

"No. We'll go another day," Nicholas said quickly. His face was, she noted, much paler than usual. "I will stay here with you."

"No. No, please. I'll be fine. It's just a little sickness, probably something I ate. Celia will take care of me."

"But I—"

"No, really." Juliana stretched out a hand toward him pleadingly. "I want you to go. You need to talk to her. We mustn't let her slip through our fingers. I will be right as rain by the time you get back. You'll see. But I really don't think we should wait."

Nicholas looked torn. "No, I can't leave you like this."

"Just a spot of wooziness, sir," Celia spoke up. "I'm thinking it might turn out to be delightful news." She nodded at him and smiled.

"What?"

"Your being just married and all. Wouldn't be at all surprising," she went on with a knowing look.

"What?" He stared at the maid, stunned. "Are you joking?" He looked back at Juliana, and now a smile was starting on his lips. "Is it? Do you think so?"

"I don't know," Juliana said miserably. She sincerely hoped that this was not morning sickness, as she wasn't sure she could bear feeling like this every day for several months.

Nicholas was grinning now, and he bent down to kiss the top of her head. "All right. I will go. But perhaps we should send for the doctor."

"It's far too early to know," Juliana murmured. She gritted her teeth as another wave of nausea swept her, and dug her fingers into the bedding.

Nicholas went to the door, promising to be back as soon as he could. Juliana mumbled something in reply, and as soon as he was gone, she turned gratefully to Celia, who was holding out a chamberpot, and proceeded to empty the contents of her stomach.

NICHOLAS RODE rather than taking the carriage, eager to get to Bridgewater and back as soon as possible. He was torn between elation at the thought that Juliana might be pregnant and a deep fear at the fact that she was so ill. He had seen the paleness of her face, the sweat that beaded her brow. *Surely morning sickness did not affect one so badly, did it?*

His desire had been to stay by her side, to help her in whatever way he could, even if it was only to hold her hand. But he could see in her face that she wished him gone. She was trying to act as if it were nothing, to pretend to be less ill in front of him. He could understand that; he knew how proud and independent a woman Juliana was. It would be humiliating for her to be ill in front of him. She would be happier if he was not there. For that reason, more than any other, he had agreed to go, for, quite frankly, his need to know who had killed Crandall was far outweighed by his concern for Juliana.

He had to admit, however, that it was good to be out, to be doing something active to keep his mind from dwelling on the possibilities of what could be wrong with Juliana. The sight of her pale face, the misery in her eyes, had chilled him to the core.

It was nothing serious, he told himself firmly, pushing down the terror that was trying to claw its way up his throat. Juliana was not about to die. It was a spot of bad food, as she had said, or perhaps her maid's hintings at pregnancy were accurate. She was young; she was healthy. It was foolish to even think she could fall prey to some serious illness.

Such thoughts spurred him on, and he reached the town of Bridgewater in record time. It took only a few inquiries to locate the house of Annie Sawyer's cousin, and soon he was knocking at the front door of a small old wattle-and-daub cottage.

The door was opened after a moment by a young woman. She stared at Nicholas in slack-jawed amazement. "Cor…"

"I am looking for Miss Annie Sawyer," Nicholas began.

"Annie?" The woman appeared even more astounded.

"Yes. Is she here?" Nicholas prodded gently.

"Oh! Yes! Yes, of course she is. Pardon me manners, sir. We don't usually get the likes of you come calling." She bobbed a curtsey to him and gestured him inside. "I'll, um, just get her. Would you like to…?" She glanced around the interior of the small house as if she had never noticed it before. She waved vaguely in the direction of the front room, where there were several chairs, and a few stools, as well. "Please, sit down, sir. I'll, um, fetch Annie for you."

Nicholas walked into the room and stood, waiting, looking about him. A few moments later, Annie came rushing into the room, appearing almost as dumbstruck as the woman who had answered the door. Was there, Nicholas wondered, also just a touch of trepidation in the girl's gaze?

"Hello, Annie."

"My lord! What are you doing here?" She seemed to realize the rudeness of her remark, for she quickly added, "I'm sorry, my lord, but you've fair thrown me for a loop."

"I came to ask you a few questions," Nicholas told her.

Now the wary look was definitely uppermost in the former maid's face. "Questions?" she repeated doubtfully.

"Yes. I went to see your mother yesterday, and she said you had come here."

"Me mother!" Annie looked as if she could not quite picture that meeting. "But why—I mean—"

"There were some things I needed to ask you. About Mr. Barre's murder."

He was watching her closely, and he did not miss the tightening of her face at the mention of Crandall's name.

Annie glanced away. "I'm sure I don't know nothing about that, sir."

"Perhaps you know more than you think. Certainly more than you have let anyone know."

"I don't know what you mean, sir," she retorted, the fear that crept into her eyes belying her words.

"I think you do. It looks very odd, your leaving your home this way," Nicholas went on.

Annie stared at him, nonplussed. "Odd? What do you mean?"

"Well, when someone has been murdered, and then someone in that same person's household suddenly flees the area, it is rather suspicious."

The girl stiffened, indignation flooding her features. "You saying that I killed Mr. Crandall?"

"I'm not saying anything of the sort. I am merely pointing out that your departure makes one wonder."

"I didn't have aught to do with it. Or with him," Annie told him flatly.

"Yet clearly you know something about what happened."

"I never!" Annie protested.

"Then why did someone send you fifty pounds? And why did you leave town?"

"I didn't want to work there no more, that's all," Annie protested. "A house where there's been killing done? I couldn't work there. It was too scary."

"It *is* a frightening thought," Nicholas admitted. "Still, I think everyone will agree that there were a number of people who might have wished Crandall ill. It seems likely that whoever killed him has no interest in killing anyone else." He paused, adding thoughtfully, "Unless, of course, he thought that someone else in the house could give him away."

Annie sucked in her breath. "No! I don't know nothing!"

"I think you do, Annie. It's as clear as day. I have only to look at your face. Did you see Crandall that night? Did you see who killed him?"

"No!"

"The only way to keep yourself out of danger is to tell what you know," Nicholas told her sternly. "Once you have revealed your secret, there is no reason for anyone to harm you to shut you up."

"I didn't see nothing! I just…" She sighed, then said in a flat voice, "I was going outside to set out some more food. I was carrying a big bowl, and Mr. Crandall reached out and grabbed me. I nearly dropped it, I did, and then he took it from me and set it on the table, saying wouldn't I like to be doing something more fun than carrying great heavy bowls. And I told him it was my job. He just laughed and held on to me so tight I could scarcely breathe, and then he began to kiss me."

She looked down, flushing at the memory. "He was always doing that, pinching me or putting his arm around me or grabbing at me. None of us wanted to go into a room if he was the only one there."

Nicholas studied the girl. Gently he said, "Did you fight him off, Annie? Did you pick up the poker to keep him away?"

"No!" The maid looked up at him, alarmed. "I never! I just pushed at him and told him I had to go, but he was that drunk, sir, and he kept holding on. It was like he had six hands that night. But then Mrs. Barre come in and saw us—"

"His wife?"

"Oh, no, my lord, not her. She'd've just started crying. It was the old Mrs. Barre. His mum."

"Lilith?"

Annie nodded. "Yes. She yelled at him to stop— well, she didn't yell exactly. She didn't raise her voice none, but it cracked like a whip, like she can do."

"I know."

"And he let go of me, just like that. So I picked up my bowl and ran out of the room, fast as I could. And that's all I know, I swear it. That's all I seen. But it couldn't've been her who killed him, could it? Not his mother!"

Nicholas just looked at her for a long moment, the uneasiness inside him growing and solidifying. Lilith! It had never occurred to either him or Juliana that Crandall's mother could have been the murderer.

Even now, hearing Annie's story, the idea seemed absurd. Despite her recent indications of being tired of his behavior, Lilith had adored her son. Indeed, Nicholas did not think that, other than her horses, there was anyone or anything that Lilith loved besides Crandall. She could not have killed him.

"It wasn't wrong not to tell, was it?" Annie asked. "Mrs. Barre couldn't've been the one to kill him."

"No doubt you are right," Nicholas reassured her. But his own mind, as he walked out of the house and mounted his horse, was not so clear.

Someone had, after all, sent Annie money. Clearly, whoever that person was thought she knew something incriminating. Who else would have sent the money beside Lilith? And why else would she have sent it, except to keep Annie from telling what she knew?

Nicholas turned toward home, the doubts multiplying within him. *Why had Lilith not told everyone that she had seen Crandall in the room where he was killed shortly before his murder? Why would his own mother conceal knowledge that might help them catch the murderer?*

It made no sense…unless she did not want the murderer caught.

He thought of Juliana at home, helpless and ill in bed. She would never think that Lilith could be the murderer. She might be on her guard against others in the house, but not against her.

Fear flashed through him, and he dug his heels into his horse's side, urging him into a gallop.

CHAPTER EIGHTEEN

JULIANA LAY back against her pillow with a sigh.
There was nothing left in her stomach to come up,
and there had not been the last several times, so she
had merely heaved dryly for a few minutes before the
spasms subsided.

At least, she thought, the bouts were growing
fewer, and there was more time in between them. And
the strange way her mouth kept watering had slowed
down, as well. She preferred not to test her dizziness,
so she continued to lie on her pillow, eyes closed.

She wondered what time it was. The morning must
have passed by now. It seemed as if it had been hours
and hours, but she supposed that her misery made it
seem longer than it really was. She wished, not for
the first time, that she had not sent Nicholas away.
Little as she wanted him to see her this way, there had
been several times when she had felt so scared that
she had longed for him to be there. Things were less
frightening, more bearable, with Nicholas around.

For the first time, too, she spared a thought for what he had learned from Annie. Perhaps, she thought, that meant she really was feeling better at last. Celia seemed to think she was, for she had gone downstairs to get some clear hot broth for her mistress, hoping she might now be able to keep something down.

The door opened, and someone entered, a woman by the sound of her skirts. Juliana did not make the effort of opening her eyes, assuming it was her maid returning.

But then the woman spoke, and she recognized the voice.

"Aunt Lilith?" Surprised, Juliana opened her eyes and looked at the woman approaching her bed, a small tray in her hands.

"Yes," Lilith said. "I've come to see how you are."

"Better, I think."

As though sensing Juliana's surprise, Lilith gave her a faint smile and said, "I am rather adept at nursing patients, you know. I did, after all, raise two children, and I tended to Trenton all through his last illness."

Juliana forbore to mention that it was not Lilith's nursing skills that she questioned, but her kindness.

"I have some syrup here for you," Lilith said, setting down the tray on the table beside the bed. There was a glass with a little water in it, and a small stoppered vial of brownish liquid. Juliana looked distastefully at the liquid. She had no desire to drink anything, let alone the brackish-looking syrup in the vial.

"I don't think I'm up to it," she began.

"Nonsense," Lilith said in her usual peremptory manner. "It will make you feel better. It's an old remedy my mother used to prepare for us when we were ill."

"I'm really feeling better," Juliana protested feebly, eyeing Lilith askance as she pulled the stopper from the small glass bottle and poured the bit of brown liquid into the glass of water.

"Don't be childish, Juliana," Lilith said, swirling the liquid around in the glass. "It tastes a little bitter, but you will feel much better after you take it."

Lilith picked up the glass and turned back to the bed. Juliana edged a little farther away. Just the sight of the concoction made her stomach churn queasily. She cast about for something to delay Lilith, hoping that Celia would come back in and persuade Lilith not to force the medicine on her.

Her eyes fell on the brooch at the throat of Lilith's neck, a braided length of dark hair made into an ornament. Lilith, seeing the direction of her eyes, reached up and touched the brooch. "It's a mourning brooch. I made it from a length of Crandall's hair."

Lilith's eyes glittered with tears, and Juliana felt a pang of pity for the woman. "I'm sorry."

Lilith shook her head slightly. "He was a wonderful boy. He loved me. He wasn't what everyone tries to make him out to be. And I won't have his image besmirched by those who were jealous of him."

Her face hardened as she spoke, her gaze turning inward. Juliana started to speak, to try to offer the woman some comfort, when suddenly she thought of Lilith at the wedding reception. She had had on a light gray dress, and at the neckline of it, there had been a brooch—not one like this, but a large thing made of diamonds and rubies.

Suddenly Juliana was gripped with fear. She stared at the brooch; then her eyes flew to Lilith's face. Dread filled her, and she lay frozen, staring at the other woman.

Lilith's eyes lit with an unholy fire and she leaned forward, grasping Juliana's shoulder and bringing the glass toward her. "Drink," she demanded. "Go on. Drink it."

"No!" Juliana started to roll across the bed, but Lilith grabbed her arm, holding on tightly. She set the glass down on the table and placed both hands on Juliana's shoulders, holding her to the mattress, as she climbed up onto the bed, throwing her leg across Juliana and pinning her down.

"You will. You will!" Lilith rasped, her eyes bright with madness. Her face loomed over Juliana, a harsh mask of hate. Her fingers dug into Juliana's shoulders as she pressed down on her with all her weight. Juliana could not believe how strong she was, and her own muscles were weak from the hours of vomiting.

"Let go of me!" Juliana yelled with all the strength she could muster. She cursed the illness that had left her so weak, and even as she thought it, she knew. "You! You did this to me. You gave me something this morning to make me ill." Her mind raced. "In the tea. You handed me tea."

"Irises!" Lilith made a disdainful noise. "They won't kill you, only make you sick a bit. But they were close at hand. I had to purchase some time to get the yew needles. Fitting, isn't it, that you'll die like your mother?"

Juliana went still, staring up at Lilith as the woman's words sank into her. "My mother! You killed her, too?"

"Of course I did. I knew no one would suspect. Yew seeds are quite poisonous. I ground them up, put a decoction of them in your mother's migraine medicine, and the next time she had one of her headaches…" Lilith shrugged.

Juliana's eyes filled with tears. "You killed her?"

"She took my husband from me," Lilith replied simply. "I thought if she were gone, then he would come back to me." Her gaze hardened. "But he kept on doing the same things, hanging about with harlots, shaming me, disdaining me. He got one of the maids pregnant. In my own home!"

Bright spots of color flared in her cheeks, and there was a distant look in her eyes as she went on, speaking almost to herself. "He refused to be a good husband. I tried. I gave him every chance."

"Then you killed *him?*" Juliana guessed. She had to keep Lilith talking. Perhaps the woman's grip would lessen as she talked, and if Juliana gathered her strength, she could break free from her.

"Of course I did. Differently, of course. It wouldn't do to have another person drop dead from a seeming heart attack, would it?" Lilith's lip curled. "No one suspected—why would anyone think I knew anything of poisons?" Her voice dripped scorn. "Fools! As if I hadn't learned them at my father's knee—all the plants that hurt and kill your horse. I knew what to avoid and exactly what to use to make one appear to die of a heart attack—or a disease. I gave Trenton ragwort—little bits of it every day or two for weeks and weeks. It destroys your liver, you know. Everyone thought the dropsy was from his years of drinking. It was a fitting end. I was glad to see him suffer."

The bitterness and hate in Lilith's eyes were chilling.

"But why did you kill Crandall?" Juliana asked. "You loved him."

"He was just like his father!" Lilith spat out. "I refused to believe it. All those years, all the things he did...I made excuses for him. I said it was difficult to live up to the image of his father. I said he was wronged by having that upstart inherit the land that should have been his. I blamed his silly little fluff of a wife for not being woman enough to hold on to her husband. Even when he lied and cheated, even when he stole my jewelry to pay his gambling debts—I loved him too much to admit it. And then..." Her mouth worked as she remembered, her eyes filling with tears and her voice roughening. "I saw him with that maid, grabbing her and wrestling with her, and she was struggling with him, begging him to let her go. And I knew then—I could not escape it. He was just like his father—vile and lascivious...a filthy lecher. And I could not have it! I could not!"

Lilith's grip on Juliana's shoulders eased slightly, and Juliana seized the moment. Heaving upward with all her might, she brought her hands up, ramming them as hard as she could into Lilith's stomach. She knocked Lilith to the side and rolled away from her across the bed.

But before she could reach the other side, Lilith was on her, clawing and grappling. Juliana wrestled with her, struggling to free herself, but Lilith's strength was insane. The two of them rolled across the bed. Lilith swung with her fist and connected with Juliana's cheek, sending tears of pain starting in her eyes. Juliana kicked and swung, then rolled away, but this time Lilith pounced on her from behind, sitting on her back and pressing her down into the mattress. With both hands, Lilith grabbed Juliana's head and forced her facedown into the soft feather mattress. Juliana kicked and flailed backward, but her movements were ineffectual. The pillowy mattress surrounded her, the soft material forming to her face, choking off her air.

Faintly, in the distance, she heard a pounding and Nicholas calling her name. There was a tremendous thud against the door. It was locked, she thought dully, black spots forming before her eyes. She would never see him again, Juliana thought. She would never be able to tell him that she loved him....

The door slammed open, and an instant later the heavy weight was gone from her back. Juliana rolled over, gasping for air, as Nicholas and Lilith crashed to the floor on the other side of the bed.

Celia was by Juliana's side immediately, helping her up from the bed, and the rest of the family and servants crowded in behind her. The butler and Sir Herbert rushed to Nicholas's side to help him with Lilith, who was still struggling and screaming incoherently.

Nicholas handed the woman to the other two men and turned back to the bed.

"Juliana!" he cried and went to her side, taking her into his arms. "My love, thank God! Are you all right?"

"Yes," Juliana breathed, clinging to him tightly. "I'm all right now."

"WHAT WILL THEY DO with her?" Juliana asked.

It was the next day, and she was sitting up in her bed, fully recovered from her illness of the day before. Lilith had been accurate in her assessment of the effect of the irises upon her. After Lilith's attack, Juliana had gradually recovered, sleeping away most of the afternoon held securely in her husband's arms. Indeed, Nicholas had not left her until an hour ago, when he had gone down to talk with the magistrate about what was to be done with Lilith. Even then, he had sent Winifred in to watch over her until he returned.

"She's apparently gone quite mad," Nicholas said,

perching on the edge of the bed beside her. "She confessed to killing Crandall, as well as Trenton and your mother years ago. Then, when they took her to the gaol and approached her cell, she fell into a gibbering state, screaming and kicking and making no sense whatsoever. According to the judge, she has been sitting in her cell ever since, staring fixedly at the wall and not moving. He doesn't know what to do with her, and he came to ask me my opinion."

"What did you tell him?"

Nicholas's face hardened. "For what she did to you, I'd say kill the witch."

"She's insane," Juliana said softly. "And what a hell she must be living in now. She killed the only people she ever loved."

"She deserves no less," Nicholas replied harshly. "But I cannot escape the fact that the trial would be an ordeal for you. It would be a terrible scandal."

"And poor Seraphina! 'Tis bad enough that her brother was just murdered a few days ago, however awful he was. And now to find that her mother murdered him *and* her father! We cannot do that to Seraphina. Silly as she is, she is not a wicked person. And Winifred would suffer. She told me when she was in here earlier about Sam Morely and how much they love each other. She said that they plan to marry as soon as a decent period of mourning is past. She seemed so happy. But if there was a trial, and everything about Crandall and his mother and father was exposed to the world, it would ruin her happiness and cast a stain upon the family name. And she might feel she could not marry Mr. Morely with that sort of scandal attached to her. It seems horridly unfair that Lilith's wickedness should cause Winifred any more grief. Must they try Lilith and sentence her to hang? Is there nothing else they can do with her?"

"I knew that would be your feeling on the subject," Nicholas replied, faintly smiling. "The magistrate wants to have her locked up in an insane asylum. It's a terrible fate, but at least it would be better than hanging."

"I could almost feel sorry for her," Juliana said.

"I could, as well—if she had not tried to kill you. That I cannot forgive her." Nicholas reached out and pulled Juliana to him, holding her close. "I hope to God I never have to live through another few hours such as I did yesterday. All the time I was riding, I grew more and more certain that Aunt Lilith had indeed killed Crandall, and I thought about you lying here, weak and vulnerable. I began to wonder about your illness, and I remembered that she poured the tea yesterday at breakfast."

Nicholas kissed the top of her head and murmured, "I've never been so frightened in my life. I don't know what I would have done if I had lost you."

Juliana wrapped her arms around him and hugged him tightly to her. "I love you," she murmured. Then she sat up and pulled back to look at him. "I know you do not want a marriage of love. But yesterday, when I thought that I was going to die, I regretted so not having told you. I love you. I'm not asking you to love me in return. But I cannot go on pretending that what I feel for you is not love. I have loved you for as long as I can remember."

Nicholas slowly smiled. "And I have loved you just as long. I know what I said. I was an idiot. I thought that I had never loved. But it is because my heart was always filled with you. I could not love any other woman. Somehow I always knew that I would come back to you. I did not call it love. But that is because it was so much more than what people speak of when they talk of love. You were my life, my home. My center."

He wrapped his arms around her, covering her face with kisses. "I love you, Juliana."

She melted against him, tears welling in her eyes. This, she thought, was what she had spent her lifetime waiting for. "And I love you."

Turn the page for a sample of
A DANGEROUS MAN
coming in September 2006
from New York Times bestselling author
Candace Camp and HQN Books.

CHAPTER ONE

ANTHONY, LORD NEALE, sliced through the seal on the note that the footman had just handed him and read through it quickly. He sighed. His older sister Honoria was informing him that she planned to visit him that afternoon. Knowing Honoria, he suspected that her carriage would arrive not long after the messenger.

He was aware of a cowardly impulse to send a note to the stables asking the groom to saddle his horse, so he could ride out and pretend he had not been there to receive Honoria's message. But he knew, with a sigh, that he could not. It had been only six months since Sir Edmund's death. Annoying as his sister could be, he could not bring himself to be rude to a grieving mother.

Tossing the letter onto his desk, he rang for the footman and sent a message to the kitchen, informing the butler that his sister would be with them for tea…and perhaps supper.

He walked over to the window and stood looking out. It was his favorite view, offering a sweeping expanse of the front yard, the drive and the trees beyond, but at the moment, he scarcely saw it. His thoughts were turned inward, to his nephew and the young man's death six months ago. He had not been close, he supposed, to Edmund; he was not, he admitted, close to any of his relatives—a fault, no doubt Honoria would tell him, in his own nature. But he had been quite fond of Edmund, and had thought him a man of great talent and promise. He had been saddened by the news of his death, and he was certain that the world would be poorer for the music it had lost.

It had been clear for years that Edmund would not have a long life. He had always been sickly. But to have lost him this way, in a sudden accident, seemed wrong. He could not help but wonder if the young man would still have been alive if it had not been for that stubborn woman he had been foolish enough to marry.

At the time, despite his dislike for Eleanor Townsend, now Lady Scarbrough, Anthony had approved of their moving to Italy, thinking that the warm, sunny clime would be better for Edmund's consumption than the damp winters in England. Nor, he had thought, would it hurt the young man to be farther away from his mother's frequent complaints and demands.

But ever since Edmund's death, Anthony had been weighed down by the guilty thought that he had failed his nephew by not trying to persuade him to remain in England. Only Anthony himself knew how much of his decision not to talk to Sir Edmund about the move had been due to his reluctance to go to Sir Edmund's house, where he might once again run into Lady Eleanor.

Anthony felt the same uneasy sensations he always did whenever he thought of Lady Eleanor: a volatile blend of annoyance and sharp physical hunger, as well as a fierce stab of anger at his seeming inability to control those emotions. The devil take the woman, he thought. She was impossible in every way, not the least of which was impossible to forget.

It had been a year since he had first seen her, but he could remember every moment of it perfectly....

ANTHONY WAITED in the foyer of Eleanor Townsend's house wishing he were somewhere else... anywhere else. He regretted telling his sister he would talk to the woman Sir Edmund intended to marry.

Anthony had not wanted to do as his older sister asked; everything within him rebelled at the idea of messing about in his relatives' lives. He was a man who preferred to live his own life free of others' interference, and he liked to return the favor.

At the sound of footsteps, he turned and went utterly still. The woman walking toward him was stunningly beautiful.

She was tall and statuesque, with thick jet-black hair and vivid blue eyes. Her firm jaw and prominent cheekbones were, perhaps, a trifle too strong, but those features were softened by a soft, full-lipped mouth and large, compelling eyes. She was dressed in peacock blue, too bold for a proper maiden, and she carried herself with confidence, head up and gaze straight.

A wave of pure physical desire swept through him, so intense and hot that it stunned him. He was a man used to being in control of himself, and at thirty-five years of age, he considered himself long past the adolescent days of being swept this way or that by sheer lust. But this woman...

He took an unconscious step toward her, then stopped, realizing what he was doing. By sheer strength of will, he tamped down the surge of desire.

Clearly, he thought, this was the woman who had captured Sir Edmund's heart. And, just as clearly, his sister had been correct in her assessment that Miss Eleanor Townsend was a fortune-hunter. There was no way a woman like this would be marrying his inarticulate, inexperienced nephew out of love. Indeed, it was astonishing that she had not set her cap for a wealthier man or one of higher title.

She was a beauty of the kind that could inspire poets or start wars. And she had the confident carriage of a woman well aware of her power. Had she been some timid soul, a sweet girl fresh from the country, he could have believed she had fallen in love with his nephew, dazzled, perhaps, by his genius, or filled with the maternal urge to take care of him.

But this was no naive girl. This was a strong woman in the full flush of her beauty. It was ludicrous to think she could have fallen in love with Edmund.

Fond as he was of Edmund, Anthony knew full well what he was like. At twenty-four years of age, he was still a boy tightly under his mother's thumb. He was vague and inattentive, more concerned with the music in his head than with the world around him, and completely at a loss in social situations. All in all, he was not the sort chosen by a woman who could have any man she wanted.

Anthony, much to his regret, was quite familiar with manipulative beauties and the ways in which they ensnared men too weak or lonely to see past their looks.

"Lord Neale?" Eleanor Townsend said, and there was a certain wariness in her eyes that made him feel even more certain that she was an adventuress. An innocent female, surely, would not be so guarded when meeting her fiancé's relatives. "You are Edmund's uncle?"

He nodded shortly, irritated by the fact that her voice, low and throaty, with just the trace of an American inflection, made his loins tighten. "Yes."

Her eyebrows rose a fraction at his response, and he knew that he had sounded rude in his abrupt reply.

"Why don't we converse in the drawing room?" she suggested, gesturing down the hall. "I am sorry that Edmund is not here."

"I didn't expect him to be. I came to see you, Miss Townsend."

"Indeed? I am honored."

Anthony did not miss the slightly ironic twist to her voice as she said the words. She sat down, motioning him to do likewise, and waited, watching him coolly.

Lord Neale shifted uncomfortably beneath her gaze and finally said, "You cannot marry Edmund," realizing even as he said it that he had overstepped the bounds. He felt a flush starting in his cheeks. *Damn the woman!* She made him feel as awkward as a schoolboy.

"Indeed? Why not? Is there some impediment?" she responded, her voice cool and faintly sarcastic.

He expected indignation, and he was aware of a curious disappointment at her lack of dismay. It was obvious that she expected him to say something of the kind.

"Only common decency," he snapped.

"I would think it more indecent if Edmund resided in my house without benefit of marriage, wouldn't you?" Eleanor replied, her blue eyes challenging him.

The look in her eyes was like a spark to tinder, and anger flared to life in Anthony, quick and hot.

"You must have known his family would object to this engagement," he retorted.

"Of course. No doubt it will be quite a loss to you," Eleanor told him.

Her tone carried a sting. Anthony was not quite sure what she meant by her words, but her contempt for him was clear. It would be useless, he knew, to try to persuade or reason with her. So he went straight to the point.

"I am prepared to pay you."

"Pay me?" Eleanor's eyebrows soared, and her voice became almost a purr. "You are offering to pay me not to marry Edmund?" She crossed her arms, considering him. "Just how much are you prepared to offer?"

For an instant he thought she would accept. Hope surged up in him, mingled, strangely, with a kind of disappointment, and he named a figure far higher than he had originally intended.

Eleanor rose to her feet, her movement not quick but with a kind of regal grace and power that made him realize suddenly how mistaken he had been in thinking she might accept his offer. He had, he saw, gravely underestimated his opponent.

"It is interesting to learn," she said bitingly, "that your concern for your nephew is solely monetary. I shall not tell Edmund about your offer, as he inexplicably admires you, and I do not like to see him hurt."

She was fairly vibrating with fury, her blue eyes blazing at him, and, much to Anthony's surprise and self-disgust, lust coiled in his loins in response.

"I am sorry," Eleanor went on in a clipped voice that clearly said she was no such thing. "But I must decline your offer. It is too late. Sir Edmund and I were married yesterday by special license."

ANTHONY HAD NOT SEEN Eleanor, Lady Scarbrough again. Two months later, she and Edmund had sailed for Italy. A year later, Sir Edmund was dead.

If you enjoyed what you just read,
then we've got an offer you can't resist!

Take 2 bestselling
love stories FREE!

Plus get a FREE surprise gift!

Clip this page and mail it to Harlequin Reader Service®

IN U.S.A.
3010 Walden Ave.
P.O. Box 1867
Buffalo, N.Y. 14240-1867

IN CANADA
P.O. Box 609
Fort Erie, Ontario
L2A 5X3

YES! Please send me 2 free Harlequin Flipside™ novels and my free surprise gift. After receiving them, if I don't wish to receive anymore, I can return the shipping statement marked cancel. If I don't cancel, I will receive 2 brand-new novels every month, before they're available in stores! In the U.S.A., bill me at the bargain price of $4.24 plus 50¢ shipping & handling per book and applicable sales tax, if any*. In Canada, bill me at the bargain price of $4.94 plus 50¢ shipping & handling per book and applicable taxes**. That's the complete price—what a great deal! I understand that accepting the 2 free books and gift places me under no obligation ever to buy any books. I can always return a shipment and cancel at any time. Even if I never buy another book from Harlequin, the 2 free books and gift are mine to keep forever.

131 HDN DZ9H
331 HDN DZ9J

Name	(PLEASE PRINT)	
Address	Apt.#	
City	State/Prov.	Zip/Postal Code

Not valid to current Harlequin Flipside™ subscribers.

Want to try two free books from another series?
Call 1-800-873-8635 or visit www.morefreebooks.com.

* Terms and prices subject to change without notice. Sales tax applicable in N.Y.
** Canadian residents will be charged applicable provincial taxes and GST.
  All orders subject to approval. Offer limited to one per household.
® and ™ are registered trademarks owned and used by the trademark owner or its licensee.

© 2004 Harlequin Enterprises Ltd.   FLIPS04R